The Book of Fire

Brought up in London, Christy Lefteri is the child of Cypriot refugees. Her novel, *The Beekeeper of Aleppo*, was an international bestseller, selling well over a million copies worldwide and published in over forty countries. It won The Aspen Literary Prize, was runner up for The Dayton Literary Prize and won the Prix de l'Union Interalliée for Best Foreign novel in France. It was also adapted as a play for The Nottingham Playhouse and toured the UK. *The Book of Fire*, Christy Lefteri's latest powerful novel, was shortlisted for the Viking Award for Fiction with a Sense of Place at the Edward Stanford Travel Writing Awards.

Y070182

The item should be returned or renewed by the last date stamped below.

Dylid dychwelyd neu adnewyddu'r eitem erbyn y dyddiad olaf sydd wedi'i stampio isod.

Newport
CITY COUNCIL
CYNGOR DINAS
Casnewydd

PILLGWENLLY

To renew visit / Adnewyddwch ar
www.newport.gov.uk/libraries

Also by Christy Lefteri

The Beekeeper of Aleppo
Songbirds

CHRISTY LEFTERI

The Book of Fire

MANILLA
PRESS

First published in the UK in 2023
This paperback edition published in the UK in 2024 by
MANILLA PRESS
An imprint of Zaffre Publishing Group
A Bonnier Books UK company
4ᵗʰ Floor, Victoria House, Bloomsbury Square, London, WC1B 4DA
Owned by Bonnier Books
Sveavägen 56, Stockholm, Sweden

A CIP catalogue record for this book is
available from the British Library.

ISBN: 978-1-78658-159-4

Also available as an ebook and an audiobook

1 3 5 7 9 10 8 6 4 2

Typeset by IDSUK (Data Connection) Ltd
Printed and bound in Great Britain by Clays Ltd, Elcograf S.p.A.

Manilla Press is an imprint of Zaffre Publishing Group
A Bonnier Books UK company
www.bonnierbooks.co.uk

For Evie

1

THIS MORNING, I MET THE man who started the fire. He did something terrible, but then, so did I. I left him.

I left him, and now he may be dead. I can see him clearly, exactly as he was this morning, sitting beneath the ancient tree, his eyes blue as a summer sky.

The man I left to die was never the type to come to the Kafeneon for a Greek coffee and bougatsa. He kept himself to himself, so I'd only ever greet him in passing, usually as he walked from his massive villa down to the sea and I went up to the top of the mountain with Rosalie, our greyhound. Even then, he hardly made any effort. He smiled with distracted eyes and didn't bother to say a word.

He was a property developer who had moved here from the city. None of us in the village liked him that much, even before the fire. And we have been justified, really.

Was it Aristotle who said that man is a political animal? Not that we are all born to take an active interest in party politics, but it is in our nature to live in a *polis*, a community. So, as a joke, we called this guy Mr Monk, because he seemed to live like the monks in the monastery in Olympia, except that he was rich and very well dressed. I can't even remember his real name.

In mythology, Zeus gave Hermes two gifts for humankind: shame and justice. When Hermes asked if he should distribute these gifts to some and not others, Zeus said no. Every single person should possess these gifts, so that they could all learn to live together. Even in the distant past, people understood the importance of community, so they infused their stories with these morals. Zeus even said to Hermes that if someone was without a sense of shame or justice when doing wrong, they should be put to death by their community.

But that was centuries ago, and we've come a long way since then, right?

Mr Monk stole the world. At least, the part of the world that I call my own. He obliterated beautiful mornings.

For many years, I was in the habit of waking early as the sun rose over the firs. I'd open the window, summer or winter, to take in their smell, to watch them stand so tall and silent. In the winter, they appeared like ghosts through the fog, and in the spring, they were green and fresh and bright, and heather bloomed by the thousands in their shadows. In the summer, light fell upon them so peacefully. At such an early hour, everything was soft and harmless. I used to make a cup of tea and stand for a while, looking out of the window.

My husband was nearly always still asleep. He was the type to work into the night. Only the birds could be heard. Nothing else. Autumn was my favourite season, the way the trees looked like flames upon the hill and the air was crisp. I loved sensing the coming cold, the whisper of it on the wind.

He took all this, the man who started the fire.

The point is that Mr Monk lacked humanity.

To live our lives with a sense of justice in our hearts would inevitably mean seeking fairness in the way people are treated by others – or indeed by us. It's not that Mr Monk hasn't acknowledged what he's done; it's just that he has been trying to get away with it. As for shame – shame is a tradition in Greece! But perhaps Mr Monk would not feel bad for doing wrong had he not been caught in the act. My question is, does he feel guilt? Is he suffering for what he has done to us all?

Then, there's this: yesterday, ash rained down from the sky. My daughter and I both saw it. It is January now, five months since the fire. We were standing at the window that faces the forest. All you can see from that window are the endless skeletons of pines, some taller, others merely stumps. Over this fell the ash.

'It looks like snowflakes,' I said to Chara, who was standing by my shoulder; I could hear her breathing, but she said nothing. My lovely, sweet Chara, too old for her age. Her name means *joy*. Chara with a silent C. She loved it once, loved how its happiness was a secret kept from all who didn't know its origin, like a secret summer garden. There are many secret places in her mind, even at such a young age, and some are not full of light or colour or ancient trees: some are dark; some are empty; they are stark.

The ash began to settle on the fig tree in the garden, the only living tree, where my husband, Tasso, sat quietly, staring out towards the slope of the mountain, his bandaged hands resting on his lap, palms facing up, as if he were waiting for something to fall from the sky. I saw him shudder from the cold, but he did not move to come in; instead, he inclined his head and looked up. Rosalie sat by his feet, as always. His protector.

'The ash is settling,' I said, as if Chara couldn't see it herself.

'It's snow, Mamma,' she huffed and walked away.

I heard her footsteps along the old wooden floor, then silence.

Was it really snow? I looked more closely, strained my eyes. Indeed, it was. It glimmered, sparkled beneath the midday light. It brought new life. Of course, ash would not be falling from above months after the fire. But my mind was playing tricks on me.

I found Chara in her bedroom, sitting cross-legged on the bed, her back facing the mirror, naked from the waist up, her tiny ten-year-old breasts just appearing, round and soft, egg-like, brand-new. She doesn't pay them any attention. At her age, I was dying to buy my first sports bra from C&A. But Chara doesn't want to focus on her future; her eyes are on the past.

She was peering over her shoulder, eyes fixed on her reflection.

'I can't really see it,' she said. 'How does it look now?'

4

We do this every day: record the changes with words. In the last two weeks, less has changed.

I sat down beside her and ran my fingers along her scar, which stretched from shoulder to shoulder and down her spine.

'It's such a beautiful tree,' I said, 'almost exactly like the ancient chestnut tree in the forest. Can you feel the bark?'

She nodded.

'And the branches?'

'Crooked and long,' she said.

'Without leaves,' I added.

'And no chestnuts yet.'

'It's a bare tree,' I said. 'You can see its bare beauty, its grooves and curves and all its potential for new life.'

Chara was no longer looking over her shoulder; her gaze had settled on the magnolia flowers on the duvet cover. She was lost in thought. Then she said, 'Thanks, Mamma,' and turned to give me a kiss on the cheek. It was the most tender kiss. A whisper. It held secrets of both love and resentment, hope and fear. It was so soft, as if she was afraid to assert any of those feelings too strongly.

Since the fire, her love has become delicate: she lives life as if she is holding a butterfly in her palm, afraid that it will die. Before the fire, she was fierce, yes, with everything out there – or at least as much of it as she could already understand; her love was wild and ruthless. If she believed something, she would make sure she was heard. If she felt something, she expressed it with passion. This was how I had taught her.

Now, she is as quiet and subdued as our surroundings.

5

I thank the heavens that my daughter is alive. But she is a ghost of herself. The fire has stolen her, too.

So, this morning, I was out for a walk, as usual. Rosalie must have smelt him, because she ran off the dirt-path, panting; I followed her paw prints.

Mr Monk was leaning against the ancient chestnut tree, staring up at the sky. His blue eyes.

No. I can't think about this now.

Seeing him has brought it all back. It's pressing in on me, the fire. It's seeping in around the door-frame of my bedroom; it's making the necklace around my neck tingle with heat, turning the whites of my eyes red, filling my lungs.

But I won't cry. I have cried too much.

Maybe I can write it down. Maybe, that way, I can allow myself to remember without burning. Remember it as if it is a story from long, long ago. A fairy tale with a happy ending, like one of those in the beautifully illustrated books on the shelf in Maria's Kafeneon.

I will call it *The Book of Fire*.

The Book of Fire

Once upon a Harry Lime.

This is how my dad started every story, even if the story was as true as the nose on his face. Once upon a Harry Lime, once upon a time. Because he was Greek and far from home, he wanted to belong so much that he used cockney rhyming slang whenever he could slip it in, even when it sounded ridiculous. Yes, I remember those days when he came home from playing the bouzouki in smoky London tavernas, wearing that tattered fisherman's hat and reeking of cigarettes. He went out and played music all night, so that he could soothe people's souls and bandage their hearts – people who wanted to be reminded of home, because none of us ever want to forget where we came from. That's what he said. I would hear the key in the lock and wake up to get a hug, and he would tell me a story so that I could get back to sleep.

He would never return to live in his homeland, but I would go in his place, following the man I loved because it already felt like home.

Once upon a Harry Lime, there was a beautiful village inside an ancient forest.

How I wish I could start the story like this and tell you that it all took place a long time ago.

Once upon a time, before the fire, there was an ancient forest.

Before the fire, there were pines and firs that reached up to the sky and a thousand-year-old chestnut that my great-grandad sat beneath at the end of a hundred-day journey. Story goes, he was so exhausted that he stayed beneath the gigantic tree for days, leaning on its twisted bark, in the cool shade. So he rested there among rock lizards and dormice, white-breasted hedgehogs and beech marten, rabbits and deer, red foxes and jackals. He ate juicy purple figs and blackberries. At night, he listened to the howl of the wolves as they roamed the highlands.

Once upon a time, *mia fora ke ena kairo – don't forget your Greek, young lady,* my father would say to me – there was a beautiful village inside an ancient forest on the slope of a mountain that looked down upon the sea.

In this village, there was a bungalow surrounded by fig trees, olive trees and a wildflower meadow. Over the decades and centuries, there were many joys and many losses that could be peeled back like the fine translucent layers of an onion.

There lived a woman who was a musician; people said she was a very good musician, but she didn't often believe it. She taught children how to read and play music, and when school was over for the day, they would visit her house one by one, a book of songs tucked beneath one arm and their instrument in the other.

8

Her husband was an artist. He had the darkest eyes in the world, which twinkled whenever he looked at her. She lit up his darkness, he often said, and this was true. His eyes reminded her of a clear night sky with a million stars. He loved to paint the forest; in fact, he *needed* to paint it, and – if it was up to him – he would have painted it forever.

They had a young daughter whose name meant joy, who had grown up playing in the woods. Through the seasons and the years, she spent so much time there, climbing trees and getting to know the brooks and the creeks, that she was almost like one of the creatures who lived there.

One summer's day, once upon a time, long, long ago—

No. One summer's day – in fact, one day in the summer – a scorching dry day, early in the morning, they all sat at the round table in the garden, having breakfast: yoghurt and honey, cereal and fruit and a big loaf of crusty bread from the bakery. The woman drank tea with milk in it, like her mother used to back in England, and the man drank Greek coffee in a tiny cup, and the girl downed a huge glass of milk. In a while, the man would take his daughter to a roller-skating party in the courtyard at the centre of the village, and the woman had a student arriving: a ninety-three-year-old grandma who was learning to play the drums. They owned a drum set, which they kept in the shed with some of the larger instruments, like the double bass and the harp.

There was quite a wind that day, and it blew the napkins from the table, and they fluttered to the ground.

'Look. Like birds!' the girl said, for she noticed everything, like her father.

'You know, I was brilliant at roller-skating,' the father said.

The girl raised her eyebrows and dunked a piece of bread into her father's coffee.

'If you don't believe me, watch this.' He stood up and did some moves. 'And this is how you brake. Are you watching? You need to learn. Come and try!'

'Let her finish her breakfast – you'll be late to the party,' the mother said. 'Show her when you get there.'

The dog, a beautiful greyhound, was at their feet, waiting for crumbs to fall.

'I had no idea you could roller-skate,' the mother said.

'I've never mentioned it before?'

The mother shook her head and smiled. 'Unless I wasn't listening.'

'I was on them every day. I would even go to the city so I could use the ramps.'

'This is so unlike you! You're so ...'

'So what ... ?' the girl said.

'I don't know. Your pappa is so gentle, I guess, and quiet – it's so unlike him.' She glanced at her husband, and his eyes twinkled, and her long fingers tapped on the table as if she was playing something in her head.

'Well, I guess we all have a side to ourselves that doesn't seem to fit into the rest of us. Like an extra jigsaw puzzle piece. I even used to make my own roller-skates.'

'Huh?' the mother said.

'Huh?' the girl said.

'Woof!' the dog barked, and they all glanced at each other and burst out laughing.

'Oh my god,' the girl said. 'I reckon she understands everything we are saying.' And she ruffled the dog's head and kissed its nose.

And then the dog changed. It was very sudden, as if an invisible person had whispered something disturbing into its ear. Its ears went back, its tail down, and it whimpered. Something had frightened it.

A shiver went through the mother's body, and she stopped tapping her fingers on the table.

'What is it, my love?' the man said to the dog.

The dog ran to the end of the garden, where the forest began. It lifted its head and sniffed the air, then came back to the man and whimpered again, looking into his eyes. Then the sounds began: the sounds of the animals. Birds screeched, wolves howled, and the forest seemed to crack and pop.

'What's happening?' the girl asked.

'Don't worry, sweetie,' the man replied.

But the mother began to worry, especially when she saw that her husband looked frightened. They could not soothe the dog. They rubbed its ears and gave it some bread, but it would not take any. Then the birds flew over, in hundreds and thousands – a black mass like a huge cloud, filling the sky as they fled.

The family all looked up towards the slope of the mountain, which was covered in trees, and saw a tower of smoke.

'Oh my ...' the man mouthed, unable to even speak.

And that was when they saw the trees alight, glowing orange and red as the cracking and the popping became louder. And the sound of the animals became louder, too, coming down the mountain.

They all froze, in exactly the way we imagine we would never do: their limbs stiff, their eyes wide and full of fear. It happened so fast: in a few moments, the smoke was thick and black – a wall, rising high, consuming the sky where the birds had been, swallowing the blue.

They began to feel the heat. They felt it on their skin, in their eyes, in their lungs. The mother even felt the tingle of the gold necklace around her neck.

Then came the sirens, like the sirens of war.

'Let's go,' the mother said, and when the others failed to move, she called, 'Now!' to wake them from their stupor.

They ran out of their bungalow, holding nothing, black smoke blanketing the sky above their heads. And as they ran, the mother looked back, one last time, to see a tall fir light up like a giant candle as it swayed and tipped towards the house. She felt herself swaying like the tree; she felt like she was alight. Her husband pulled at her arm, and they ran, the dog ahead, turning to make sure its family was following. They ran down towards the sea, down down down.

They were suddenly stopped by a police officer, who held open his arms and stood in their way.

'What're you doing, man?!' the husband said. 'Get out of our fucking way!'

But the man was like a robot; he didn't move and didn't listen.

Police cars flashed around them. The officers had herded around fifteen people into a circle, like sheep, and there they stood, some hugging, some alone, all stunned.

'What are you doing?!' the husband said again, sweat dripping down the sides of his face. He held the girl's hand on one side and his wife's on the other.

'You need to stay here,' the officer said. 'Instructions are to stay put. It's safer.' The officer was young and frightened, the whites of his eyes red.

A plane flew overhead through the smoke, low, and they felt its rumble in their chests.

'Don't be ridiculous – the fire is coming! We need to get to the water,' the husband said. 'Let these people go!' And he pushed past the officer before anyone else could stop them.

But after just a few yards, the husband stopped in his tracks and let go of his wife's hand. 'Keep going! I have to go back. I have to look for my father.'

'You can't!' the mother cried. 'It's too dangerous!'

The girl became more frightened and clung on to his arm.

'I have to. Please keep going – you have to get to the sea.'

And he prised his daughter's hands from his arm and went back up, veering to the east where the smoke was less dense, where his father lived alone.

The mother and the girl and the dog could do nothing but continue to run down towards the sea, the greyhound leading the way, until they reached a dead end. A huge white villa blocked their path.

The sky was black now, like a black sea above them.

They had to turn back and run up the path they had taken; then they continued along the road, running parallel to the sea, and took the next path that headed down. But that, too, was blocked by high locked gates – the garden of another house.

13

The mother stopped now. Her lungs hurt; she could taste the smoke. She leant forwards and coughed, hands on thighs. The girl began to cry, and the dog pulled her skirt, urging her not to stop, not to give up now.

The wind was so strong, igniting the fire and pushing it down the hill, ever closer. Their skin felt hot, their eyes running. They followed the dog and ran back up to the main road, where a house was aflame and a car was aflame, where birds lay dead in the street. People in cars were trapped along a narrow road – at least five cars, bumper to bumper, blowing their horns. One woman jumped out of the driver's seat, dashed to the passenger side, where she took a child into her arms and abandoned the car. Others stayed put. Animals ran past, also heading down to the sea. The mother saw a couple of rabbits, a lone jackal and, in the distance, she was sure she saw a wolf dashing between one garden and another.

They had paused for too long – only a few seconds, but it felt too long. The girl was taking long gasps of air, preparing herself to run again.

'Come on!' her mother said.

They kept running and saw some people taking the next path along – a family, an old man with a young boy in his arms, a woman holding the hand of an older woman, two children gripping each other tightly.

The mother and the girl and the dog joined this group, and without words, they all headed again down the path and reached yet another gate. This one was not as high as the previous one.

'We can climb over,' the old man said. 'We have no choice.'

The mother turned to see the fire was about to reach the house they had just passed; the electricity pylon behind it was falling on the roof.

'Mamma,' the girl said, 'the fire is so fast – it's too fast for us.'

'No, it's not,' the mother said.

The old man was strong; he was a machine. He steadied himself and used his hands to help each person up and over the gate. One by one, they placed their feet in his palms and heaved themselves over the gate.

'Grandad,' the little boy called, reaching up with his hands.

'Go, my boy. I'll follow. Go with this nice lady here.'

And the lady took the boy's hand, and the boy went with her reluctantly, crying as he ran. The people ran as fast as they could through the garden of this villa, while the mother stopped to help the old man over the fence, but without something to climb on, he was stuck.

'Grab something!' the mother said.

'There's nothing here,' the old man replied.

The mother scanned her environment. There was a rock garden close by, and she tried to lift one of the rocks to throw it over the fence, but it was far too heavy. The girl was helping her mother, the dog panting, urging them to run, when they heard the old man's voice.

'There's no time,' he said. 'Please, young lady, go. Please leave me.'

And she looked through the fence at the old man's eyes; they were severe and true and full of tears. She reached out her hand, and he did, too, and she touched his fingers through the gate.

'Go,' he said.

And so they continued, and as she ran she cried, for there was something about this old man, something about the sincerity in his eyes, that reminded her of her own father. They ran through the green garden, trampling over the flowers, until they reached, on the other side, a gate. This time it was not locked; they pushed it open, and a path led them down to the sea.

But the fire had now reached the house whose garden they had just run through; it had happened so quickly. The fire had opened its mouth and swallowed it up, and the windows glowed, and the walls began to fall. The dog ran ahead, looking back every few seconds, barking whenever they wavered even a little. The girl was coughing as she ran, but they could see the sea now, shining. They just had to reach it.

They went down down down as the heat pressed in on them, a colossal monster breathing flames just behind them, and at the point when they reached the edge of a low cliff, the girl began to scream. The heat had penetrated her skin, and later, much later, she would tell her mother that she felt as though she were melting.

'Jump!' the mother called and held tight to her daughter's hand.

They jumped at once into the water, the fire a massive wall along the cliff.

Once upon a Harry Lime, once upon a time, there was a mother and a father, a girl and a dog, who lived in a bungalow, in a beautiful village, in an ancient forest that looked down upon the sea.

2

I PUT DOWN MY PEN AND stand up with my fingers still resting on the desk. My legs are weak; there is a tremor in my chest every time I inhale. I look at the wall-clock and see that it is now noon. I have been home now for about an hour. There is a part of me running back to Mr Monk: a ghost of myself who is heading through the dead woods to find him, to call for help, to make sure that he is alive. There is a fragment of myself who never left his side.

But there is also *this me*. The me who knows that Mr Monk should not walk the Earth, does not deserve to. The me who is longing to see real joy in my daughter's eyes. The me who misses my husband, because he is lost and broken and burnt. The me who thinks about the people who died huddled together and the others who didn't make it and the ones who are living alone now, longing for their loved ones, and the homes and the animals that have all gone.

From where I am standing, I have a clear view of the garden. Tasso is sitting outside, silently beneath the fig tree.

This is where he sits all day long. Both his hands are bandaged and resting on his lap, palms facing upwards. I have tried to get him to come inside, believe me, because it is winter now and without the trees to shield us from the wind, there is a chill that I've never felt before on this land.

I realise that my hands are shaking, that my writing in the journal does not look like my own. I wish I could return to yesterday; I wish that I had not followed Rosalie into the woods.

This morning, I took what remained of the path up towards what used to be the denser parts of the forest, where a tiny brook once joined a stream. I wasn't intending to go further than that. It was close to where our bungalow once stood.

We are living now in my father-in-law's house, one of the rare properties to have escaped the flames. My father-in-law, Lazaros, was never found after the fire. Apart from the people who died huddled together – the group the police held back, who we broke away from, because Tasso knew we would otherwise die – there were others who have never been found. At the beginning, we still hoped. People searched, of course: volunteers from other towns, groups with cadaver dogs, scouring the remains, trying to find the twenty-one people who were still missing. Only three of those were discovered and identified.

I still wait for Lazaros sometimes, expecting him to walk through the door, with his eyebrows raised, complaining about one thing or another, demanding that I make him coffee. I would plant a kiss on his cheek and tell him to sit down and have a rest before he gave himself a heart attack, for I loved him like my own father. Tasso waits for him, too. I know it. But I know that he is gone. He is part of the earth now; that is how I like to think of it.

Lazaros's house is a fairly large place with a terrace that looks over a garden. The house itself is warm in the winter and cool in the summer, because it is made of stone. There is a big kitchen with large windows and a living room with shelves full of bric-a-brac, mini statuettes of gods and goddesses, vases, crystals and tiny glasses that look like they were made for elves. Hanging on the living-room walls are fifteen of Tasso's pictures. These are paintings of the forest, one of his mother and one of my grandfather's old bouzouki, the very same instrument that my father used to play all those years ago in London. If my father-in-law hadn't insisted on keeping these paintings at his house, they would have been burnt in the fire, too, along with all the others. There is a low wooden fence along the perimeter of the garden; it is so low that the forest used to brim over it, spilling onto my father-in-law's land. Only one tree survived the fire – the old fig tree that sits in the middle of the garden.

Ours was a village of around five hundred inhabitants, perched in the foothills of a mountain about thirty kilometres from the sea. Many years ago, way before I was born, a main road wound up the slope with a number of small footpaths branching off it. There was a square surrounded by firs, where people used to sit in the shade to drink coffee and chat by the Byzantine church. There was one small shop in the square, but that was the extent of the village. The inhabitants then

19

were farmers and resin collectors. There was a man who made the best feta cheese for miles around; his wife knitted blankets. It was like something out of a storybook.

In the 1960s and '70s, city people who had left the countryside after the Second World War dreamt of returning to build a summer home or to live in the shade of the pine trees. They would be close enough to the city and still on the mainland – only an hour or so by car – so this was a perfect location. Villas slowly invaded the inland wooded areas. They were built anywhere and everywhere, illegally. When I first came here, in the summer of 1989, I could hear construction workers drilling and banging in the distance, wherever I went. The entire infrastructure revealed something anarchic and mischievous. It was a hodgepodge of cafés, tavernas, villas. More and more shops appeared; there were at least twelve dotted about on the footpaths that led down towards the sea, selling all sorts of things – giant beach-balls and Turkish delight, plastic buckets and spades and wicker hats. To the east, on a residential street, is Maria's Kafeneon, which became the hub of the town and is one of the few buildings that withstood the fire.

Still, no matter how many shops and villas were built, one thing always stayed the same: if you followed the road all the way up to the top, you would feel like you could reach the sky, and if there were some clouds floating above, you could stand on your toes and stretch up and pretend to touch them. The landscape below changed over the years, but when I stood at the top of the mountain, I always felt like I was at the top of the world. I did this when I was a girl, long before I emigrated here, when I came to spend my summers in my dad's old village.

Now, that road doesn't even exist. I could still make my way to the top of the mountain, of course, but I haven't ventured that far yet, not since the fire.

I clench my fists to stop my hands from shaking. No matter how strongly I have planted my feet here on the ground, on the wooden floor of this bedroom, I keep thinking about Mr Monk and the ghost of me, the one who is still by his side.

I won't go back. I have no reason to. But I keep seeing him leaning on the old chestnut tree, so nicely dressed, his silver Cartier watch catching the light.

I am still wearing the shoes I had on when I walked through the dead woods, and there is soot on the floor by my feet. I look back and see black footprints leading from the bedroom door to where I stand.

It is 12.30 p.m.

It was 9.30 a.m. when I left the house this morning to take Rosalie out. But today, as I walked, she ran off. It made me anxious. In the past, we used to stroll around freely. I recognised all the tree landmarks; I always knew exactly where I was. Now, I have to be cautious, or I will get lost.

'Rosalie!' I called, but she would not return. I saw her disappearing among the tree-stumps in the distance, her grey fur shimmering in the sunlight.

I was on open and barren land. This was once a field of wildflowers and herbs; it once smelt of rosemary and lavender and thyme. At the end of it, the forest began. Now, the soil is parched, with black stumps of trees jutting out like daggers. Some barely reach my knee; others are six foot high.

I followed her paw prints into these woods. I placed my hand on one of the tall branchless stumps, and then I looked at my palm and saw that it was as black as the land. I came across the ruins of a house that was once the bungalow where Mr and Mrs Chrisofos lived. Only one wall remained standing, and it was crumbling and burnt, and leaning against this wall was a metallic bedframe. I walked on and saw what appeared to be parts of an oven and a sink.

I spotted Rosalie again further along; it seemed as though she had paused for me, looking back, and when she was sure that I had seen her, she continued and ignored my calls. So I followed, deeper still – past the remains of another house, once the holiday home of a couple whose name I could never remember.

Death scattered all around. Death beneath my feet: the ashes of insects and animals and leaves, the ashes of colour, of a million greens and a million browns, the ashes of sounds, of scuttling and sighing, of rustling, of birdsong. I've become accustomed to noticing everything – colours and sounds and changes, big and small. This is Tasso's influence, because I've been with him for so long. He would always point out stuff as we walked. *Look at the way the sunlight falls through the leaves, Irini, just there.* Or, *Look at the colour of the sky today. It is like stone, or bone, or topaz.* Or, *Look at that flower – it's ever so slightly more open than it was yesterday.* Or, *Listen to the scuttling of that animal – I'm pretty sure it's a baby rabbit.* As a result, even when

22

he isn't by my side, my eyes and ears are more open to the world, to its shifting musical rhythms.

I remembered Tasso as I walked, the person he used to be.

Then the forest came alive, just as it used to be. Flowers sprang from the ground and bloomed; tree-stumps grew into full trees, tall firs and stooping pines. There was a rabbit running into a hedge.

Tasso was walking ahead of me, holding an easel.

'Come on, keep up,' he called, 'or I'll miss the morning light. The clouds are gathering – look.' He was wearing a huge rucksack full of paints, holding a wooden easel in one hand and his phone in the other.

I walked faster.

'Come on.' He looked back. 'Or I'm just going to go on ahead of you.'

'Go for it!'

'Will you know where I am?'

'I'll find you.'

He disappeared among the trees, and I slowed my pace to take a breath.

The alive forest vanished before me.

The acrid smell of old fire hit my throat. I wanted to turn back. I kept calling for Rosalie. For god's sake, where had she gone?! Here and there, small lumps of snow glimmered in the morning light.

Then I spotted her in the distance, sitting beside someone. My first thought was: who else would be stupid enough to be out here in the dead woods? As I approached, I saw that it was a man. I thought he was sleeping on the trunk of the thousand-year-old chestnut. It was the way he was sitting, the way his head rested on the tree, the way it tilted slightly upwards, as if he had drifted off deep in thought.

Seeing this tree made me freeze in my tracks. The tree is so large and so old that it survived the fire, half of its trunk black as charcoal, the other half bold and brown, its body twisting out into branches as it always had. This was where my great-grandfather had sat after his long migration from Turkey in 1923; this is where I had my first kiss and where Chara had taken her very first steps. I could see her for a brief moment, her tiny feet in those tiny white trainers her grandfather had bought her, crunching over the leaves, her arms outstretched, smiling, coming towards me.

Rosalie sat on her hind legs, next to the sleeping man, tongue hanging out, proudly waiting for a treat. I fumbled around in my bum-bag to give her one, and then I realised who this man was.

My heart began to thump hard, and my skin burnt, and I began to sweat as if the fire was around me. I remember pulling at the collar of my jumper, just pulling. It was strangling me. Looking at him made it hard to breathe. I was inhaling thick black smoke.

The Book of Fire

Once upon a time, there was a beautiful village, which held a million stories of love and loss and peace and war, and it was swallowed by a fire that blazed up to the sky. The fire ran all the way down to the sea, where it met with its reflection.

At first, the coolness. This is what the mother felt as her body fell into the water. The smooth blue coolness of the water on her skin, submerging her, enveloping her, drawing out the heat. She opened her eyes while she was under and saw the bubbles of her breath floating upwards. She felt her daughter's hand, firmly in hers. She would never let her go, especially now.

When she came up for breath, she turned immediately to see her daughter's face, glistening with water. On every part of her skin, on her cheeks and her gasping mouth and tightly shut eyes, red fire was reflected, as if she were made of flames.

This is an image that will never vanish: her daughter glistening all over with flames, her daughter's entire face alight with water and fire.

How could she ever forget this?

Why did she ever have to see it?

It was as if the world was burning upon the body of this young girl, her girl.

But it was not only her daughter – other people's children floated in the water, only their heads visible. They were floating in the reflection of the flames, while the fire blazed along the shore, along the port, and beyond into all of the forest and up all of the mountain. They both had to tread water to stay afloat; they could not reach the ground.

Their dog emerged from the waves now and went straight for the girl, licking and licking her face as if it was attempting to lick off the flames. The actions of the dog made the girl open her eyes and wrap her arms around its body as it paddled and kept them both afloat.

'I love you so much,' was the first thing to come out of the girl's mouth, and she spoke with a voice that was fifty years older, as if she had seen already the darkness of life. It was the first time she spoke in that way. It just came out of her mouth – in fact, it gushed out like a waterfall; the change was in its intonation, its force, its depth of gratitude and pain, and the dog blinked in response and continued its steady paddle.

The mother heard this change; she heard it through the sound of the flames. It reached her through all the noise.

The mother kissed her daughter's face while they treaded water side by side, but she could not say a single word. It was as if all of the words in all of her mind and heart had fallen out of her into the water. She reached out and squeezed the girl's hand, to make sure that they were truly alive, to let her know that she loved her more than the Earth, more than the universe.

She remembered a conversation they used to have when the girl was tiny. This is how it used to go:

'I love you,' the mother would say.

'I know,' the daughter would reply.

'How do you know?'

'Because you tell me every day.'

'Do you love me, too?'

'Well, yes, of course.'

'How much do you love me then?'

'More than the world!'

'How big is the world then?'

'Bigger than our bungalow!'

'How much do you love me now?'

'Bigger than the oooniverse.'

'How big is the oooniverse?'

'Bigger than Pappa's chilly-night jumper.'

She wished she could speak to her daughter now, say something to override the sound of the waves and the sound of the screams and the sound of the flames.

They treaded the water. They were getting tired, but they could not get nearer to the land, because of the heat of the fire and the thick smoke.

'I feel like my mouth has lots of salt in it,' the girl said.

For now, the water held them safely enough, keeping the fire away.

Where was her husband? The mother scanned her surroundings. They were about ten metres from the land.

The fire made a wall along the edge of the cliff. It had come right up to the sea; it had burnt all the way down the mountain to the cliff that ran adjacent to the port. There were once trees here and houses on the leafy slope. Now, they were all aflame.

Around them, other people treaded water. She could barely see their faces through the smoke, but she sensed their fear, and she heard whispers, moans and sometimes screams. Somewhere beyond, a young child cried and cried and cried. There must have been a hundred people, maybe more. Could her husband be among them? He wouldn't be able to see them. Maybe he had changed his mind and followed after all?

She called his name. She called again, but her voice was lost among all the other voices. The wind rose; the fire along the cliff blazed. The sea lapped around her chin and entered her mouth; she spat out salty water and heaved.

Then she heard her daughter cry.

'I'm so scared,' the girl said.

'I know – I know you are. I am, too.'

'My body is burning – it hurts.' And the girl cried, but the tears were lost among the glittering flames on her face.

'Where does it hurt?' the mother said, desperate.

'My back. It's stinging – it's stinging so much. It's on fire! And my face is hot – it's so hot.'

'Let me see,' the mother said, and she turned her daughter around in the water to face the other way. She held her breath. The back of the T-shirt, soaked, was black; it seemed to be stuck to her skin. She wanted to peel the material away, but she knew this could be dangerous and painful. She exhaled and released a sob.

'What is it?' the girl said.

'Nothing, sweetie. Nothing. It's just a bit red.' She swallowed her tears so that her daughter wouldn't hear her cry.

The mother turned the daughter to face her again, and they both continued to tread water, keeping themselves afloat. 'Take a deep breath, as deep as you can,' the mother said. 'One, two, three.'

And they both gasped, inhaling smoke and heat, and plunged into the water. Holding hands, they opened their eyes. The girl's long hair floated around her head. The mother's green dress floated about her waist. They held on to each other's hands and looked into each other's eyes. The girl's eyes were wide, but they were calmer here under the surface of the water, in this cool underworld that didn't belong to them, that in any moment would spit them out to face again the world from which they had come. If only they were mermaids, then the entire world could burn around them, and they could live far below among the corals and shells and the fish. Slowly, bubbles rose around their faces. The bubbles were small and gentle. They were controlled. *Let's stay under for as long as we can*, they seemed to be saying to each other. *Let's stay here for as many long seconds as we possibly can.* And for those seconds, they floated light and free. One more second. Just one more. And maybe another.

But no.

Time has run out. This world does not belong to us.

And out they emerged, into the orange and the red and the black, their mouths open wide like drowning fish. They spluttered and coughed. The dog licked their faces, first the mother's, then the girl's, then it stayed close to her, so close, alert and vigilant.

'How do you feel?' the mother said, once they had caught their breath.

'I don't feel OK, Mamma. I feel strange.'

The mother nodded and looked around. She saw a lifeboat floating further out, full of people. To her left was a man on a speed boat, pulling children onto it. Before she could even think, the boat was full to the brim and speeding away. Maybe he would be back? In the distance, emerging from the fog, were dinghies and life rafts. They just had to get to them – then they could sail away to safety.

'Do you think you can swim?' the mother asked.

And the girl did not speak this time; she merely shook her head with huge dark eyes as the water lapped at her chin.

'OK, sweetie,' the mother said.

The girl looked tired, her eyes weary and red.

'We have to keep moving,' the mother said. 'We cannot stop moving.'

The daughter nodded and scrunched her eyes, mustering energy from within. They had to keep paddling, but the mother's energy was dwindling too. They could not go closer to the land; the smoke was much thicker there, and they would be far too close to the fire. Embers fell around them; they glimmered and glittered. The mother looked around.

Where was her husband?

She longed to hear his voice. Where was he? She wanted to touch him, to know that he was alive. She imagined him high up on the mountain, surrounded by flames.

She dispelled the thought. She focused on her daughter. 'Let's talk about something else.'

The girl gave her a disbelieving look. 'Like what?'

'Anything,' the mother said. 'Anything at all. Any ideas?'

The girl shook her head. 'You should come up with something, since it was your idea to think of something in the first place.'

'OK, clever clogs,' said the mother, frowning, distracted by the lifeboats in the distance, the flames along the shore, the dark sky. Her mind was on the people in the water and on the reflection of the fire.

The dog paddled and paddled as close as it could to the girl. The girl rested her hand on its back.

'OK, then,' the girl said, 'I'll start. So, do you remember the little badger that got bitten by the neighbour's cat? I looked after him all week. He's in my bedroom. He's probably died.' The girl's eyes filled with tears, and the flames moved within them.

Her mother took both her hands in hers and held them tightly. 'Put your arms around my neck and relax,' the mother said. 'Just completely relax. I've got you.'

The girl put her arms around her mother and rested her head on her shoulder, so that the waves lapped at her chin.

'The water is all red,' the girl said.

'Just close your eyes.'

'OK.'

'Are they closed?'

'Yes.'

There was silence between them now. The mother could barely breathe from exhaustion; she felt sick, but she worked her legs and arms hard as her daughter clung on to her to keep them both afloat.

'Where's Pappa?' the girl asked.

'I don't know, sweetie.'

'Is he OK?'

'I don't know. I hope so.'

'And Grandad?'

'They will both be OK.'

'I'm frightened.' The girl paused, thought for a moment, and said, 'You must be so tired, Mamma. I can paddle by myself again.'

There was silence, because the mother felt that she had lost her voice. She tried to speak, but nothing came out of her mouth – no sound. Her voice was lost, burnt with the flames.

'Can you tell me a story?' the girl asked as she treaded water again. 'Like you used to when I was a little girl.'

So she thought to tell the only story that came to mind in that moment.

The mother mouthed the word *once*. No sound. She could see the word – she could feel her mouth moving – but nothing came out.

Once.

The word grew.

Once.

It grew in her mind; it became so big that she looked up to free her vocal cords and the word filled the entire sky:

'*ONCE!*' she called, exhaling as she did so.

'OK, Mamma,' the girl said. 'You didn't need to scream.'

And the mother laughed, and so did the girl. The mother could see a flash of joy in the girl's eyes. She was so grateful that they were alive, that she was here to feel the aliveness of her daughter, to hear her laughter, the familiarity and the beauty of it.

'You're sooo weird,' the girl said.

'I know,' the mother replied with exaggerated resignation, just as she always did, just to make her daughter laugh once more – but this time, there was silence.

'Once upon a Harry Lime,' the mother said.

'Oh yes!' the girl said. 'I remember!'

'Once upon a Harry Lime, there lived a boy called Vassilios in a Greek village in Turkey. He was fourteen years old.'

'The story of my great-great-grandad!' the girl said and smiled.

The people around them hovered like ghosts among the smoke. There was no sky anymore – no up, no down. The sea and the smoke seemed to merge. The mother could feel herself shivering, despite the heat from the fire.

'Yes! Anyway,' she said, trying to sound as normal as possible, 'his father was a master luthier. He made an array of string instruments, long-necked lutes, like tambours, tzouras and the bouzouki. He owned a tiny old shop, where Vassilios worked as his assistant. Together, they created masterpieces. Vassilios knew he had to keep the tricks of the trade a secret. The first thing he learnt to make was—'

'The sound box,' the girl whispered.

33

'Yes. Which he carved from one piece of maple. His father called this type of wood—'

'Sfendamos.'

'Well done, and—'

'Kelembek in Turkish. They spoke both languages.'

'Even at such a young age, Vassilios was an expert and was steadily becoming a master like his father, because this is all he did, day in and day out, carving the wood until it turned into a beautiful instrument that contained within its heart thousands of songs.'

Her words were interrupted, suddenly, torn from the air with a scream that sliced through the fire and the darkness.

The girl lifted her head, and the mother turned to face the shore, where a young woman stood on the edge of a rock. She had her back to them, and she cried out to the flames:

'Nichola!'

'Nichola!!'

'Nichola!!'

And the sound of her screams and the sound of this man's name tore the mother up. Who was he? Was he this woman's husband, her son, her brother, her father, her lover? Where was he? Had he been eaten by the fire?

Then she began to search the flames. The panic rose again in her chest. Where was her husband? She longed to see his face appearing through the smoke, to see him coming towards them, wrapping them up in his embrace. She wanted to stand on the rock like that young woman and scream out, too. And in the darkness and the heat, she was in awe for this woman, for how she poured from herself all that love and all that fear.

3

I PUT MY PEN DOWN, BUT this time I do not stand up.
I do not want to look out of the window and see Tasso
sitting there, looking so lost. It turns my stomach when
I see him like this. I feel sick, because I do not recognise
him. The man out there is a stranger. Sometimes, I think
that I do not love this man, this intruder who has planted
himself in the garden. I want to go out there and say, *Who
are you? What did you do with the man I love?*

I look at the clock. It is 1 p.m. I open up my palms and
steady them. I imagine that I am holding a bouzouki. I feel
the warmth of the wood, see the glimmer of the mother-of-
pearl on the body of the instrument. My left hand moves
along the neck; my right plucks the strings. I play the opening
stanza of 'Roza' by Dimitris Mitropanos, then my fingers
freeze. The bouzouki vanishes.

I should not be playing anything. How can I allow myself
to use my hands to create music when Tasso cannot paint,
when his hands are burnt and useless? Now, I love him again,

suddenly. I am afraid this love will vanish like the bouzouki. For the moment, I feel this love on my skin like sunshine. Then I imagine how he must be sitting out there, the slope of his back hunched in the chair, the sadness in his eyes, the deep lines on his face from all that thinking and turning things around and around in his mind. This is what Mr Monk did to us all. He took away music and love and beautiful mornings. This is why I cannot go back.

This morning, in the forest, I found Mr Monk leaning on the thousand-year-old chestnut, gazing up at the sky.

'Good morning,' I said, but he did not reply. 'Good morning,' I insisted.

And when again there was no answer, I went closer. His eyes were closed and his head was tilted up as if he fell asleep staring at something in the clouds.

Take a good look at him, I said to myself – yes, take a good look at the man who stole so much.

I stared at his freshly shaven face, the curve of his jaw, the fine lines about his eyes and those laughter lines, mocking – how they were mocking! – even now that his face was as still as the dead woods.

Mr Monk used to live at the top of the mountain. I used to be able to see his house from my living-room window, higher up: a gleaming white villa that was once embedded in the trees like a cruise boat on the waves of a green sea. He had a pool, too. It glinted, mirror-like, among the trees. Mrs Gataki would gossip about him sometimes over iced coffee, while she fanned herself with the crime thriller she was reading.

'Daughter,' she would begin, though I am not her daughter. 'He thinks he's above everybody else,' she'd whisper loudly as she sucked on her thin cigar, a million wrinkles appearing around her lips. 'Never underestimate these kinds of men. They are up there for a reason, and they would eat you alive if they could.'

She said this before the fire happened. And she was right. He wanted to clear the land to build a boutique hotel inside the forest. What he was *intending* to do was to burn five acres to claim a piece of land that was not granted to him.

'But you know,' Mrs Gataki said, months later, after 300,000 acres of forest had been destroyed, 'we live in a world where we can have anything we want, and some people have learnt not to accept no for an answer. Consequences mean nothing – they've probably never had to really face any. *I* am of a different generation, and *you* have a good, sensible head on your shoulders, but Mr Monk ... Well, what can I say? All greed and no kindness. Unfortunately, that gets you somewhere.'

Like I said, Mr Monk was a solitary man, kept himself to himself. He was always alone and paid no interest to anyone or anything around him. On the weekends, however, someone would visit him in a red Beetle, which I would spot appearing through the trees on the country path.

Rosalie was standing beside him now, sniffing at the ground. I wanted to approach him, nudge his shoulder to wake him up, ask him what he was doing here. But I couldn't help myself – I just stood there, staring at this man who had taken so much from us. I couldn't turn away. I looked at him in the same way that you might masochistically – or perhaps with some kind of morbid curiosity – fix your eyes on something horrific or frightening.

Yesterday, I went with Rosalie down to Maria's Kafeneon, where all the villagers still gather – the ones who did not flee on the boats that came in the night. They are the ones who, like us, will not leave the forest, the ones whose houses have either escaped the fire – though there are not even a handful – or who are still living in half-burnt properties, or who have moved out of the village, not too far, staying in hotels or hostels like refugees.

The resident cat rubbed himself against my leg, purring. I stroked his ears, feeling the bare, burnt tips, running my hand along his back and up to the stump of his tail.

The cat appeared a week after the fire, charred and almost dead, but not quite. Maria, the owner of the Kafeneon, nursed him – nursed him as if he were a baby. Now, the cat never leaves the café, not even to hunt.

I smelt the coffee and sighed. I was safe here.

Maria's is the only place in the world where you don't have to ask people how they got burnt, where their scars came from. Everyone knows. Maria runs the place smoothly. She makes sure everyone is OK. This is my haven. Everyone here understands each other. There is no need for formalities or anything like that.

Silver teapots and tea lights hang from the wooden beams. Grapevines shelter the tables from the sun.

I headed for the daybed with the floral blanket. It sits beneath the massive mirror with the latticed frame in the alcove at the back alongside the bookcases and lit-up globe.

The TV was on in the background – it hangs on the wall by the entrance to the kitchen. A black-and-white film was playing, a silent movie, and when the adverts came on, they were too bright and too loud, but no one moved to turn down the volume.

I ordered my coffee from Maria. 'The usual,' I said, and she knew. There is a comfort in this, especially when you have lost so much.

However, as much as I wanted to hold on to that feeling, another took over: the place was so quiet in comparison to how it used to be. Mr and Mrs Chrisofos would have once been sitting at the table beneath the vines; she would continually play solitaire with a deck of cards, and he would lean back in his chair, slowly drink his coffee, order another as soon as it was finished, and make casual chit-chat with all the locals.

There were so many people missing now. Ghosts flickered in my mind wherever I looked. At the table by the lantern would have sat the retired schoolteacher, Kyria Petrou, with her laptop, forever typing something. I wished I had asked her what she was working on.

Mrs Gataki arrived. She came straight towards me. She sat in the green armchair, greeted me and applied a thick layer of bright-pink lipstick to her wrinkled lips. Holding her latest crime thriller, she fanned herself with it, as always, even though it wasn't hot. I could see the cobweb of burnt skin reaching out of her white blouse, up her neck, smoothing out her wrinkles into thicker creases, then opening up again like a flower and crawling up the side of her jaw to meet a gold heart-shaped stud – the earrings she always wore.

I couldn't get used to it. I kept picturing her without these scars, like a hologram flickering over her – her former self.

She greeted the locals around her with a smile or a raise of her tattooed eyebrows. There was old Nicholas with his cane and his worry beads. There was the professor, in the denim knee-length shorts he always wore, playing a game of tavli with Mrs Dimitra, the woman who once owned the convenience store. She wore a thousand rings and bracelets. She used to jangle when she picked up the jars to place them on the shelves. A few young men sat together, drinking Greek coffee and eating milk pies. They used to work at the garage, which also burnt down. Their fingernails were still black with grease. They raised their hands at us both, and we smiled in response.

'Daughter,' Mrs Gataki said, then, 'Oh,' she added, looking at the TV. 'Gosh, *The Adventures of Villar*. From the 1920s. The oldest Greek film to be saved and restored – did you know that? The Greek Film Archive's department of restoration and conservation did a great job. We must always conserve our portraits. I used to watch this with my grandad. Look at them dance!'

I glanced up at the TV. A Black jazz band was playing, and the people danced under its rhythms, its richness and beauty, by the seaside.

'Just look at them play their beautiful music, and look at them dance!' Mrs Gataki said this as if the thought of these things was such a rare treasure, and her eyes lit up.

My heart sank. I focused not on the dancers at all, but on the musicians, probably from New Orleans, and on the instruments that they held so naturally in their hands, at the saxophone and trombone. My instruments were all destroyed in the fire. My piano and bass, my clarinet and harp – all gone. Then my heart sank further as I thought of my great-grandfather's bouzouki, the one he carried with him from Turkey to Greece in 1923. I cherished that instrument. It used to hang on the wall of the hallway, and I would take it down once a month to clean and tune it.

I watched the people dance and the musicians play, and I felt a deep sadness. We cannot restore anything that has been burnt to ashes.

Maria brought my coffee and, without even asking Mrs Gataki what she wanted, set a small, clear cup of mint tea on the table.

The musicians played; the people danced.

'Daughter,' Mrs Gataki said, 'I don't like talking about myself – you know that more than anyone – but I had a terrible night. I tossed and turned until 6 a.m.'

'What was on your mind?' I asked.

'It's not that I'm thinking anything. It's the loneliness. It's the missing. My husband ...' she paused. 'Even the sounds of the trees – they are missing, too.'

'I know,' I said. 'I feel it, too.'

'At least your husband is still alive. At least you have him there. I can't bring my husband back.' She didn't say this with bitterness but with an immense sadness, stressing the words *at least*, putting weight on them so that they seemed to break open in her mouth like an egg, out of which poured a well of darkness.

41

'Yes,' I said. 'You are right.' I wanted to add, *But he is far away — he's no longer with me, and you have no idea how much I miss him.* However, I felt it wasn't right to say these things to her. Her husband didn't survive the fire.

I expected her to continue, to say what she normally said: *They need to pay for what they have done to us — the government, the police, the fire brigade. We need to get justice for their negligence. The police trapped all those people, Irini! How many people died huddled together? Was it fifteen? They should have still been living with us here. The police trapped them there and they died holding on to each other like the people of Pompei. The fire brigade were not prepared. They were underfunded, yes, but they could have still responded better. They failed us, daughter! You do know that, right?! And the government ... pah!*

But she said none of these things. She remained silent and watched the musicians play and the people dance in the black-and-white world on the screen by the kitchen, where sweet smells wafted towards us. And if only, I thought, we could allow ourselves to become completely lost in that world.

'It's people's greed that is the problem,' she said finally. 'We know that for sure, don't we?' She raised her purple tattooed eyebrows as if in shock. 'I am not surprised, however!' she continued. 'Fires are started time and again so they can build illegally. It's been going on for years, because the authorities take no action against it. They are saying it is the illegally built summer houses that are to blame. Pah!'

She took a big gulp of her tea, without waiting for it to cool, and her eyes and face reddened from the heat. Then she reached into her clutch bag, which was on the table beside her, and took out a long brown cigarette. She held this to her lips without lighting it. She wore a fine layer of glittery lavender eyeshadow, which shimmered on her lids beneath the light of the screen.

Then the dancing people were no longer on the TV. The film had been interrupted by the news, with an update about the ongoing inquiries into the fire brigade's response to the fire – at one point they showed footage of the prime minister making his speech immediately after the fire.

'As prime minister of this country I assume full responsibility for this tragedy, this is what the prime minster of a country should do. But, I urge you *all* to do the same. We have to show respect for the truth, no matter how hard it may be. There were many contributing factors, including the changing climate. This region is one of the fastest warming anywhere ...'

Suddenly, one of the young men from the garage stood up and dashed a slice of milk pie at the screen. '*Malaka*!' he called. 'Say what you want when it suits you!'

The other men calmed him down and brought him back to his seat. Milk pie dripped down the prime minister's face.

I looked over at Mrs Gataki. She was leaning back in her chair as if she had written the scene and was satisfied with the way it had unfolded.

'What do you expect?' she said, fanning herself once more.

I felt the anger in that place. I felt the heat as if the fire was still burning in the surrounding forest. And it got inside me, the fury mounted. Our home was taken from us by criminals. The government allowed it to happen. They might as well have dropped a bomb on us. To make matters worse, the fire brigade did not respond as they should have. The government did not send adequate firefighting forces quickly enough; they allowed the fire to flare up and burn everything in its path. Why were they so complacent, so badly prepared? Then, when the police arrived, they told people to stay put; that was their fatal advice.

But none of this would have happened in the first place if it wasn't for Mr Monk.

So, you can imagine how I felt when I saw Mr Monk in the forest this morning. But while I stood there, waiting for him to wake up, perhaps to sense that someone was staring at him, all of a sudden, I saw something that I hadn't noticed before. Around his neck was the noose of a thick white rope. I hadn't seen it until I came closer – it had been hidden by the collar of his coat. The end of the rope was not visible; it seemed to hang behind him.

I went closer. The skin around the noose was red raw. Instinctively, I looked up and saw that a large branch above his head had broken in two. Part of it was next to him on the ground like a severed limb.

I took a step back and froze. My hands began to shake. I saw myself as if from a distance, standing in this forest, facing Mr Monk, who was either dead or alive, as if I was looking at one of Tasso's paintings. So many times, I have imagined myself walking inside Tasso's paintings, the ones he did before the fire, when the forest was alive and full of all sorts of creatures. They would appear in his paintings – splashes of colour, but I knew exactly what they were. How

I wished I could walk into the paintings that hung on the wall and melt into the softness of the oils – become a dash of colour, a fragment of light, with the other creatures of the woods.

Rosalie sniffed around Mr Monk's head. She tugged at the fallen rope that hung over his shoulder, and I told her to sit. This was not the time to play. This rope was the culmination of a very dangerous game played by a greedy man.

4

I'VE LOVED TASSO FOR NEARLY my whole life.

Those hours when I was in the water stretched out into an eternity. I still live there sometimes, in that eternity, where he is neither alive nor dead, where I will either feel his arms around me or never feel them again – where his black eyes will twinkle or turn to ash. All I knew then as I treaded the water with our daughter and our dog was that I would never love another man the way I love him.

But now, I don't know how I feel. I stand up and see him sitting there, beneath that tree with his bandaged hands on his lap. The tree is bare. His eyes are fixed on something in the near distance. I wish he would stand up and come here and help me and put his arms around me, tell me everything will be OK. But that man – the man who was capable of sadness and joy and empathy – that man has gone.

I remember Tasso scanning the forest with his eyes, before the fire, with a slight shift of his head, like a wild animal. I remember one summer, just before Chara was born, he was mixing colours on the palette, applying them gently but briskly onto a blank canvas. While he painted, I sat on a fallen bark, playing my bouzouki, and then I lay flat on my back on the soft ground, staring up at the sky through the leaves. I listened not only to the sound of the forest but to Tasso mixing his brushes in the glass of water or opening the bottle of turpentine and pouring it into the old coffee cup. Now and then, I took a peek at what he was doing. Some artists prefer to keep their work hidden until it is finished, but he didn't mind me looking. He could see colours where others see only shifting shapes: a splash of purple where the shadows sleep beneath the trees; a streak of pink on the tips of the leaves where the sun rests; and there was light where it seemed that light shouldn't exist. In this painting, there was a subtle glow emanating from around the roots of the chestnut tree as it met the soil; it was so subtle, like a sheen, but it told me that life existed in places I did not expect.

I am suddenly surrounded by the smell of pine and heather and thyme and the crackle of chestnuts as they fall onto the conifer needles.

Then another memory comes to me. Once, after Chara was born, he painted us both while I was feeding her. It was a day in spring, and he painted our flesh, mine and hers, and the woods around us, our skin picking up the colours of the forest, and within the colours of the leaves and the trees was a whisper of our skin in its shadows and light. Chara and I had become part of the forest.

I want to go outside and tell him what I've just remembered. I want to shout and shake him and tell him to wake up. What

47

right does he have to lock himself away? I wish he would get up and paint what exists now, paint it with all its darkness, all its honesty.

But his bandaged hands rest on his lap, in the same position, palms facing upwards. The bandages are thick; they seem to weigh down his entire body, as if they are made of concrete. Tomorrow, the nurse will visit to change them.

Before the fire, he would wake up late after working on his paintings until the early hours. I would hear him turn on the shower and then pad along the old wooden floor with his bare feet. After that, he would come down and make breakfast for us both. I would always wait to eat with him. He would warm up koulouri in the oven and spread it with butter; he would lay the table with olives and yoghurt, honey and fruit. While he was doing all this, I would slowly make some Greek coffee. We did all this in silence usually. This was my favourite part of the day, so gentle and quiet and rhythmic.

Once we'd finished breakfast, he would clean up the kitchen, and he was meticulous, making sure the white marble worktops were gleaming before he folded the tea towel, neatly placing it by the sink. This was when I knew he was finished. Often, by this time, I would be at the kitchen table, planning some of my lessons for the afternoon. Then he would gather his sketchpad and paints and head out, to capture a new scene or improve one that he had already begun.

In the daylight hours, he would explore, observe and sketch. It was at night, when I was asleep, that these scenes would really emerge and come to life. I loved waking up in the morning, going to the large shed at the back of the house and seeing what he had done during the night. I found his paintings to resemble dreams at times, the types of dreams that are so real you cannot tell the difference, that contain a certain indescribable freedom and a deeper kind of know-ledge that our conscious mind does not possess. It was as if, during the night, he went to places in his head and in his memory of the forest that I could never reach.

When he returned from the forest in the afternoon, I would be almost ready to start teaching, but we had about half an hour or so to sit down together and have a drink. In the winter, we sat in the living room by the fire; in the summer, we sat outside by the lemon tree in our garden. I loved the smell of the lemon blossom. He would always pick one of the blossoms and hand it to me to smell; he would place it so delicately in my open palm. Then he would watch me while I dug my nail into the blossom and breathed in the scent.

'Gosh,' I might say. 'It reminds me of my garden back in England.'

He would laugh at this. 'That's such an unlikely thing for this lemon tree to remind you of.'

'I know, right!'

He was a creature of habit, and I didn't mind that at all, because in all our rhythms and repetitions, new and beautiful things emerged.

'You know, my mum loved those blossoms, too,' he said once, in the early years of our marriage.

'No, I didn't know that.'

He had a strange habit of telling me something brand-new that he'd had many opportunities to mention before but for some reason never had. He was constantly unravelling to me.

'Do you know that painting of the lemon tree at my dad's house?'

'Sure. It's beautiful.'

'That was the first painting I did after my mother died. I made it for her.'

'I didn't know that.'

It was during this conversation that he suddenly became very sad.

'Are you thinking about her?' I asked.

'No, it's not that.'

'What then?'

'It's just that every time I go out into the forest, I see how it has changed.'

This reminded me of what he had said about his mother all those years ago, before she died, when we were both still teenagers. He had said that every time he saw her in the mornings, he realised that she had changed, that she had died a little bit more through the night. At the time I found this so sad and so frightening that I searched for these changes in her myself, but I did not see them. But Tasso saw something, some small thing that had altered and sent warnings to his heart. In this conversation, he was saying something similar about the land.

'What do you see?' I asked.

'The earth is drier. The roots of the trees are drier; the leaves and flowers are growing differently and at the wrong times ... My dad is right.' I knew he wanted to say more, but he stopped speaking. He was never great with words.

But from that day forth, his paintings changed; they seemed to gradually lose their glow, and I did see it. I did see the changes in his landscapes.

This was just before Chara was born. Later, he would get up early just for her. He would always call her *agabi mou*, my love.

'What would you like for breakfast, *agabi mou*?'

'Cereal!'

'Which one, *agabi mou*?'

'The one with the holes!'

'The one with the holes?'

'You know, Pappa – the one that's like baby doughnuts!'

'Do you mean Cheerios?'

'Yes!'

'Didn't we have this conversation yesterday?'

'Yes, but I forgotted.'

Then she would grab his stubbly face with both her hands and give him big slobbery kisses on both his cheeks.

'Oh my god, it's like chicken-bum kisses!'

She would giggle and giggle and giggle. Later, she would ask him, 'What does that even mean, Pappa? Chicken bums don't kiss!'

However old she was and no matter what discussion they were having, he would pour the cereal and the milk for her and sit down beside her while she ate. She loved this time with him.

These days, he stays in the garden all day, thinking. Or perhaps he is not thinking. Maybe his mind is as blank as the forest. I can't take seeing him like this, so last week I called a psychiatrist to come and speak with him, a man who Maria from the Kafeneon recommended.

The doctor came a few days ago, wearing black-rimmed glasses and a thick winter coat and holding nothing in his hands – not a briefcase or a rucksack, no notes, no laptop.

'Is he eating?' was the first thing the doctor asked me.

'Yes. Barely, but yes,' I replied. 'Though he doesn't even look at me. It's like I don't exist.'

'It's cold out here,' he said, looking around at the garden and resting his eyes beyond, upon the dark and burnt land.

'Please,' I said, and he turned to face me. 'I want my husband back.'

I was mortified that I had been so open, that I was begging this man as if he were a magician.

He simply nodded. I led him through the garden to the fig tree, where Tasso was sitting, and left them alone.

About an hour later, the doctor knocked on the kitchen door, and I let him in. He stood for a moment, rubbing his hands together. He took off his glasses. 'So, he sits there all day?' he said.

'Yes, most of the day. He comes in at night. I think the cold gets too much for him then. Did he speak to you?'

'We did manage to have a talk, yes. I have prescribed him medication for depression. It should start working within a month,' he said. 'Hopefully you will begin to see a difference. In any case, I'll be back to see him same time next week.'

Now, in the quiet of my room, there is something that Tasso said that keeps returning to me. *Every time I go out into the forest, I see how it has changed.*

I see Lazaros now, as if he is right in front of me. He is standing in the forest in the dappled shade of the trees, wearing that wicker baseball cap he loved so much.

Look at this, my girl, he says, tearing up a clump of earth from the ground and crumbling it in his hands. *It shouldn't be this dry right now and the summer is coming. The winter and spring rainfall has decreased. The winter rainfall is so important. Bone dry. Bone bone bone dry. Like dead bones. Not even alive bones!* He has a heavy grey brow, and his eyes are sharp beneath. *It is that simple. The entire earth is changing, we have neglected our home, Irini.*

He said this slowly and with a kind of restraint I had not heard in his voice before, hesitating deeply, as if these words were stones upon a great plane of water and he had to make it from one to the other in order to find his way to safety. Then he looked up, into my eyes, and a chill went through me. *The earth here*, he said, returning his gaze to the soil in his hand, becoming his normal practical, fiery self again, *it has not been saturated enough and the summer is coming. But no one will listen, it's like my tongue is growing hair!* He stuck his tongue out to show me. *I have said it so many times.*

Lazaros said the same thing to me and Tasso whenever we had a dry winter and spring, which was becoming more frequent, with such authority and certainty. Even in the changing climate, a few winters were wetter than normal, but this did not ease his fears. 'This is due to natural climate variability,' he would say, 'the drought will return, you'll see.' I would kiss him on the cheek and tell him not to worry, that he needed to learn to worry less, that everything would be OK.

This memory fills up my mind like sunlight fills up a darkened room. It is telling me something I have forgotten. It is too bright. It is too much for me.

The Book of Fire

'I'm getting tired, Mamma,' the girl said. 'I feel heavy.'

The mother was facing the daughter; they were both still treading water. Their arms and legs had not stopped moving for so long now. The mother could see that the girl was in pain; she winced and took deep breaths and looked up at the sky as if she wanted to give up.

'We have to keep our heads above the water,' the mother said. 'Keep treading. Pretend that you are on your bicycle and we are riding up the mountain, and we will soon get to the top and look up at the birds flying in the open sky.'

The girl grimaced. 'But I'm so tired.'

'Are you still wearing your shoes?'

The girl nodded.

'Lift up your foot.'

The girl awkwardly lifted one foot after the other, and the mother pulled off her shoes. They watched the shoes slip away into the depths.

The mother saw that people's clothes were floating in the water. Then she noticed that among these clothes were also bodies. She could see the arms of a man, the top of his head and his puffed-up shirt. She turned her daughter around so that she wouldn't notice.

She could hear explosions coming from the land.

'What is that, Mamma?' the girl asked.

'I don't know, sweetie.'

The heat from the flames was unbearable. She wanted to swim further out, deeper into the sea, but they needed to stay close to the others, to where the people in the lifeboats could see them.

The mother made sure that her daughter was facing away from the fire, but it was hard. She couldn't protect her, and she was becoming more and more tired herself. The dog, who was paddling away beside them, was panting heavily, its eyes red. How long had they been here? Maybe an hour, maybe more. They had drifted a little further out, but it was still too hot to bear.

The mother noticed an old lady nearby; she was helping herself to stay afloat by leaning on a box. The waves lapped at the box, and the old lady's face was just visible above it.

As they got closer to her, it became clearer that what she was leaning on was a large wooden beer crate.

'If it wasn't for this,' the old lady said, seeing that the mother had noticed her, 'I'd be dead. I always used to complain to my husband that he drank too much, and look now how the drink has saved me!'

The mother didn't respond.

'I'm not sure about my daughter, though,' the old lady continued. 'We came running down together. We kept getting stuck. I turned back, and she was gone. She vanished, as if she were never there.'

This made the mother think of her husband, and she forced herself not to scan the port.

'I was visiting her – my daughter. She comes and picks me up and brings me here once a week on Saturday, because I live in the middle of nowhere, and the only shop by me isn't that good – too expensive. We have coffee and cake out on the terrace, then she takes me to the shops, so that I can get my groceries and stuff. It's nice to have company while you're picking out tomatoes. She laughs a lot, my daughter – has a good sense of humour like her dad did. She has his hair, too, so fine and almost blonde.'

And with her words, the vanished daughter materialised in the mother's mind, and she wished she would appear again in reality with her fine, blonde hair and laughing face.

'Is that your daughter?' the old lady asked.

The mother nodded.

'Can I hold on to the crate with you?' the girl asked.

'Well, of course, my dolly!' the old lady said, her eyes waking up as she looked at the girl. 'I apologise. I should have offered, myself! And there is room for us all.'

The mother and the girl rested their arms and elbows on the crate, and they both seemed to sigh at the same time. This allowed them to rest for the first time, and they let their legs float up behind them. But now that the girl had stopped paddling, the mother could see even more clearly the pain

57

in her eyes. The girl winced and turned her head this way and that, trying to make herself comfortable. Then she rested her head on top of her arms, which held on to the crate.

The old lady's eyes were kind, and she seemed to carry a gentle sadness upon her, as if she had always carried it and it was from this sadness that her love emanated. This was the impression the mother had of the old lady, and on any other day, she would have asked her questions about her daughter and about where she lived and about her husband.

The old lady was quiet now. Perhaps she was tired of speaking to someone who was not responding, or perhaps she was just *tired*. The mother looked out into the haze beyond.

Nobody had come for them. Some lifeboats had come and gone. The mother could see one boat in the far distance, collecting more people from the sea, but no boats had come this way, not yet.

It was as if the three of them were together now, but the old lady said nothing more. Her tiny eyes twinkled from the flames, and now and then she forced a little smile, as if this were the only thing left to do.

It felt like night had fallen, but this was impossible. It had been early morning when they sat together in the garden to have breakfast. How much time had passed since then? They must have been in the water for at least three hours. The mother had watched the movement of the sun through the smoke, its soft and barely visible glow as it moved across the sky.

She was desperate to see her husband. She searched the faces of the people close to them. She forced her eyes to focus, and far in the distance, above the horizon, she saw a slither of blue appearing behind the clouds, like a slice of magic. But this sky, this beautiful sky, still existed behind the smoke. Normal life still existed beyond. She tried to hold on to this thought.

The old lady sighed, and the mother looked again at her eyes. This time, the old lady did not smile; she was staring out at the flames. The mother could see her eyes taking in their surroundings: the water and fire that had spread across the land all the way to the edge of the cliff, the fire that towered above them, the smoke that surrounded them, and the water that was deep and too warm to be refreshing.

Now that the girl had had a rest, she looked with curiosity at the old lady beside them.

'It's OK, Grandma,' the girl said, because she was taught to always address anyone older than her politely. 'It's really OK that you forgot to ask us to hold on. You're old – you can't remember things so well.'

The old lady chuckled.

'It's true,' the girl said.

'I agree, dolly,' the old lady said, and she smiled broadly and from the heart, as if for a moment this was a normal day and they had met at a café by the sea.

The dog was paddling right beside her. Its tongue was hanging out from thirst.

'Mamma,' the girl said. 'Can you say the rest of the story for us to hear?' She turned to the old lady. 'Mamma is telling a story about my great-great-grandad, who travelled from Turkey to Greece during ...' She paused and looked at her mother.

'The population exchange of 1923.'

'He was a minority!' the girl said, very proud of herself for knowing this. 'I'll tell you what I know first.'

The old lady nodded.

'When the Ottoman Empire ruled everyone in Greece, people kind of lived peacefully. I say *kind of*, because it wasn't great and a lot of bad things happened, but it wasn't as bad as what happened after. They lived in different groups, which were called millets.'

The girl glanced over at her mother to make sure that this was correct, and her mother nodded.

'The leaders of these millet thingies reported back to the big guy, who was called the sultan. Those were the rules. It worked OK. There were the Sunni Muslims – they were the biggest – and the Greek orthodox – that's what my great-great-grandad was. There were the Armenians, the Jews, the Catholics.' She counted off each one in her head, looking upwards. 'Maybe more, but I can't remember.'

The girl paused to take a breath and to make sure that she had an attentive audience.

The old lady nodded with interest. 'Well, you're a clever girl, dolly,' she said with a smile.

'Yes,' the girl said. 'My teacher says that *all* the time.'

And once again, the old lady chuckled. 'I like you. I think I have found my new best friend.'

And for the first time, the girl smiled, perhaps forgetting for a moment where she was, so that she was for a while in a bubble with her new-found friend and the Ottomans.

'The thing is,' the girl said, 'the big Ottoman guys were really, really doomed. Everyone knew it. And then – I can't really explain this bit; it's a bit too complicated – but loads of stuff changed. All the groups wanted to be the big, powerful people. Then they all started to really hate each other and to be afraid of each other – and this is always, *always* bad. Always.' The girl looked very seriously at the old lady.

'Yes, dolly,' the old lady said. 'You couldn't be more right.'

'The Turkish group wanted to get rid of the Armenians, and they did – that is a whole other story! Then the Greek group were afraid the Turkish group would do the same to them. But the Turkish group were really afraid of the Greek group, because they thought the Greek group wanted lots and lots of power – like, all of it, like wanting all the cake at a party when you should really have only one slice.'

'Well,' the old lady said, 'I've never heard it explained better than that.'

Then the girl scrunched up her face and tears dropped from her eyes. 'My back hurts a lot. I'm trying not to think about it, but it's hard.'

The old lady reached out and touched the girl's hand, which rested on the crate.

'I'll continue the story if you like?' the mother said, and they both nodded. The dog licked the tears from the girl's face, and a clear note of laughter escaped from her mouth and flew up to the black sky like a free bird.

Another explosion came from the burning land.

The mother braced herself, swallowed her fear and tore herself away from the present, finding deep in her mind the teenage boy in the old musical shop by the port.

'My great-grandfather, Vassilios, made musical instruments with his dad,' she began. 'Even at such a young age, Vassilios was an expert and was steadily becoming a master like his father, because this is all he did, day in and day out, carving the wood until it turned into a beautiful instrument that contained within its heart thousands of songs. This is how Vassilios saw it – that the instrument already existed within the wood, and that it was his job to find it. During his lunch break, he would have – even at such a young age – a few cups of strong Turkish coffee with his father. They would sit out on the street, facing the big cargo ships and glittering lights of the port and the fine layer of smog that enveloped everything and made the town appear heavenly when the sun shone bright. Their little shop was located in Turkey on the Pontic port of Samsun on the southern coast of the Black Sea.'

The mother noticed that all eyes were on her: the old lady, the dog and her daughter all stared at her, their attention fully on the story, and she felt for a moment pleased that they had managed somehow to create a pocket of normality in all this chaos. The old lady still had her hand resting on the girl's hand, and the girl seemed to be comforted by this, for she did not move an inch.

'His grandmother,' the mother proceeded, 'would bring them a tray of kiofte or some lahmacun. Vassilios's mother had died giving birth to him, so he lived with his father and grandmother in a flat above the shop. After lunch, Vassilios would take his time to sand the sound box, carefully and gently, with soft strokes, round and round until the wood was smooth and the grain looked like ripples of sand, and then he would finish it with lacquer.

'One hot day in September, Vassilios sat out on the little table alone. They were busier than usual, making some instruments for a wedding that was taking place next month. His dad told Vassilios that he would join him for a short break in a while. Vassilios sipped his coffee and ate the lahmacun that his grandmother had made, licking his fingers, looking out to sea, where a large American cargo ship had been stationed for a week. One of the naval officers walked past and nodded at him – he was on his way to have coffee with the Tobacco men. The officer usually stopped to say hello to Vassilios and to marvel at the instruments on the display table outside, but today he was in a mad rush. Vassilios was always polite to the naval officer, but he felt his insides tremble as he spoke to him each morning – he hated being reminded why the ship was there in the first place, because of the terrible tensions between the Greeks and the Turks. The Turks had already begun to move huge bodies of people, marching them away from their homes. The Turkish nationalists feared that this population – the Ottoman Greeks – would support a Greek army's landing on the coast, so they wanted to get rid of them, to destroy them as much as possible. There were robbings and killings and all sorts of things. Local Greek men had been marched off to "labour battalions". Vassilios had a friend in the next village called Nicos whose father had been taken away in broad daylight and he had never returned. The neighbours whispered. They told stories of men dying in terrible conditions after months on the road. As a result of all this, American warships were constantly present at the port.

'To calm himself, Vassilios rested his eyes on the Pontic mountains that rose to the east, the way the midday sun made them appear hazy. But something in his peripheral vision was disturbing him, and though he tried his best to focus on the mountains, his attention was being pulled away, and eventually he gave in and turned his head to see a tower of smoke rising from the next village. He put his coffee cup down and stood up. He had seen these towers of smoke before, but this time it was closer.'

The mother stopped the story here, because of the way her daughter and the old lady were looking at her. In their eyes, she could see the towers of smoke that rose from the land around them. She knew where the story was going, so why did she decide to tell this one now? They were trapped and surrounded, but the story of young Vassilios gave them something to connect to, because stories of long, long ago are palatable, especially if they tell of hardship being overcome.

'I just want to ask one thing,' the old lady said, 'and then you can continue with your brilliant story. I just want to know – because I can't take it – does Vassilios escape whatever fire it is that is coming?'

'Yes,' the mother said, and the old lady breathed a sigh of relief and nodded, as if the mother had told her that everything would be OK for them, too.

There is something about stories that allows us to process the present. We listen to tales of tribulations overcome so that we might imagine we can survive ours. Children listen to the same fairy tale time and time again because there is a puzzle in their hearts that they unknowingly need to solve.

But what no one mentioned in that moment was this: where was the old lady's daughter? Where was the girl's father? How would their stories end?

And how, later, and later still, will it all be remembered?

5

M R MONK WAS LEANING ON the tree, unconscious in the dead forest, and all I could do
was stand there and stare at him. In my defence,
freezing is our third stress response after fight-or-flight:
playing dead in the face of danger. Sure, in reality, I was
not in immediate danger, but my body did not seem to
know this. Inside I was burning. Inside existed the fire
that this man had caused. It surrounded me. I could even
smell it – I was sure I could smell it – the burning of
everything.

Rosalie kept sniffing the noose around his neck, and then
she came towards me, pulling at my trouser leg, forcing me
to snap out of it, to react, to take action.

The first thing I managed to do was feel his wrist for a
pulse. He was definitely alive. 'Mr ...' I began, realising that
I didn't know his name. 'Excuse me ... are you OK?'
I put my hand on his arm and shook it a bit.

Just then, his eyes opened, slowly, and he groaned.

'Are you OK?' I said, kneeling down. I checked my phone, but there was no signal.

His eyes were open and red, and he glanced up at me and then closed them again, wincing.

'I'm going to help you.' But even as these words left my lips, a more disturbing thought came to mind – had he attempted suicide or had he been lynched? What would he have stood on? Unless he climbed the tree? My thoughts whizzed around.

'Mr ... Did you try to kill yourself?'

He said nothing.

'Can you try to get up? I can't get a signal on my phone here. I will need to go and get help, and that will mean leaving you.'

All this must have taken about a minute, give or take. I was scared, and my heart was beating fast, my mouth dry. Now, I had become afraid that this man would die, because in those moments I had forgotten who he was; he became just another human being who needed my help.

'Can you tell me what happened?' I said, feeling more desperate, panicking about what I should do. 'Can you tell me your name?'

'The people,' he said suddenly.

'The people?'

He tried to say something more but appeared to be in too much pain.

'Where does it hurt?' I said.

The pain didn't seem to be coming from just his neck; he was scrunching up his face and hunching his shoulders.

'Do you think you can stand up?'

And there in the forest, he began to cry. He cried quietly, looking down and away from me. He looked like a young boy when he cried, of no more than nine or ten. I looked at his fine clothes, his leather shoes, his cufflinks that sparkled in the morning sun.

He squeezed his eyes shut and mumbled something unintelligible. Then he looked right into my eyes again.

And that's when it all changed.

That's when his eyes tore me apart. For, in that moment, he looked straight at me. His bright-blue eyes fixed me in my place. I was so close to him that I could feel his breath on my face, the smell of toothpaste and coffee. But his eyes. Such a bright blue. Blue as the sky.

And within them blazed the fire.

Within them, I saw Lazaros. I saw Lazaros standing in the old forest. I saw the pine trees and fir trees and poplars and plane trees and oaks. I saw the weasels and minks, the wildcats and the badgers. I saw the beautiful red deer that roamed the lowlands. I saw the birds and the rabbits and the hares and the hedgehogs and moles and rats, the lizards and the beetles, the tiny insects, the ladybirds and butterflies. I saw the wildflowers. I saw the colours of the forest as it was. As it was.

And I began to sob; the tears escaped me. I wanted to reach out and touch this life that I saw in his eyes. I sobbed from my heart, and then I shook my head and swallowed hard, wiping my tears, managing finally to control myself.

But as I was about to stand up and get help, as I opened my mouth to tell him this, I caught his eyes again, and images flashed within them. I saw then the fifteen people huddled together, the ones we had seen as we ran down to the sea from our home – they had died holding on to each other. I saw my husband's face and my daughter's. I saw the fire along the port. I saw it reflected in the sea. I saw the old lady who had died beside us in the water. I saw the woman who had stood on the rock, calling for the person she loved. I saw Lazaros again, tapping a tree, collecting resin.

This all appeared in the blue of his eyes. It all drifted across the blue like clouds in the sky. And my face began to heat up again. I shut my eyes tight and gulped down all my pain, and I got up and ran.

I ran, and I ran.

I ran away from the man who had started the fire.

6

I HEAR CHARA CALLING ME FROM the garden. I cannot respond. My hands are on my lap now, shaking again. I grip my knees, attempting to stop the tremors. My window is open a crack and Chara's voice rises up to me.

'Mamma! Mamma!'

I picture Mr Monk sitting beneath the tree. I hear his voice. *The people*, he said, *the people*.

I see his eyes and feel the fire surrounding me again. But I have done the right thing. I am sure of it. Mr Monk does not deserve my help or anybody else's.

I look out of the window, but Chara is not there. The sun has risen high.

There is so much that Mr Monk has stolen from us. I remember walking in the forest with Chara when she was a baby, supporting her head as she arched backwards with this crazy desire to look up. How she peered into the tall branches, the leaves, the sky! Her eyes absorbing all the colour. I looked down into her little face as I held her, observing the movement of her eyes: how a rainbow of greens and browns moved across their surface as if they were tiny ponds.

It was early October, and chestnuts crunched beneath our feet and dried-up blueberries rattled in dark corners. Although it was autumn, it was so hot, and I was relieved to find myself within the cool and dappled shade of the forest. I unravelled Chara from the harness and sat down on a fallen bark to feed her. I tried to guide her mouth to my nipple. She screamed. A raw sound, barely human. A sound that merged with the call of the birds, the call of the wind, and other sounds that I cannot name. And then she opened her mouth wide and latched on. It was only then that she closed her eyes and settled into the rhythms of suckling and feeding. Chara wrapped her fingers around mine as she fed. I could see her eyes rolling around beneath her lids, secure in the world of her dreams.

At this same time, somewhere else in the forest, Lazaros was tapping the trees by stripping back a slice of bark. He would have been doing this slowly and carefully, in order to not wound the actual wood. He would have been applying a special paste to stimulate the flow of sap, attaching a bag underneath, like a bib, and catching the sticky substance as it leaked slowly from the tree. Then he would have begun to collect the full bags of resin that he'd applied to the trees ten to fifteen days before. This golden resin was his livelihood. He had been doing this job since he was thirteen.

I knew all this because I had seen him do it so many times. He knew the trees, how they changed rapidly throughout the year and so slowly over the years. Lazaros observed these

71

changes; he understood that trees exist in a different time-frame to us, that we are mere visitors in their world.

Now, Lazaros appears before me, with his wicker baseball cap, stray hairs sticking out of the top. He sticks his tongue out and then frowns. *Bone dry*, he says. *Bone bone bone dry. Like dead bones. Not even alive bones!*

'Mamma!' Chara calls again, and I see now that she is standing just below and waving. Was she there the entire time?

'Mamma, what have you been doing?' She tightens her high ponytail and frowns up at me.

'I'll be down in a minute, sweetie.'

But she disappears now in the direction of the kitchen door.

Due to her injuries, Chara hasn't gone back to school yet. I've been teaching her here myself, and I am sure that she feels trapped in this place, surrounded by the burnt forest. In a month or two, she will begin school again, in the next town. She doesn't want to go to the new school; she wants to go back to her old one, but it doesn't exist anymore. She knows this, but she cries about it every day.

It is no use trying to think about anything else. I see Mr Monk again, as if he is sitting right in front of me, and this time he begins to sob.

I have never left anyone hurt before. If someone is crying, I am the type of person who will sit beside them, even if I can do nothing more, just to be there with them, though I suppose I am like most people in that.

The door-knob turns and the door rattles. 'Mamma?' Chara says from the other side. 'What are you doing, Mamma? Why is the door locked?'

'Give me a sec, love.'

I close *The Book of Fire* and hide it in the drawer. I straighten out my shirt with my palms, as if this will make me look calmer. Maybe she will see in my eyes what I have become.

I open the door.

'What's up?' I say.

'How come the door was locked?'

'Oh, I didn't realise,' I say.

From the expression on her face, it is clear that she doesn't really believe me. She frowns, but then she looks down at her shoes. It seems there is something else on her mind.

'I wanted to play with Pappa for a bit,' she says, still looking down.

I see tears fall from her eyes and drop onto the toes of her black shoes.

'He won't play backgammon with me. He promised me yesterday that today he would give it a go, but now today has arrived – and nothing. I know that he can't use his hands, but I told him that I can play *for* him. He said, "Well then, why don't you just play on your own?"'

'Has he promised to play another day?'

'Of course. Tomorrow.'

I force a smile. 'Maybe tomorrow will be better for him?'

'I don't think so, Mamma.' There is such certainty in her voice that it breaks my heart.

More tears fall from her eyes, but she doesn't look up. She has fixed herself in this position.

'Please don't cry. I love you,' I say. 'Please don't cry. It breaks me to see you sad.'

And then she swallows her tears, like she always does, and as always, I regret allowing those desperate words to leave my mouth.

I lean forwards and kiss her on the cheek and squeeze her soft hands and remember how beautiful and plump and soft and squidgy those little hands were when she was a baby. I loved her with all my soul then, as I love her with all of me now.

In that moment, she looks up at me. She is so close to me, and I look into her glimmering eyes, dark and sombre like her father's.

'Mamma,' she says, 'are you going to leave me, too?'

Her eyes shimmer with tears and fear.

'No,' I say sharply. 'Your father hasn't left you. I am not going anywhere. I am right here.'

But I know what she means. She already understands that someone can be right near you and a thousand miles from your heart.

She holds my gaze. I look into her black eyes. In the deep midnight of her eyes, I picture Lazaros standing in a dark field. His lips move and make inaudible sounds; he sticks his tongue out, and there are deep, dark lines about his mouth. I see Chara running beneath the trees. Then I see myself, standing alone, lost. What would Chara think if she knew what I have done? What would happen if all the darkness that exists in the forest consumed me and took me away from her?

I realise I am sweating. I wipe my forehead with the back of my hand.

'I need to do something,' I say suddenly. 'I have to go.'

It is as if I have suddenly woken up and, sensing this, she takes a step back and the expression on her face changes. Her tears have dried, and her focus is on me.

She nods seriously. 'Yes, Mamma.'

I want to hold her. I want to tell her to not lose her innocence, her sense of safety, her sense of wonder and playfulness, but my chest shakes again, and I exhale sharply. She is right to have lost those things – in that moment, somewhere deep down, this thought comes to me; it flickers somewhere in my mind, a tiny light in the darkness.

'I need to go,' I say to her. I kiss her on the cheek, squeeze her hand and leave.

7

I RUN BACK THE WAY I came, but this time I stop to look at nothing. I don't even need to call Rosalie; she is right there, running along with me. I run through the dead forest, deeper and deeper into the darkness, where clumps of snow melt here and there. I run until I reach Mr Monk.

He is sitting just as I left him, except one hand is now resting on the ground rather than on his lap; his palm is facing up, and now his head has fallen forwards so that his chin is hanging over his chest.

I kneel beside him and squeeze his arm. 'Hello,' I say, 'I'm sorry I left you. I'm so sorry.'

He doesn't move. I check his pulse. Nothing. I check again. I move my fingers over the soft skin of his wrist. Maybe I've missed it. I find his vein in his neck just beneath the noose and press down hard upon it with the tips of my fingers. Nothing.

I sit back, and I look around. I notice a rucksack not too far from where he sits. It's a black sports rucksack, the type that city people wear when they rush about on the metro to get to work. It is lying on its side. I crawl towards it and unzip it. Inside there is an iPad, a pencil case that contains three ballpoint pens, and a paper file, which I open up. I skim the first few paragraphs. It seems to be the dissolution of a contract for a hotel development on the island of Kea.

I put everything back into the bag. I realise now that I shouldn't have touched anything, but I can barely hold this thought.

Mr Monk committed suicide.

No. Judging by how he is dressed and the fact that he is carrying this contract on him, it is possible that he was heading to a meeting. He wanted out of this contract. He didn't want to build another hotel. If this is the case, then why would he kill himself, if he thought he was heading to a meeting?

Mr Monk was lynched.

No. I was wrong. Mr Monk did feel guilt. Mr Monk felt so guilty that he wanted to end his own life. He climbed up the tree and perched on the thick part of that branch. He tied the rope around it and placed the noose around his neck. He prepared himself. He believed the branch would hold his weight until he died. Just for a moment, before he jumped, perched up on the thick branch of the tree like a boy on an imaginary adventure – just at that moment when he hesitated, he glanced around and saw all that he had killed. He saw the destruction he had caused. He understood for the first time what his greed had done. Perhaps he imagined the people who had died.

No. Mr Monk was murdered for what he has done to us all.
No.

Stop.

I hear my own voice in my head, as if I am another, calmer person speaking to me.

Stop, please. Stop thinking now.

I feel acid rise up in my chest. My head becomes hot, and I vomit onto the ground beside me. That's when I notice Rosalie. She leans closer and brushes her nose on my face. I feel the softness of her fur. For a long time, I don't move.

I notice tiny closed buds on the living part of the chestnut tree. I glance up. That side seems to be reaching up to the sky, while the dead side appears to melt down into the ground like a waterfall of tar. The waxy buds glisten in the sunlight. Such a beautiful thing. Such a beautiful, simple thing. A squirrel scuttles up the tree, along the broken branch, stops there at the edge, glances around and down.

I shut my eyes again. I don't want to look at anything. I want to remember this tree as if it is the whole world. As if behind it is a watercolour landscape. The dead forest does not exist. This dead black forest is no longer here around me.

But no. The wind blows again, and I can smell the forest's charred remains.

I open my eyes and force myself to look at Mr Monk. Whatever it is that has happened, I am the last person that he saw, the last person he spoke to, and what did I say to him?

8

WHEN I RETURN, CHARA is curled up on a sheep-skin rug on the floor in the living room. The lights are off, and a sliver of sun comes through the curtains. Chara's eyes are wide open, and they follow me as I sit down beside her and put my arms around her.

'You feel cold,' she says, kissing my cheek gently. 'Your cheek is so cold,' she whispers. I can hear that she is getting sleepy. 'Mamma,' she says, 'did you do what you needed to do?'

'Yes,' I say.

'What did you do, Mamma?' There is a tremor in her voice. It is as if she can see into me. I can almost hear her heart beating.

'It's adult stuff,' I say, knowing that she has learnt to accept this.

I hear her sigh. 'You won't be leaving me?' she says.

'Never,' I say.

'Good. Now, I'm going to have a nap.'

I take a blanket from a basket and cover her with it, and she faces the other way, pulling it up over her shoulder, and I hear her breathing soften.

I go outside and sit next to my husband.

'Tasso,' I say. My voice is sharp and clear in the silence.

'Last night I had a dream,' he says. 'I was in the forest, and it started to bloom. The trees, everything, started to grow out of the ashes. The flowers, the animals – it all sprouted and grew, and then I saw my father. He stood beneath the chestnut tree.'

'What was he doing?' I force myself to ask. I feel acid rise to my throat.

'Nothing. He just stood there and smiled. He was happy.'

Tasso's eyes look into mine, and for a second, I get lost in them, in their darkness and light. This is the first time that he has shared a thought with me, let alone a dream, since the fire, and it has to be right now. Right now, when my heart is shaking with fear for what I have done by leaving Mr Monk in the woods to die. But tears fill Tasso's eyes, and when he closes them, the tears run down his cheeks. The sun is shining on him; it is as if light has overflowed from his eyes.

'It wasn't your fault,' I say.

I want to hold him, but I fear that he will feel me shaking.

There is a long silence. All I want is to hear his voice again, for him to agree or disagree – it doesn't matter.

'I should have kept looking for him,' Tasso says suddenly. 'After I left his house, I went to his usual spot, and the trees were all on fire. I called him ...' His voice breaks. 'We'd be here having pastries now.'

'Yes,' I say, but I think of Mr Monk.

I trace my finger along his right arm, from where the bandage ends just below the elbow. The bandages on both his hands will be removed soon. What will his arms and hands look like now? I imagine taut skin of ridges and hills, like scorched, abandoned land.

'You mustn't blame yourself,' I say. 'You tried your best to find him. What else could you have done? We would have lost you, too.' And at these final words, the anger returns to me. The fury that I have harboured inside me. 'What would we have done if we had lost you? Did you not think of that when you left us? I know you wanted to save your father, but you could have died, too.'

He turns sharply towards me. I feel my face heating up. But he does not respond. I want him to speak, to say anything that will let me know that he is still alive inside.

Instead, he looks back out over the skeleton of trees, across the land. I follow his gaze, high above to the misty slope of the mountain, where empty crumbling houses sit in crevices. We could not see these houses before; they were hidden behind trees flaming green in the sunlight.

His head lowers. And he is lost again. Even my anger doesn't bring him back to me.

His eyes seem to focus on a fallen pine and on the lavender flowers that have managed to push through the dry earth – a splash of violet, a memory of life. He does not see this right now; I am sure of it. No, his heart is moving to a different rhythm. His eyes see what his heart remembers. The scene before us is nothing more than a reflection in his eyes.

I think of Mr Monk. I think of what I have done. I imagine myself through Chara's eyes. If she knew who I really was, what kind of a person her mother really was, would she still love me?

The sun is setting, and we are now in the shadow of the house.

'I need you,' I say suddenly to Tasso, and he slips out of this dreamlike state and forces his gaze on me.

His eyes are then fully on me; he is completely present, like he used to be, and he must be able to see the terror in my eyes, for he says, 'What is it? What happened?'

'Nothing,' I say. I suddenly can't take the intensity of his gaze. It is too much for me.

'Don't give me that. Do you think I can't feel you shaking?'

He gives me that look I know so well: *You've told me you need me,* he seems to be saying, *and I've snapped out of my dream to be here for you.*

'Mr Monk,' I say. 'You remember him?'

'Mr Trachonides. Yes, of course. The guy who started the fire.'

'Yes. The man who caused all this. The man who destroyed us.'

Tasso blinks but says nothing.

'Well, I found him dead in the woods ...'

'When?'

'This morning.'

Silence.

'There was a rope around his neck.'

'My god,' he says. 'He killed himself.'

He looks right into my eyes, and I say nothing.

'Have you called the police?'

'No.'

'Why not?'

'I can't bring myself to—'

'—treat him like a human being?' he interrupts.

I say nothing.

'So, you just left him there?' His voice is loud and low-pitched. Tasso is never angry with me, but I can feel his fury, the fire in his eyes. 'You left him there?' He is quieter now.

I say nothing.

'Irini?'

'Yes, that's what I did. He destroyed us – don't you understand?'

'And who made you judge and jury?'

These words are clear and sharp. They hang in the air.

'Mr Trachonides is dead,' he says eventually, in a slightly softer voice, 'but it won't change anything. You need to call the police.'

'Yes,' I say. And I have never before felt so small in his presence.

'You know that if you don't call them, then I will.'

'I will,' I say. 'Right now.'

I get up and go to the kitchen. I call the police and wait. I sit at the kitchen table and look out at the veranda, at the fig tree where Tasso is sitting. And beyond that, where the forest no longer exists. And his words come back to me: *Who made you judge and jury?*

The memory of Lazaros holding the dry soil in his hands fades into shadows.

If Mr Monk had not started the fire, we would not be here now. It is that simple. Do we need a judge and a jury to know what this man has done? Do we need a courtroom to know that he has destroyed the forest, killed people and animals, caused us to remember forever the fire and the pain?

9

TWENTY MINUTES AFTER THE CALL, three police officers knock on our door. It is 4.30 p.m.

I told Chara before they arrived.

'The police will be coming soon, Chara,' I said, 'so don't be alarmed.'

'Why?' She looked up at me, scared.

'Because,' I began slowly, 'this morning, when I took Rosalie out for a walk, I found an injured man in the woods.'

'How did he get injured?'

'I'm not sure,' I said. 'I will probably need to go back out to the woods to help the officers find the man.'

I was suddenly worried that she would realise I had left this injured man in the woods alone, but she didn't say anything.

'Mamma?' she said.

'Yes?'

'You need to stop calling it the woods.'

'What would you like me to call it? The forest?'

'Not that either, of course.'

'What then?'

She thought for a while. 'I have no idea. There is no good word. We should make a new word.'

'Mrs Diamandis?' the officer says when I open the door, and I nod.

'I am Lieutenant Makris, and this is Officer Adonis and Officer Andreas.'

They all flash their cards, and I lead the men out into the garden, where Tasso is still sitting beneath the tree. He greets the officers politely and seriously. Before doing anything else, the lieutenant looks up at the fig tree with reverence, as if it is Christ resurrected.

He is a tall man with a long, crooked nose; it looks like it was once broken and left to heal on its own. He has kind eyes, I notice. They are green – a rare type of green, the colour you might see on a cat or on a tree when the leaves are just turning yellow. His eyes twinkle and, despite the grave situation, I feel a warmth emanating from him. It is in his stance; it is in the way he seems quiet and patient and thoughtful to his surroundings. This makes me relax, but only a little. I see that he has a fine gold chain around his neck, with a shimmering heart pendant hanging over the shirt of his uniform; there must have been a diamond in that heart once, because there seemed to be a gap where a gem used to be.

'We would like you to accompany us to the forest,' Lieutenant Makris says, 'to show us where you found the body.'

'Yes, of course.'

I am dreading going back there.

'Officer Adonis will stay here. He will wait for us in the living room, if that's OK with you?'

I wonder why one of the officers needs to stay here, but I do not say anything.

The officer standing beside him, a fresh-faced young man, smiles at me warily.

Lieutenant Makris looks around, as if he is expecting to find something. 'It's cold out here,' he says, rubbing his hands together. 'Why aren't you inside, keeping warm?' he asks, looking at Tasso, but Tasso looks up at him, blinks and does not say a word.

'My husband comes out here in the morning,' I say. 'He needs to be outside.'

The officer looks down at his bandaged hands and nods. He understands the injury, but he also understands something more, and his eyes shimmer so that the green becomes brighter.

Then his gaze drops, and I see him picking at the skin of his thumb; it is raw, as if he has been doing this a lot.

'I lost my wife in the fire,' he says suddenly. 'These are terrible times for us all.'

'Yes,' I say, and Tasso nods.

I feel that I want to embrace this kind, sad man. I also feel that I can't say much more. I keep picturing Mr Monk, leaning up against the tree.

The winter sun rests softly on the dead forest. The lieutenant's eyes dart in that direction.

I show Officer Adonis where the living room is, and he stands diligently by the door. The lieutenant is glancing around at the paintings on the wall, and as if he is, in fact, surrounded by the fresh and ancient beauty of the forest, he takes a deep breath and releases it with a sigh. When he catches me looking, he turns away.

Then I lead him and the other officer through the gate at the side of the house and back to the path, where their car is waiting with another officer inside.

The lieutenant opens the door for Rosalie and me to get in and says, 'I went to his exhibition last year – your husband. His landscapes of the last decade – they were magnificent. When I went home, I felt ... how shall I put it? I was so enamoured with the beauty of the world that it frightened me.' He falls silent, and then, 'Can you tell him that, your husband? Can you tell him what it means that he does what he does?'

'Yes, of course.'

'Thank you,' he says. 'I couldn't tell him myself.'

He closes the car door and gets into the passenger seat, and we drive in silence as far as we can into the forest, until it is impossible to go any further.

The officers hold on to their walkie-talkies as we walk along the path I had taken. 'This was the way we were going,' I said, 'before my dog ran off a little further down.'

And just as I finish the sentence, Rosalie runs ahead of us and veers off the path as she did earlier today. This time, she goes more slowly and keeps stopping to check we are close behind.

Her grey fur looks silver, the winter sun shining down upon her. There are no branches and therefore no shadows. This time, she is not running through the dappled shade like she used to before the fire. She is bright and beautiful in the open, on this plane of forest that we are walking upon. The smell of old fire is overwhelming now, worse than it was earlier. We enter an area where there are many trees still standing, but all are dead. It really is like walking in a graveyard. I try to figure out which were the pines, which the firs.

Finally, I spot the chestnut tree. Rosalie turns back to look at us. Her eyes flash.

The tree breaks my heart. I focus on the parts that are still alive, the side where the branches reach up to the sky. I focus on the tiny buds. I do not want to look down and see Mr Monk again.

I hear Lieutenant Makris tell me with a stern voice to stay where I am, to not approach the crime scene. *Crime scene.* Two of the other officers return to the car to retrieve some yellow tape and, when they return, immediately cordon off the area.

Rosalie stays obediently by my feet, observing all this happening around her.

I hear the officers chatting. There is a beeping sound, a crackling from the walkie-talkie. The lieutenant is saying things about the time. He is describing what he sees in front of him. He speaks into the walkie-talkie while staring ahead. I focus on him for a while. I do not want to look at Mr Monk. I dread looking at Mr Monk, who is dead now, because of me.

Rosalie comes and sits beside me. Then my eyes move involuntarily to where I know Mr Monk is sitting.

There he is, exactly as he was when I left him: his head hanging over his chin, his hand resting on the ground, palm open and facing upwards, and for a moment, I think of a flower. I wish this hand was a flower. But then my eyes return to his face. His lips are swollen now and red. His face is so still. I wish he would move; I wish he would speak like he did before. But then again, if he could speak, what would he say? Would he tell them that I left him to die? Would he tell them that I stole his last chance of life?

His cufflinks catch the light. I focus on them. I want to cry, but I hold it in.

My mouth is dry, and I struggle to take a deep breath; I feel that my lungs are full of ash. And, in all this, with everything that he needs to do, Lieutenant Makris glances over and comes towards me.

'Are you OK?' he asks. 'This is a terrible thing to see.'

I nod but say nothing. He asks one of the officers to fetch some water from a bag. He hands me the bottle, and I take a small sip, then another. He watches me.

'Do you know who this is?' he says, gesturing to Mr Monk.

I nod. 'He is the man who started the fire.'

The lieutenant sighs, but it is a very quiet sigh. Then he glances around. He looks at the sky. He looks at the dead trees. He rests his eyes on Mr Monk for what feels like a very long time.

Then he turns to me.

'Will you be OK to come to the station tomorrow?' he says. 'I know it's hard, but we need to ask you some questions, seeing as you were the first on the scene and the person who discovered the body.'

'Yes, Lieutenant,' I manage to say. 'Yes, that's fine.'

But it is not fine. It is anything but fine.

'We will call for you tomorrow afternoon,' he says. 'Today, go back to your family and have some rest.'

Then Lieutenant Makris is on his walkie-talkie again, calling for backup. 'We will come out and meet you – it might be hard to find,' he says. 'Possible suicide.'

My hands begin to shake.

Possible suicide.

Crime scene.

The lieutenant is clearly thinking what I was thinking.

The shirt I am wearing is drenched, though it is a cold day. I feel like I want to lie down on the ground and cry, but instead, I hold my breath and dig my nails into the skin of my palms.

I have never hated myself before. Until now, I have never understood what self-hatred meant. Because if I was another person looking at me, I would despise me.

The Book of Fire

The mother and the girl and the old lady and the dog were still floating in the water together. There was so much smoke that it was as if a thick fog had gathered around them. The mother could no longer see if there were life rafts in the water. There were three orange lights in the distance, and when she felt frightened, she focused her eyes on these. They reminded her of a distant time, of headlights through the fog on the streets of Walthamstow. For the first time, she missed the safety of the city, its solidity, the concrete and the highways, the street lamps and shop shutters and red postboxes. She missed its sounds, so familiar, so consistent: traffic, car horns, thumping bass, police sirens, fire engines. Those sirens, those city sounds meant safety. She wished she could go back there now and find her mother kneading bread and her father absent until the early hours, his instruments lining the walls, sheet music and vinyl records along the bookshelves – all those things that made the structure of her world.

Then she remembered the forest that wound itself through the east like a thick green snake and how she could nearly always, as she walked beneath the canopy of trees, hear the hum of the city beyond. She felt so afraid that she wanted the past to come and rest its hand upon her and say *You are safe. You will be safe just as you always were before.*

'Are you OK, Mamma?' the girl said.

The mother saw that her daughter's eyes were intently on her, but she could not reassure her daughter that she was safe; these words could not leave her mouth. 'Yes, my love,' she said finally. 'I was just somewhere else for a minute.'

The old lady was getting tired, and the light seemed to be dying from her eyes.

'My back hurts, Mamma,' the girl said, shivering in spite of the immense heat.

The mother's eyes filled with tears, but she looked away so that her daughter would not see her cry.

'I know!' the mother said. 'Let's do a little dance!'

The girl raised her eyebrows in disbelief.

'I'll pretend to play the violin, and you do the dance I taught you last week – do you remember it?'

'The Ballos dance?' the girl said.

Her mother nodded and sang, holding an imaginary violin under her chin with one hand while she leant on the crate with the other. The girl tapped her feet beneath the water as she held on to the crate.

The old lady smiled feebly, but there was such little life and energy in any of them that the song died to a whisper, the violin vanished, and limbs were limp and tired in the water.

'Just tell the story, Mamma – that's all we can handle right now.'

The mother noticed that the old lady was not responding as much as she was before, and this worried her.

'OK,' she said, reaching out and squeezing the old lady's hand. 'Are you both listening?'

The old lady gave a little smile, and the flames twinkled in her eyes.

'So, the young lad Vassilios,' the mother began, 'worked as an assistant for his father, Thanos, who was a master luthier, making string instruments of all kinds. Their little shop was located on the Pontic port of Samsun on the southern coast of the Black Sea. One hot day in September, if you remember ... ?'

The girl and the old lady nodded.

'The boy saw a tower of smoke rising from the next village. He put his coffee cup down and stood up. He had seen these towers of smoke before, but this time the tower was closer.

'Then he heard a loud rumbling sound. Was it an earth-quake? The ground seemed to tremble beneath his feet. The sound got louder and louder, and in the next moment there appeared a herd of buffalo in a cloud of dust, their large heads down, horns curved upwards. The cattle were being driven through the streets by soldiers. All the shop owners came out onto the street. Next to Vassilios was the dress-maker, and she stood with a garment draped over her arm and a needle in her fingers. They watched in silence. Vassilios felt his father approach behind him. He came closer to his son and took his hand. Vassilios heard the dressmaker call out above the racket, "The Turks have looted the neigh-bouring village! Do you see?!"

'Well, of course they saw. They saw and heard and felt. There was no escaping this reality, and the boy's father gripped his hand tightly until the last buffalo went past. When all was quiet again, Vassilios raised his head to look at his father and saw that his glasses were covered in a fine film of dust. Vassilios waited for him to speak, but he said nothing. This was unusual and worried Vassilios even more than his father's usual truthful observations.

'Vassilios wished his dad would say something, name that bad thing that was happening. But instead, the dressmaker spoke up. She dropped the needle and pointed at the street. "They are coming for us. You'll see! We are the minority, and we will be wiped out. They did it to the Armenians and they will do it to us!" Her chins trembled. There was no satisfaction in the words. Her voice was more like a cry, full of fear, and she had a loud voice, a voice that carried itself across places, through walls.

'And just when Vassilios thought his father would elaborate, Thanos turned to Vassilios and said simply, "Wait here – I'll make us a nice hot coffee," and he disappeared into the back of the shop. When he returned with the coffees he told Vassilios all about the rivalries between the Turks and the Greeks. "Things are never as simple as they seem, always remember that in life. It is dangerous to see things in black and white, even – and maybe especially – during troubled times," he had said. "Each side hates each other because of memories and traumas on both sides, some are real and some are imagined, and these become national narratives. They demonise each other. The 'other' is always to blame and it fuels people and groups and governments with fire. This never leads to any good on this earth." Then he fell silent and went inside.

'With his father's words in his mind, Vassilios watched the dust settle. He looked down at his shoes and saw they were filthy. He then turned to the instruments on display and saw that they, too, were covered in dust. The dust had even settled on the strings and inside the sound box. He was too angry to listen to what his father had said. Look what the Turks had done! It made the instruments look ghostly, as if he were seeing a picture of them taken in another time. And beyond, he saw that there were three towers of smoke, each one closer than the last.

'That's when he saw that a young girl, about a year or so younger than him, was standing beside the display table. She wore a red dress that was completely covered in dust. She stood so still, staring at him, wide-eyed with large dark eyes, that Vassilios wanted to shake her.

'"Are you OK?" he asked her.

'"Not really." Her bottom lip trembled, and her eyes darted to the smoke, which now hovered above them. Vassilios instinctively put his hand on her shoulder.'

The mother stopped talking, because she saw that the old lady's eyes and mouth were open wide. Her head lay on her arms, which rested on the crate. The mother nudged the old lady, but she didn't move. She yanked her from the box and held her in her arms and pinched her nose and breathed into her mouth, again and again. She gasped for breath herself and called for help, but nobody came.

From the corner of her eye, she could see her daughter treading water beside her, her eyes upon them.

'Help!' the mother called again into the smoke, into the unknown, shouting as loudly as she could, but nobody came.

The mother breathed into the old lady's mouth as she stared blankly up to the sky.

'Mamma,' she heard her daughter say, 'please don't let her die.'

The mother took a deep breath and exhaled again into the old lady's mouth, holding her tightly in her left arm, leaning down over her. She tried one more time. No movement. She tried again. Nothing. Without looking at her daughter, she heaved and lifted the old lady's body onto the crate, so that her torso was leaning on the box. She held onto her arms to make sure she didn't fall off.

Then she dared to look at her daughter. The girl treaded water and stared with wide, fearful eyes. The mother checked for a pulse, just to be sure. She checked the old lady's wrist and beneath her neck, but there was no life left.

The mother shook her head, and the girl cried, and her tears fell silently and shivered with fire.

10

Lieutenant Makris asked one of the female officers on the scene to take me home, but I refused. 'I could do with some fresh air,' I told him, and he smiled, though his green eyes were serious and sharp.

I headed back with Rosalie. I kept my eyes down, and for some reason I counted my steps, which I have never done before. I lost count and started again. Then the old chestnut tree flashed in my mind, fully alive, with my great-grandfather sitting beneath it, gorging on blue and purple fruit. Then I saw Tasso, so close to me, kissing me beneath the tree, his lips soft and tender. Then I saw Chara, so tiny, releasing her hand from my grip and toddling towards the tree, glancing up at its massiveness and falling back onto her bum.

Rosalie walked obediently beside me and led me out of the woods and out of my memories. Every so often, she looked up at me, urging me forwards.

I sneaked into the house and sat for a while alone in the bedroom.

It is dark now. Chara is fast asleep, and Tasso is outside with Rosalie. My body is heavy with the realisation that Mr Monk may have still been alive if I hadn't left him there. I am so exhausted.

I go downstairs and make some coffee. I look at the box that contains the tablets the doctor prescribed for Tasso. I open it up and take one from its compartment. I head outside with the tablet, a glass of water and the coffee.

I sit beside him. His shoulders are hunched; it makes him look like he's resigned himself to some greater power, that he has understood something about the world and has given in or given up, or both.

'Did you take the police to him?' he says.

'Yes.'

He says nothing more. There is silence for a long time.

'You need to take your medication,' I say.

He nods. 'Just leave it on the table. I'll take it later.'

'How will you take it by yourself?'

He glances down at his hands. 'You are right.'

I hold out the tablet as if it is a magic pill, hoping he will open his mouth so I can pop it in.

'Will you remind me tomorrow?'

'Why not now?' I ask, but he doesn't respond.

I want to argue with him, but instead, I pick up the mug of coffee. 'Do you want some?'

He nods, so I bring the cup up to his face so that its rim is just touching his lips. Then he leans forwards, and I tilt the cup upwards. He slurps the coffee and I close my eyes, and with this sound and the familiar smell of coffee, just for a minute, I am sitting here with Tasso beneath the fig tree while he drinks coffee with his father, his bag of paints and easel beside him, about to head out to begin a new painting.

'I still can't believe you left him,' Tasso says suddenly, breaking the silence between us. 'I mean, what possessed you?' His voice is full of anger again.

I find that I can't reply. How can I explain to him everything that went through my mind? If I did, would he understand?

Then his eyes slide towards me, and he says, 'Look, I'm sorry. I know it must have been tough.'

'More than you even think.'

'Why's that?'

I think for a moment. 'I'm just not entirely sure . . .' I pause.

'Of what?'

'I'm not one hundred per cent sure that he committed suicide.'

'What makes you say that?'

'A hunch.'

'Just a hunch?'

'The . . . all the . . .' And I find that I cannot say the words, that they are too close to home.

'All the what?' he asks.

'All the anger.'

He nods and stays quiet for a few moments. Then he says, 'Have you told the police what you think?'

'They're interviewing me tomorrow.'

He nods.

'In the afternoon, after the nurse has removed your bandages, the officer said he will come and collect me. The psychiatrist is also coming tomorrow – you haven't been taking your medication.'

Tasso looks down at his hands; he stares at them with such sadness in his eyes, such fear, that all I can do is reach out and put my hand on his knee, then lean forwards and brush my face gently against his stubble and whisper in his ear, 'I love you.'

I wait for his response, but his answer is nothing. I sink into the chair. No sound from his lips, not even a gesture.

I think about how the outside world has the power to penetrate us, to get deeply inside us – like how the dark forest exists inside Tasso. Or is it the other way around? Could it be the other way around? Could there be something destructive and barren in all of us that bleeds out into our land?

And then I hear the howl of a wolf. The first time since the fire. A surviving wolf. I imagine it alone on the hillside. I imagine it beneath the moon, alone in all that darkness.

11

WHEN I FIRST LOVED TASSO, I loved *everything* more: the whole of life, the whole of the world, the whole of the universe. It kind of feels as though I've never not loved him. And now he is so far from me, and it breaks me.

Our dads grew up in the same village. Mine moved to London when he was eighteen to find work and decided to stay when he met my mum.

We lived in a semi-detached ex-council house in Walthamstow, just by the greyhound racing stadium. There was a parapet entrance and a clock tower and Charlie Chan's nightclub under the totalisator board, which showed the scores of the betting shop. At night, the red and black doors in the underground car park were flanked by doormen. There were so many people queuing up to get in, fake teeth glowing in the blue neon lights. The people in the queue were mostly footballers, gangsters and east London's glitterati. That is what Dad told me, anyway.

Late at night, I would hear fights from my bedroom window, the music of the raves thumping every time those double doors opened – that's how close we lived. My dad would take me to the betting shop during the week to pick a dog. In the bookies, he would slip into his cockney accent. 'Awight, mate,' he would say to the guy behind the counter, 'here's a pony. Let's see if I'll get some bees and honey.' He would place twenty-five pounds on the counter, rub his hands together and wink beneath his hat. Then, on Sundays, we would head down to the dogs, to watch them race around the whippet track.

Mum worked at the local bakery, making meaty white loaves and hot cross buns. Dad was a postman. While he walked fourteen miles a day, he would often close his eyes – that's how well he knew those streets – and pretend that he was heading down the path from his old village to the sea. He loved where we lived in London, the hustle and bustle, the markets, the high-rise buildings, the mixture of cultures – my dad loved all that stuff; he was like a real Londoner, but he never ever forgot his home. I know the exact road he was imagining.

In Walthamstow, our local park was made of concrete, and our back garden was not much bigger than the shed. Yet Dad managed to keep a big barbecue in there and grow a lemon tree from seeds that were sent to him in an envelope. The tree and the barbecue took up nearly the whole garden, so there was no room at all to play. At first, he grew it in a pot, then when it become too big, he re-planted it in the garden. He watched it diligently, fearful it wouldn't survive. But the tree seemed to like the urban heat. In the city we didn't get much frost, and when we did, the warmth from our poorly insulated house made it melt away. That tree was his pride and joy. It blossomed in the spring and produced several small lemons each year. He would pluck one off the branch, dig his nails into the zest, pulling off the rind with his big hands, hold it up to his nose, squeezing the lemon so that a soft spray was released. Then, as the Victoria line train rumbled right by our fence, he would inhale the citrus scent, as if he were breathing in an entire country.

'Smell that, Irini. Come here and smell it. That is Greece!'

Then his eyes would shimmer, not from happiness but with longing.

Tasso lived an entirely different life. His father had flocks of goats and a whole olive orchard with trees that were hundreds of years old. I was mesmerised by their twisted branches and silver leaves. His father, Lazaros, worked in the forest. He spent his entire life collecting resin from the trees.

When I first met Tasso, one scorching summer, he was lying on the ground in the shade of the porch-canopy with a book on his face. My mum, my dad and I had to step over him to get into the house. His mother nudged him with her foot, and he jumped up, immediately alert.

'Welcome. I'm happy to meet you,' he said, shaking each of our hands in turn. He was thirteen, lanky and dark with sharp, grubby elbows and knees. He had shining eyes that were so black they reminded me of the night sky.

His mother tremored in the sunlight, as if she didn't quite exist in this world. We knew that she was unwell; Dad had mentioned it in the car as we drove the winding path to their house. When I met her, she was hunched from a crooked spine, which I later learnt was slowly crumbling. Her cheekbones shone in the light, and her nose was small and bony, almost like a beak. Looking at her, as she stood or sat still, you may have questioned whether she was living – so pale was her skin, so fine and translucent. It hung on her bones like a veil – yet she walked around the house, watering the plants, lightly on her feet, as if something or someone were carrying her.

Tasso was always close by. I had a feeling that he was always ready to catch her. When she finished with the watering can, his hands were outstretched, and she placed it in them. In the kitchen, when she made Greek coffees, he passed her the silver pot, the cups, the spoon. She accepted each item, deftly continuing with her task. In the meantime, he placed a sweet preserve of green walnuts dripping with black syrup into small cups of water. Then he waited patiently – Greek coffee needs to be heated slowly – until his mother placed the coffees, along with the sweets, on a tray for him to take to the living room.

'What a lovely helpful boy!' my mother announced.

My mother was so different from Tasso's mother, who was so light and ethereal. My mother walked with heavy flat feet and looked slightly lost and her large buttery hands always seemed ready to thump a slab of dough. She was a tall woman, so tall in fact that my father would jokingly call her *camel*, because her name was Camilla, and she would laugh at him and say *Dimitri, camels are not tall – you are thinking of a giraffe!*

'Such a lovely, lovely helpful boy!'

Ekaterini nodded in agreement. 'When he hasn't fallen asleep on the ground somewhere.'

I found this at odds with his attentiveness, his vigilance.

'Sometimes, his dad goes out and finds him on the forest floor. Once, he found him up a tree, hugging a branch in his sleep, like a koala.'

Ekaterini's voice was stronger than her body; it was smooth but weighty. It had not been affected by her illness. Her soul, it seemed, had remained intact.

But there was something more to Tasso's interactions with his mother than being a helpful boy: an intimacy, a rhythm, as if they were dancing together and each knew the other's moves by heart.

My own mother lived quietly in the shadows of life, like a bug might live beneath the fallen leaves of a grand tree in a great forest. She kneaded bread. Bread was safe. Kneading was safe. She dug her white knuckles into the dough, and I watched her, hypnotised by the rhythmic force of it. Sure, we would go on outings, we would visit places and have long Sunday drives, but she was never really with us. It was never entirely clear to me why my mother was the way she was, living so quietly, so far away, and from time to time bursting out of herself with a laugh or with eyes alight with joy. *What a lovely helpful boy!* I still remember her eyes when she said this, the glow in them.

And then of course she would withdraw into herself, and I would try to work out what it was about that person or that conversation that had woken her up. All I knew was that her mother – whom I had never met, as she died a year before I was born – had had some kind of psychotic illness that created for my mother, then in her youth, a confusing, chaotic environment. My father told me this once during one of his night-time stories; it came up somehow, but I don't remember why. All my mother ever said was that her mother had been a beautiful woman, so beautiful in fact that she glowed like an angel. She told me this once when she found her mother's gold wedding band in a jewellery box as she tidied up the storage cupboard one winter's day. Her eyes lit up, and she said, *Your grandmother was beautiful. She glowed like an angel.* It was that simple. No complexity; no memories. Then she put the ring away and shut the box.

But I have a sense now that she had learnt to live in the shadows of this beautiful, glowing, unpredictable woman, and as a result, she did not stay hidden completely but learnt to be unpredictable herself. I spent my youth waiting for those rays of sunshine.

I recall this now, because it has to do with the forest. You see, when I discovered the forest – and I felt at that young age that I had truly discovered it – when I did, I felt a constancy and safety that I had lacked. The forest's rhythms were not secrets; there was sense to them. They would continue as they were, whether I was there or not; I could not make the forest happy or sad. The forest was what it was in spite of me.

We stayed there for only a week that first summer. I was eleven years old. We spent most of the time outdoors. While my parents went off to visit Dad's childhood friends, Tasso introduced me to his world. In the thyme-scented forest, we watched Lazaros running his hands along the rough barks of the trees, feeling gently – as if they were the limbs of a human being – for those wounds that appeared like volcano craters upon the scales of the trees. Then he would break away a tiny piece of the crumbling wood, look at the sun-orange substance, smell it and insert a tiny tap into the tree with a bag attached to catch the golden liquid.

'The tree excretes this to protect itself,' Tasso told me. 'If there is any damage at all, or if there are too many branches or brambles scraping its bark, it has a way of helping itself to heal.'

'It's like the tree is crying,' I said, and he laughed and roughed my hair as if I were so much younger than him.

'Dad will sell buckets of that stuff, and people will make glue, varnishes, soaps – all sorts of things.'

Whenever I entered the woods with Tasso, I felt that I was swallowed up by the forest – into its shadows and light, into the smells of conifer and earth.

'Come with me; I want to show you something,' he said.

He led me into the thick of the woods. He pointed out the trees: the alpine pines, Cephalonia firs, eastern planes. He showed me the wildflowers, the peonies and primulas. He told me to walk and breathe as quietly as I could, so that we wouldn't disturb anything. He didn't run through the forest like most boys of his age; instead, he trod gently and carefully.

I followed as quietly as I could. I tried to take long, quiet breaths through my nose. But I was not used to walking on rocky, uneven ground, especially not in my flip-flops, so I stumbled along behind him, and he turned to shush me with his eyes whenever I made too much noise.

'My god, you walk like an elephant,' he said. 'You'd think we were traipsing through the city, the way you're going. A forest needs a special kind of care.'

'I'm trying!' I said, too loud, and the leaves rustled all around me.

'Look at that,' he whispered.

I could feel his intensity and excitement from the way he grabbed my hand. His grip was full of energy. There, above us in the maple tree, was a peregrine falcon.

'You will never see these birds in the city,' he said, and I set my eyes upon it, its blue-grey feathers and yellow-rimmed eyes and beak and yellow feet. 'Do you see the vertical lines on its chest? That means it's a teenager – sort of our age. When it becomes an adult, those lines will become horizontal.'

The next moment, it opened its large wings. I watched it through the gap in the trees, up in the sky, as it made a spectacular dive, attempting to catch another bird mid-flight. I gasped. The other bird swerved higher still. I'd never bothered to stand so still and so quiet to observe a bird before. I'd only ever shooed away the London pigeons that sat on the roof of Dad's old banger. This was different. I was doing nothing but looking. For a few minutes, the world was empty apart from this blue sky and the two birds that flew now in opposite directions. Tasso was silent beside me. He squeezed my hand.

I held my breath, hoping the birds would return, but the sky was empty.

Then he let go, as if he had never been holding my hand, and continued silently and stealthily into the woods, and I had to run to catch up until we reached a clearing in the trees.

'Don't make any sound at all, OK?'

I nodded.

There, before us, was an animal that I'd never seen before. It had a delicate face and legs, like the fox that visited our garden in Walthamstow, but with a German Shepherd's long, alert ears. 'What the hell is that?'

'Shush. It's a jackal,' Tasso whispered.

We were hiding behind a tree. He crouched down, and I did the same. From the bushes emerged another jackal, slightly bigger.

'That's her mate,' he whispered. 'They stay together for life, living and hunting together. Both parents take care of the pups for as long as they need it. Keep watching.'

And then the little pups came out, and I saw for myself how they were a family. How they played! I wanted to laugh as they ran and jumped and tripped up over each other. But I pressed my palm over my lips, and I laughed into my chest. I watched as the mother and father stood close by, keeping an eye on them.

I crouched there and looked. I didn't need to do anything. I didn't need to react. I didn't even need to laugh anymore. I simply took it all in, this family loving and living and playing in the way that was natural to them.

12

IN THE MORNING, THE SKY is clear and beautiful. I wake up early and stand at the window like I used to. I imagine the forest as it was. I picture it so clearly that I can almost hear the rustle of the leaves. But there is nothing there. It is all gone, and my heart sinks as it does every morning. So I focus on the sky and the fine clouds that drift peacefully across it. Tasso is still asleep.

On my phone, there is a text message from Mrs Gataki: *Daughter, meet me for a coffee at the usual place? Have you heard about Mr Monk?*

Yes, I reply. *I have heard. I can't come to Maria's today. Busy day! But I can meet you there tomorrow at 11 a.m. if you're around?*

Yes, she replies, *see you there*, and she adds a heart emoji.

When Tasso wakes up, we sit in the kitchen and have breakfast. I make myself a cup of tea; I make Tasso a Greek coffee and Chara downs a huge glass of milk. There is creamy yoghurt and fruit, and we finish off the seeded bread that I made last week.

The fig tree outside is alive with sparrows; they sing and sing and sing, and the entire tree vibrates with their sporadic chirping. I stand by the door and look out. I miss the other trees. I miss their presence, their comfort, their shadows. But this one tree here is bursting with life!

'Tasso!' I say, and he glances at me, but before I can say anything more there is a knock at the door.

Chara goes to open it and leads the nurse into the kitchen. As usual, she doesn't look around, doesn't say anything pointless about the weather; instead, she looks Tasso directly in the eyes and says, 'Right. Are you ready?'

Tasso had his skin grafts four months ago; the nurse has changed the dressing six times since then. She always checks diligently, with so much care and attention, to see how his hands are healing, making sure the bolster is OK – secured to the surrounding skin with stitches – to ensure that there is no infection, not too much bleeding, although a little is always expected. Then, each time, she covers each hand again with a thinner bandage than before and encourages Tasso to be patient and have faith. But he does not follow her advice, and he carries his bandages as if they are weights. I began to see them as if they were slabs of white concrete.

But now, as the nurse gently unravels the white material, I can see how fine it is, how soft, and I suddenly feel anger. I want to shout at Tasso, to chide him for losing faith, for making everything darker and heavier and deadlier than it already is. Instead, I focus on that white material and remember the moon and the sails of the glowing boat.

Then she carefully removes the stitches on his right hand, one by one, and takes off the bolster, and there is Tasso's hand. Where the graft has been applied, the skin is red in places and black and grey in others; there are grooves and creases that don't belong to him. Tasso looks away immediately, but my eyes are fixed upon this hand. This hand that I don't know. This hand that I have never held. Tears fill my eyes. But it is not a dead hand, I remind myself. It is a hand that is very much alive, and I want to reach out and hold it. When I have this thought I look at Tasso, who is now crying.

'It's all right, son,' the nurse says, giving him a pat on the back. 'You've done well. It's healing very well. I'm not concerned at all.'

But it seems that Tasso's thoughts are elsewhere, for he says, 'Thank you, nurse. Thank you for everything you have done, and I'm glad to hear that. But it's not that. It's that I'm thinking of all those things that cannot be brought back to life.'

'Yes,' she says. 'I know what you mean.' She purses her lips so that all the skin around them creases, as if she is holding in too much, as if whatever is inside her is pushing to escape, to burst out. She grimaces, and just for a moment, she shuts her eyes. Then, without warning, and with a sudden fresh smile on her face, she says, 'Right, on we get then. We still have another one to do.'

Tasso and I watch her quietly as she gets on with the task of removing the bandage, followed by the stitches and the bolster. When she is done, she advises Tasso to begin using his hands, to not be afraid of them, and she gives him an

113

antibiotic cream to apply three times a day: morning, after-noon and bedtime.

When she leaves, Tasso sits beneath the fig tree as usual. I sit beside him quietly. He places his hands on his lap like he always does, palms facing upwards, but they are free of their white cages now. I wish he would move them. How I wish he would hold my hand. But the skin on his hands, the new skin, is delicate.

'Things will get better now,' I say.

'Yes,' he replies, but there is no hope or conviction in his voice.

I focus on the sound of the sparrows in the tree. They chatter and chirp and flap their wings, and it is as if the tree itself is dancing. I look at the leaves and how they glisten in the midday sun and the beautiful ridges in the branches and the bark, and for a moment I think: yes, maybe, life will get better. I will focus only on the things still living; I will ignore the darkness and deadness that surrounds them.

But then I think of Mr Monk. I remember how his skin felt on the tips of my fingers as I checked for his pulse.

The people. His voice comes back to me. *The people.*

But who are the people, Mr Monk? Which people? The people who died in the fire, the people you killed with your greed, or the people who killed you? Am I one of those people?

I know the police will come soon. I get up and go inside. I can do nothing but pace around the house, going from room to room, waiting for the interview, so I decide to clean, to wipe away the dust that rests so finely on the furniture. I use an old cloth and a duster. The furniture begins to come to life – the console table and the coffee table, both made of walnut; the golden wood beneath shines again.

The psychiatrist arrives. Once again, he wears his black-rimmed glasses and holds nothing in his hands, not even a phone. This causes me anxiety. Should he not be making notes, recording everything, diligent to remember anything that Tasso says so that he can make him better?

'How has he been?' the doctor says, standing in the kitchen and glancing out of the window to the garden. He expects to see Tasso still out there, and this makes my heart sink. How can I have hope, if the doctor doesn't?

'He hasn't taken his medication.'

'I see. May I?' he says, signalling to the kitchen door, and I show him out to the garden and return to the kitchen, waiting quietly, wondering what they might be talking about, wishing that the doctor would take Tasso's hand and pull him out of the dark.

When he returns from the garden sometime later, I stand up immediately.

The doctor looks at me for a moment too long. He is a middle-aged man with sharp eyes.

'Can you help him?' I say, and once again he takes off his glasses, folds them shut and grips them in his right hand.

'The first thing is that he has to have some tiny desire to help himself. It doesn't have to be big – it could be a pinprick of light in the darkness. Someone who talks to me, who shares things with me, might believe that it's all hopeless, but just the fact that they are telling me what ails them – that simple thing in itself – is a pinprick of light. From what I understand, losing the forest is like losing a part of himself. I noticed his paintings as we passed through to the kitchen ...' He pauses and nods again twice, as if he is thinking something through. 'He didn't tell me this, but it's clear from what I see. However, it's not just the loss and the trauma that makes him suffer – as if that in itself is not enough – it's also the guilt. He *did* mention his father. He believes that he didn't help him. In a sense, he is punishing himself. Helping himself would mean ending this punishment.'

My shoulders drop. My heart sinks, and perhaps noticing this, the doctor looks at me right in the eyes.

'He did *mention* his father, though,' he repeats. 'He handed me that tiny bit of information, as if he opened a shell to reveal a pearl.'

A few minutes after the doctor leaves, there is a knock at the door. When I open it, Lieutenant Makris is standing alone, holding his hat. 'May I come in?'

'Yes, of course,' I say.

I see his eyes glimmer as he enters the living room. Once again he looks around as if he has just walked into the forest. His eyes don't rest on any single painting; instead, they flow around the room, absorbing it all. I hear his deep intake of breath, his resigned sigh, watch the way his arms hang by his sides as if he is immobilised, the hat almost slipping out of his fingers. And this stillness goes on too long for me; the old forest presses in from all sides – the colours, the million colours of the forest. Although I see these paintings every day, something seems to happen when I am looking at them in the presence of someone else, when someone else is moved by them – it feels as if they come to life, as if the leaves are moving and the sun is shifting within them, as if a soft breeze billows through trees.

'Can I get you a coffee?' I ask.

His eyes suddenly go wide, as if I have just woken him. 'No, thank you very much.' They sparkle with unshed tears. 'I thought it would be more convenient for you if I came to get you myself.'

'Thank you, Lieutenant.'

'Seeing as there are no buses coming into this area anymore ...' But although he is trying to focus on me, his eyes wander back to the paintings, as if they are magnets, and now they rest on one in particular, the one of the chestnut tree, standing majestically with all its years etched upon its twisted bark – this one single tree against a soft background.

'I'll escort you to the station,' he says, bringing his attention back to me. 'First, we'll interview you, then we'll take your fingerprints and a DNA sample.'

'Why?' I blurt out and immediately worry that I sound too anxious.

'Nothing to worry about. You were the first on the scene, so this is part of our standard investigation procedure.'

'Investigation?'

'I'll tell you what – let's do this properly down at the station.'

'OK,' I say. My mouth is dry. Does he know that I left a man to die? It's almost as bad as killing someone yourself.

I know this. I put my shaking hands behind my back, clutching them together, to hide them from him.

Now that he has said what he wanted to say, he looks around the room again. This time, however, anger sweeps across his face. 'They spend so much money on the military, to buy arms against Turkey. Hasn't that always been the case? And they neglect the land – they don't put provisions in place ...' He pauses, as if he has said too much, and in that moment, his shoulders drop and the anger falls from his face, and he looks up again at the painting of the chestnut tree.

'Extraordinary,' he says, exhaling, the words filling the room. 'Extraordinary,' he says again, quieter this time and with the words fall tears.

I can do nothing but watch him – the creases around his eyes deepening and darkening, his shoulders shaking as he stands and sobs. The light that shines through the window catches the gold of the heart pendant around his neck.

Not knowing what else to do, I touch his shoulder very gently.

'Oh god,' he says. 'Oh god, forgive me. This is so unprofessional. I'm so sorry.' He quickly pulls himself together, tugging himself out of the pain, until his face and eyes are bright again. Then he clears his throat and looks into my eyes. 'Please accept my apology.' He bows his head. 'This is *extremely* unprofessional of me. It's just that ...'

'I know,' I say. 'You don't need to explain.'

He takes me to the station in the next town. It is an old, shabby building overlooking the shore. He leaves me in a small room and goes off to deal with a very quick but urgent matter. A junior officer fetches me a cup of tea and two biscuits, and I am left alone in this room that feels like a cell, with concrete walls and halogen lights and a metallic bin in the corner.

But there is a small window, so small that it feels almost unreal, as if it is really one of Tasso's paintings. The window is filled with the sea and a bright-blue sky. The water ripples and sparkles beneath the afternoon sun. As I wait, I watch the sun sink, ever so slightly, and the colours change so that the sky and the sea are tinged with orange and pink.

'I'm ever so sorry.' Lieutenant Makris arrives. 'These things always take longer than I anticipate – always some complication or other.'

I glance at my phone and realise that I have been here an hour already.

Now, a woman enters the room; she is not wearing a uniform but a dark-navy suit, a white shirt. She shakes my hand and introduces herself as Detective Daphne Lamprides. She opens a rucksack by her feet and takes out a notepad and pen, which she places on the table.

'Are you ready?' she asks.

I nod.

'Can we start the recording please?'

Lieutenant Makris presses the button of the recording device, then says the date, the time of the interview and the names of the people present.

'Mrs Diamandis,' Detective Lamprides says, 'I understand that you discovered the body of Mr Michael Trachonides yesterday, Tuesday 23rd January 2018. Is this correct?'

'Yes, it is.'

'Do you remember what time it was when you found his body?'

'Around half past 3.'

The detective opens the notebook and scans something with her eyes. 'Can you be more precise?'

'Close to 3.30, give or take five minutes.'

'The police received a call from you at 4.10 p.m. Why did you take so long to call the police? You found a dead body – I would have thought the first thing anyone would do is call the police.' For the first time, she makes direct eye contact; her face is serious, her hair tied in a slick bun that makes her eyes appear sharp, slightly stretched at the temples. She has a long nose and beautiful thick eyebrows. Her lips are soft and there is a gentleness to her voice when she says, 'It's OK – just tell me what you remember. We're not here to catch you out. We just want to get the facts straight, that's all.'

And in that moment, I wish we had met at Maria's Kafeneon, over coffee and a gossip. But we haven't. We are here in this tiny room because Mr Monk is dead, and I had a hand in it. The seriousness of the situation is oppressive, and I try not to shift in my seat, not to bring my hand up to my mouth to bite my nails, not to jiggle my leg beneath the table.

'There was no signal where I was in the woods, so I returned home, told my husband what had happened and then called the police.'

'So, you had a conversation with your husband before calling?'

'Yes.'

'What did this conversation entail?'

'Why am I being asked these questions?' I say without thinking, placing both my palms on the table.

The detective glances at my hands.

'You were the first on the scene.' Lieutenant Makris speaks now. 'So we have to ask. In a way, at first, everyone is a suspect.'

'I'm a suspect?'

'Yes. But we are here to ascertain what happened and to rule that *out.*' He raises his eyebrows at the last word, and I feel like a schoolgirl.

I picture myself running away and leaving Mr Monk alone to die.

I say nothing.

'Shall we carry on?' he says.

'Yes.'

'So,' says Detective Lamprides, sounding slightly exasperated, 'I'll return to my previous question. Do you remember what you and your husband spoke about before you called the police?'

'Yes. He told me that he'd had a dream about his late father, who died in the fire, and then I told him that I'd found Mr Trachonides dead in the forest. I was shocked and scared. He told me to call the police, and I did. Straightaway.'

Her eyes are fixed on me. I hate lying. But I've known since I left the house that I can't tell them the truth. They might take me away from Chara. I cannot risk that, not now, not with everything that has happened, not with how lost her father is.

My mouth is dry, my tongue sticking to the roof of my mouth. I try not to move, not even to swallow.

The detective jots something down in her notepad.

'Can you describe the events that occurred on Tuesday 23rd January 2018? Can you lead us through what happened from the moment you decided to leave your house?'

'Yes, of course,' I say, swallowing hard now, and they both stare at me. For a moment, I catch a glimpse of the sea outside the window, its soft continuous ripples, the gentle glow above the horizon, the sky that is darkening now. 'I decided to go for a walk with Rosalie, our greyhound. I take her for a walk every day. We used to walk into the forest but now – well, now, there is a very faint path that still exists, so we follow that. It stops me from getting lost now that everything is unrecognisable.'

'What time did you leave your house, do you remember?'

'It was around …' I pause. 'Three p.m.'

I feel sick. Heat rises in my chest, and I'm worried that I might heave and vomit just like I did when I realised that I had left Mr Monk to die. I can feel my hands shaking, and I sit on them.

Lieutenant Makris has noticed something, for he says, 'Would you like a glass of water?'

'Yes, please. It's just, remembering all this, it's …'

'I know,' he says and smiles a warm, kind smile. He fills up a plastic cup from a water dispenser and hands it to me.

I gulp it down, place the empty cup on the table.

'Ready?' he says.

'Yes.'

'Let's go from where we left off. So, you went for a walk with your dog, Rosalie, around 3 p.m.?'

'OK. We were walking, and suddenly, Rosalie just dashed off, into the dead woods. I was on that flat bit of land where the meadow used to be. I didn't want to follow her, believe me, but I did, because she'd never run off like that before. She's always close to me. I believe she smelt Mr Trachonides. Greyhounds are hunting animals.'

I glance up. The detective is once more writing in her notepad, and the lieutenant looks at a clock on the wall directly opposite the window. It has large, ornate hands and a diamond pattern on its face. It seems so out of place in this room.

The lieutenant nods slightly, urging me to go on.

'Then I spotted Rosalie sitting beside someone. It was strange – I didn't expect there to be another person inside this place. It was a man, leaning on the old chestnut tree – you know that beautiful ancient chestnut in the middle of the forest?'

I glance at Lieutenant Makris, and he acknowledges the question with a slight movement of his head and widening of his eyes.

'I thought he was asleep. He was leaning against this tree, which is half dead, half alive, and it looked like he was fast asleep. His chin was hanging over his chest. My dad used to sleep like that on the sofa. My first thoughts were that he had come into the dead woods out of guilt or shame. That he'd sat there alone to think and had dozed off. But while I stood there, waiting for him to wake up, perhaps to sense that someone was staring at him, I suddenly noticed the rope

123

around his neck. And then I went closer and saw that the skin around the noose was red raw. When I looked up, I saw that a large branch above his head had broken in two. Part of it was next to him on the ground.

'This all happened very fast. I think at that point I was just trying to take in what I was seeing. Then I froze. I was shaking. I remember how much I was shaking. Rosalie was near him, sniffing around his head. I remember that she tugged at the fallen rope that hung over his shoulder, and I told her to sit, but she came over to me and tugged at my trouser leg. I think she knew that I was in shock – she was trying to get me to move, to do something. So, I knelt beside him and said, "Hello", but he didn't respond. Then I squeezed his arm to see if he would react. But he didn't move, so I checked his pulse. I couldn't feel anything, and I started to panic, so I tried to find the vein in his neck, and that's when I fully realised that he had died.'

'OK,' says the detective. 'You say you saw the rope and fallen branch. Did you notice anything else that you think might be important?'

'There was a rucksack close by, which the police must have found.'

'Did you touch this rucksack?' she asks.

'Yes.'

'Why?'

'I was looking for his phone. I was hoping that it might be in there and that I might be able to use it.'

'So, you opened the bag and presumably moved it from its original position?'

124

'Yes. I'm sorry.'

'No need to apologise,' the lieutenant says. 'It was a highly stressful situation. We're just trying to establish what happened, and we need to have as clear a picture as we can.'

'And what did you find inside the bag?' the detective continued.

'His phone was not in there – well, I didn't find it in there. There were some files and stationery, that sort of thing.'

'Did you squeeze his right or left arm?'

'What do you mean?'

'You say you squeezed his arm, hoping for a response. Was it his right or left arm?'

I think for a moment, imagining myself doing it. 'Left.'

'Can you be sure?'

'Yes, because I am right-handed, and I reached out with my right hand.'

'And when you checked his pulse?'

'Again, I put my fingers on the wrist of his left hand.'

'Did you touch any other part of Mr Trachonides's body, his clothes or his personal items?'

'No.'

'Can you just confirm to us where we might expect to find your fingerprints?'

'Like I said, I checked his pulse on his wrist and neck. I touched his arm. I also touched his rucksack and the items inside it.'

The detective puts the pen down and closes the notepad. She glances over at the lieutenant, and he gives a slight nod.

'Well,' she says, 'I think we have everything we need here. Is there anything you would like to add?'

'No,' I say.

'Fine. Interview ending 18.03, Wednesday 24th January 2018.'

The lieutenant turns off the recorder. 'You did well,' he says. 'We will be in touch if we need anything else. But for now, take a minute. Someone will come and collect you shortly to do the tests what we spoke about. And don't worry.' He smiles, his green eyes twinkling. 'Go home and relax with your family, and try not to think about all this.'

I notice again the heart pendant around his neck; it is just visible beneath his white shirt. I look out of the window at the sea and the sky, which are both much darker now. Now, a slither of gold rests upon the horizon above darkness.

The Book of Fire

Once upon a time, a mother and daughter, an old lady and a dog floated in the water in the reflection of the flames. They were as far out as they could possibly go without becoming invisible to others. They needed to be seen so that they could be saved. However, no one was coming for them. In all this chaos, no one had even looked at them. And the old lady was now dead. It was too late for her. She hadn't been able to hold on any longer. The smoke was too thick, the air too hot. Perhaps her heart had given up. The crate was still holding her up, and the girl held on to both her arms to make sure that she stayed there, that she did not slip away down into the water.

The old lady was gone from this world, with all the memories of her daughter and her Saturday visits to the grocer's. There must have been so much more, of course, so many memories, conversations, dreams, fears, traumas maybe, losses, hopes, wishes, songs. Yes, always songs. People always have memories of songs. Our memories dance with music.

The mother thought about her father, how he knew that *everything* worth knowing about the world was to be found in the strings of the bouzouki. Wordlessly, they told a thousand stories of joy and of sadness. When he played the instrument, he saw the way people moved to the melody, sometimes with their heads down, dancing a song of sadness, other times full of happiness. These were stories without words; they spoke a universal language that anyone could understand. The mother had always felt this, and what came to mind now were the silly things he used to say with that fisherman's cap on his head and the bouzouki strapped to his back. He was always nearly ready to head out to play music, or else he would take her with him to the bookies or for a walk in the local park on Sunday mornings, or get her to help him tend to his lemon tree – pulling off the dead leaves, spraying it with water when it was hot – or cook a barbecue in the tiny, almost non-existent garden.

One day, she thought, she would die, and her memories of him would die with her: the way he told stories, the way he lifted her in the air and kissed her.

The mother stared at the old lady. She wished she could bring her back to life and ask her about *her* father, ask her to share a memory of him so that it could live on. She felt a sinking of her heart, as if her heart was a boat. A sail-boat. Yes. A sail-boat that could either drift away or sink.

The entire port to their left was now up in flames. The boats that were harboured close to the land were alight. But, further out to sea, there was a boat moving towards them.

It appeared through the smoke, its white sail ghostly and angelic and beautiful. To the mother, it seemed to glow.

She called and called to this boat. 'Hello!' she yelled. 'Please help us!' She waved her hands in the air, calling again and again and again.

But she realised it was no use. She was too far away to be heard.

She took a breath. The boat itself she could not see – that was lost in the darkness of the smoke – but the sail glowed like the clouds with the sun in them. Perhaps, she thought for a moment, it is not a real boat. Maybe it is a heavenly boat, coming to take the soul of this old lady. If there was such a thing as heaven, then the old lady's memories would not be lost, and the world around them that was burning would continue to exist up there, all the spirits of the trees and flowers and animals – they would all be up there, adorning heaven with their beauty. If only. God, if only.

The mother realised that she had drifted away from her daughter in her mind, and she focused on her again. She suddenly saw how tightly she was holding on to the old lady's hands. Her knuckles were white.

'Darling,' the mother said, 'you're going to exhaust yourself. She has gone. We have to let her go.'

'I know, Mamma.' The girl's voice broke. 'But she's my friend.'

'I know, my love.'

'And she is such a lovely lady.'

'I know.'

'She wants to see her daughter again.'

The mother did not reply.

They remained silent for a few minutes more. The girl held on tight, the dog beside her. Even the dog seemed to be fading, the light in its eyes dwindling in spite of the flames within them.

'She is not coming back,' the mother said.

The girl remained quiet, then said, 'I don't mind being tired.' But her face grimaced, and the mother could see that she was in pain. It seemed this pain came in waves; at times, the girl appeared to be numb to it, her eyes glazed over, and then it would return, and her eyes would widen, then shut tight, and her whole body would tense up. This was one of those times.

The mother did not want to panic, show too much concern to alarm her daughter, so she said simply, 'But we have to reserve our energy. It's so important. I think you should let her go now. Just let her rest. Allow her to go. We have to, my love.' She used the same tone her husband would have used.

The girl thought about this for a while, then said, 'No, I won't let her go. I will not let her go, OK?'

'OK.'

'I don't want her to be lost down there. Why don't you understand?'

'I really do, more than you know.'

'So why are you saying these stupid things?'

Yes, why was the mother saying them? She could not stand to see the old lady's dead face. She could not stand to see her turning blue. She was worried that her daughter would get too tired and fade away, too.

'I will hold her then. Shall we take turns?'

The girl nodded.

'Very well,' the mother said, taking over, adjusting herself so that she was opposite the old lady with most of her torso on the crate, as she pulled her up as much as possible and held her under the arms.

The girl rested one hand on the dog and one on the crate. The dog licked her face and paddled.

'She is really thirsty,' the girl said.

The mother nodded, worried for the dog.

Then she looked at the old lady. She saw her face close up, the deep and fine wrinkles that criss-crossed her round, cherry-like cheeks, the fine hairs above her lip, a light layer of turquoise eyeshadow on her lids that revealed something new about her, something she had not noticed earlier. She was so close to her. So close to death.

The last time she had felt the coldness of death was when her father had died and she had sat on his lap that spring day and laid her head on his chest. She had felt his body go cold as she watched the blossoms fall from the trees outside. She'd somehow felt that his body had become heavier, as if his blood had filled with lead. Now, whenever the season changed from autumn to winter, when frost came dancing on the wind, she would be reminded of life slipping into death. Because that was how the seasons changed – a slip of one into another.

And yet, however much it broke her heart, she knew that the death her father had experienced was gentle and kind. She had often wondered whether death could ever be described as kind, but now she had seen something horrific, cruel and callous and violent. Was it death that was these things – or people? This thought ignited in her and turned to smoke, drifting away from her. Not that she hadn't known these things existed in the world, but now that she was in the middle of it, she was wrapped up by it, the flames like the hands of a darker, more ominous reality holding her tight, strangling her, force-feeding her poison, darkness and heat.

She shook her head, rattling away these thoughts. Then she looked out across the dark water and saw that the sailboat was coming closer. She was sure of it; that glowing white sail was larger now, more luminous as it reached out to them through the smoke. Could she be imagining it? But she could see the hull more clearly now, that it was painted a leaf green, that there was a name in red written across it. Then she swore that she could see someone on the deck, reaching out over the edge of the boat and dragging another person up. It was a child, and they held this child in their arms and kissed its face. It was all clearer, so it must be coming closer. She noticed that a large man stood on the cockpit, pulling at the ropes to adjust the mast.

'Can you see that?' the woman said to her daughter.

And the daughter followed the path of her mother's gaze until her eyes, too, rested on the glowing sails. 'Is it coming this way?' she asked, her eyes wide with hope.

'I think so,' her mother said. 'It's the first time a boat has come so close.'

'But there are other people in the water!' the girl said. 'It could veer off to the left or the right. We might not be seen, and then everyone might forget us.'

The mother remembered that feeling from childhood, where a single fear would grow and become an eternal catastrophe. 'No. Don't think like that.'

'Why not?'

'There's no point. You will get yourself all panicked and scared for no reason, because you can't change the outcome by worrying.'

The girl did not reply. Her eyes trembled with fear and fire.

A father and a son had drifted very close to them, and the mother could hear their conversation. The boy had his arms wrapped around his father's neck. He must have been five or six, and he was sobbing, and the father was pleading with him to stop.

'Please,' he was saying. 'Please stop. Come on. Come on. Come on. It's OK – it's all going to be OK. Everything will be OK. You'll see. Tomorrow, we will go back home.'

'Mamma!' the boy cried into his father's face, and the father's eyes were open wide with what the mother could only describe as agony.

Then he must have noticed that someone was staring at him, and he shifted his gaze and caught her eye. It was only for a second, and he looked down, but within his eyes, she had seen the whole world melting.

'The boy has lost his mamma,' the daughter said to her mother.

'Don't worry – they will find her.'

'Just like we will find Pappa?'

The mother paused for a moment. 'Yes,' she said, as resolutely as she could muster.

She held tightly to the old lady's arms. She tried not to look at her face. She focused her eyes on the sails instead. They reminded her of the moon. Yes, they reminded her of the moon on those clear nights when she had first moved here and she had gone on long walks in the forest with her husband at night. He would point up through the trees at a full moon or half moon or new moon and say nothing. He would just point. There was no need for words. There it was: this beautiful solitary figure in the starry night sky. She loved the moon. She loved him as if he were a person.

After her dad died, she had adjusted her bed so that she could see out of the window at night; she always left the curtains open. Then she would set her Snoopy alarm clock for 2 a.m., roughly the time that her dad would return home and tell her a story. She would wake up to the sounds of music from Charlie Chan's, glass breaking and laughter and police sirens, and she would focus on the moon, so far away, on its white glow. If it was a cloudy night, she would find the part of the sky where the clouds were translucent. And once again, she would feel safe.

She and her dad had never discussed the moon – it wasn't anything that he had ever even mentioned – but after his death, she watched the moon to stop her heart from breaking, to fill her heart with light in the darkness, just like her father's music and stories had done.

She had told her husband this when they met again all those years after their childhood summers. Yes, she had told him, and every time they walked in the forest, he had pointed up at the moon and said nothing. But there was something else: he had kept hold of her hand, tightly, safely, and that was all. That was all that was needed.

'Mamma,' the daughter whispered, 'look.'

The mother realised that the boat was even closer now. In fact, it was just beside them. The man on the deck was pulling the little boy out of his father's hands, and once again, he held the child tight in his arms and kissed his face and she heard him say, 'You're safe now. You're safe now.' He put the boy down on the deck and reached out a hand for the man. Then the large guy steered the sails and they drifted towards the mother and daughter.

First, the man pulled the girl onto the deck, then he reached out for the old lady. The mother looked up at him and said, 'She has died.'

The man nodded and called out for the big guy to help him, and they both leant over the deck, but they couldn't manage to pull her up, so heavy and limp was her dead body. So the big guy jumped into the water, took her from the mother's grip and lifted her so that the other man could reach down under her armpits, around her waist and heave her up.

Then it was the mother's turn, and when she was out of the water, she exhaled and began to cry.

'That's all we can take for now,' the large man said. 'Let's get these people safe and we'll come back.' And the mother noticed how red his eyes were, how his hands shook, how his white shirt was torn and burnt, how his lips were red and cracked.

She looked around the small deck. She grabbed hold of her daughter's hands, both of them, and held them tightly in her own. The girl kept her eyes closed and tears rolled down her cheeks. The mother checked to make sure that the guy had brought the dog up to the deck, and yes, there it was, by the girl's side, but it was not sitting alert as it normally would be, but lying on its side, wet and panting.

The old lady had been laid down on the other side of the deck, and one of the two men had covered her face and upper body with a coat. There was a middle-aged man sitting on his own, looking numbly out at the water. There was a teenage girl sitting by herself, with a blanket around her shoulders, a family huddled at the far end by the rudder: a woman, a man and a baby. He was rocking the baby. The woman was leaning on his shoulder, knees pulled up towards him, shaking. She held the baby's little hand. He rocked and rocked and rocked.

Then she noticed the boy who had been calling for his mother. He was crying in his father's arms. The sound reminded the mother of a song; it was a song her father had once played, and she had thought then in her youth that it was the saddest song she had ever heard. It didn't seem to have a verse or chorus; it was the same bars repeated over and over with some rifts in between. That was how the boy's sobbing sounded. Rhythmic and mournful and eternal.

She had asked her dad while he played, *Does this song have an ending?*

No, he had replied, glancing up at her with his cap sideways on his head and a smile in his eyes. *It goes on forever.*

13

THE FOLLOWING MORNING AT 11 a.m., I go to Maria's
Kafeneon to meet Mrs Gataki.

I arrive early and spend some time alone in
the back of the café by the bookcases. I love the old fairy
tales, the beautifully illustrated books that Maria keeps
on the shelves. I pick up a book of *Aesop's Fables*. There is
a picture on the first page of a wolf playing a flute and a
goat dancing to the music; they are both standing in a
woodland of ancient trees.

I turn to the tale about the astronomer. I remember this
story! Yes, this is one my dad used to tell me. He would
chuckle at the end and say, *Good warning, that.*

It is the story of an astronomer who goes out at night to
observe the stars. Every night, he puts on his coat and cap
and heads out to see all the la-di-das up in the sky. One
night, as he wanders through the quiet suburbs, looking up,
all his attention fixed upon the stars, he accidentally falls
into a deep well. He is hurt and bruised, and he calls out

for help. A neighbour comes to his aid, and when he learns what happened, he laughs – although that is my dad's version, and perhaps he did not laugh – and says, *Listen, mate, you're trying so hard to figure out what is in heaven that you do not manage to see what is on Earth.*

I loved this story. Even as a child, I understood how we can miss things, how we can neglect one thing for the sake of another. Now, it is as if something has been whispered in my ear, some unintelligible words, and my eight-year-old self is standing beside me, tugging at my sleeve.

I close the book, hastily. Out comes dust and the smell of ancient stories. I place it back on the shelf and cover the spine with a small vase from another shelf so that I do not have to look at it.

You do not manage to see what is on Earth.

The words come back to me.

You do not manage to see what is on Earth.

But *of course* I manage – of course I *manage*. It is *all* I have been doing.

However, the words do not leave me until Mrs Gataki taps me on the shoulder with an amused look on her face.

'You're away with the fairies,' she says in English. It is one of the few phrases she knows in English, and she says it at least three or four times a week. According to Mrs Gataki, most people are away with the fairies, apart from her.

I glance quickly over at the shelf, where the book of fables is hidden by the vase, and wonder for a second if it's really such a bad thing to be away with the fairies.

We sit at one of the high tables on some stools. I look around for the first time. The men from the garage are over on the other side of the café, sitting on the comfy sofa and drinking Greek coffee. The cat is lying on the armrest, being stroked by one of them. The professor is here, reading at a table beneath the lanterns; he is on his own this time. He glances up and nods a greeting and then gets back to his book. The TV is on again, but the volume is off, and it flickers above the door of the kitchen.

Mrs Gataki fans herself as usual with another crime thriller and looks at the menu. She has her hair up in a bun today, revealing fully her scars, which stretch like cobwebs on her neck. I notice that she is wearing only one heart-shaped stud earring, but before I can say anything, a voice says, 'Ready to order?'

I look up and Maria is standing beside us, pen and notepad in hand. Her hair is so short, but she still tucks non-existent strands behind her ear. She is wearing an A-line skirt, the kind people used to wear in the eighties. One of her legs, her right leg, is covered in scars: intricate swirling cobwebs, like the ones on Mrs Gataki's neck.

'I'm starving,' Mrs Gataki says. 'I think I'm going to have an omelette.'

Maria jots this down and looks at me.

'Just the usual please,' I say.

'No food for you?'

I shake my head. 'Not today.'

Suddenly, the thought of eating makes me feel sick. Why did I come here? I glance around again, resting my eyes first

139

on the professor and then at the men on the sofa. Perhaps one of these people is responsible for what happened to Mr Monk. It's not impossible or even unlikely.

I glance over at the professor again; he has closed his book now and is checking something on his phone. He senses almost immediately that I am looking this time and raises his head. He creases his brow in a question, and I flick my hand and smile as if to say *sorry, just daydreaming*. Then I look over at the garage guys.

The people, Mr Monk said. Could they have been *the people*? Could they have dragged him down to the dead forest and hanged him? Or did Mr Monk want to take his own life? Did he feel either so much shame or so much guilt, depending on the capacity of his heart, that he could not live anymore? I remember him crying, how he sobbed like a boy beneath the tree. I remember how I ran, how I ran and left him there to die.

Then I look around again and think of the people who should be here. Lazaros, sipping his coffee, going home with a bag full of pastries. Angela and Paul, who used to live up near Mr Monk's house – they were always in here reading broadsheet papers together, swapping them from time to time. And Calliope, the biology student, who used to travel to the university in the city and work in the convenience store on the weekends. She would pop in here and chat to the garage guys. There are so many more. They flicker in my mind like ghosts.

'I don't think even the fairies can reach you today.' Mrs Gataki is staring at me with raised purple eyebrows.

'Oh gosh, sorry – I'm just tired. You know, the nurse came to remove Tasso's bandages yesterday.'

'That must have been hard.'

I nod. 'It's OK,' I say. 'At least he is alive.' I say this to acknowledge her dead husband before she says it herself.

'Yes, that is very true, although we have got into a state of alive-or-dead thinking and that is not good in the long run.'

But this is exactly what she is doing! I smile at the irony but say nothing.

We are both quiet for a while. She takes her phone out of her bag and places it face down on the table. There was a time when her husband would call; now, it remains silent.

'So,' she says, 'Mr Monk.'

'How do you know?'

'How does anyone know anything in these areas? Close friend who is a retired policewoman.'

'I found him. It was me who found him,' I say quickly, without even thinking it through; the words just spill out of my mouth.

Her eyes narrow. She brings both her hands down to her lap, placing them gently on her skirt. Then she takes a short breath and says, 'My god.'

Maria brings our coffees, and we both remain silent for a moment or two.

As soon as she leaves, I say, 'Do you think he was killed?' I am about to tell her about the interview at the police station, but I change my mind. I can't bear the thought of discussing it. She will ask me a million questions.

'I don't know,' she says, looking down at her hands, then she looks up at me with sharp eyes. 'I'm interested to know what you think. You're the one who found him.'

I picture the chestnut tree – half dead, half alive – and Mr Monk leaning upon its twisted bark. I see the noose of the thick white rope around his neck and his red raw skin and the large broken branch on the ground beside him.

'I don't know what I think,' I say. 'I can't decide what I think.'

'Well, maybe it doesn't matter,' she says, 'whether someone else killed him or he did the job himself. The good thing is that he is dead.' And when she says these words, a cold feeling rises inside me, as if ice has trickled through my veins. 'Not that it will bring my husband back.' She almost whispers this, and I hear her voice crack, ever so slightly.

I place my hand over hers. Her skin is like very fine creased silk. I remember my mother's robust hands for a second, how she pressed down on the dough, putting the force of all her weight and all her emotions into kneading, never saying a word to anyone, ever, about what was on her mind. I remember my father's hand when he died, and for a while as I lay on his chest, I held on to it, knowing that I would need to let it go and never hold it again. I remember Tasso's hands. His new hands. His different hands.

I imagine Mrs Gataki's old husband rattling around in her mind, like he had once rattled around in their old house, watering the flowers, dusting away the cobwebs. *He will never really leave you, Mrs Gataki* – this is what I want to say. I want to tell her this, that her husband will remain with her always, but I'm anxious about her response. She will say *Enough with the clichés, Irini – they never help. You should know that.*

She has not attempted to move her hand; she has remained quiet with my hand over hers, breathing slowly.

'You understand, my love, don't you? That's what I like about you, Irini – you always get it.'

But do I get it?

I do not know what I get right now.

14

WHEN NIGHT FALLS, I HEAD out to the veranda to call Tasso in for dinner, and I see that Chara is sitting beneath the fig tree with him. The sky is clear; the stars and the moon are luminous. Chara has a blanket around her shoulders, and Rosalie is sitting on the ground between her and Tasso. On the table, she has the backgammon board open.

'OK, your turn,' she says to Tasso, and I see him nod but he doesn't move. Chara looks at his unbandaged hands. She throws the dice and waits as they tumble around on the board. 'Four and six!' she calls, and he seems to nod again and smile, but his attention is constantly pulled to the open land, to the silhouettes of half trees, broken trees, burnt trees, to branches now and then jutting out of the land.

Chara moves the pieces for him and says, 'Well, that wasn't bad. I think you might beat me this time. It's definitely not looking good for me.' Then, 'Right, my turn!' and once again she throws the dice.

I can't help thinking that everything that Tasso ever was is lost now, that his old self has been consumed by the flames. All the little beautiful, complex intricacies of the person he once was do not seem to exist anymore. He is a hollow man now.

Tasso's mother, Ekaterini, told me that as a baby he had a fascination with clocks. He would stare at people's watches, gaping at the time ticking by, as if he knew what it meant. Sometimes, he would grab people's wrists – anybody's, strangers', a random person's in the queue at the grocery store or the bus stop. Once, he even grabbed the wrist of the priest during holy communion – on that occasion, he wanted to chew the face off his watch.

But she didn't have to tell me this about him. I already knew. I'm not sure how I knew – it's not as if he was walking around staring at people's watches as a grown man – but there was a curiosity in him that was so intense it was as if he was always staring life right in the face.

Often, Ekaterini would sit with him for hours, holding the wall-clock, watching him while he watched the time. That woman had such patience.

'He was different from the start,' she said to me once, as we sat beneath the fig tree in the garden. Even though her back was bent, she would look up with open and curious and sparkling eyes. She would tilt her face upwards, as if she were soaking up the sun, even if it was drizzly, and on that particular day the sky was full of clouds, and she was only a few months away from death. 'We need people who are different, always,' she continued, 'to help us all see things more clearly, and then we have a responsibility to hold on to what we have understood, but people spit these things out like the pips of olives.' Her words frightened me – I was young and scared even then that I would love him too much, that I would never find anybody else like him, even if I travelled the entire world. She had a way about her, too; her voice was so quiet, but you listened.

On that day, Tasso was standing about five metres away, sketching us onto canvas. Sometimes, he'd be hidden behind the easel; sometimes, I would see his dark eyes fixed on us. I wanted his eyes to be on me. I felt safe. I felt seen. I was only a girl of twelve but feeling his gaze on me, studying me, trying to capture something about me, made me imagine what I might be like as a woman. I caught a glimpse of myself then.

He completed about thirty paintings of his mother that year, trying to conjure her from different angles, in different locations, holding on to her with each stroke of his hand.

'Your name means peace,' she said.

'Yes, I know,' I said, trying to be as polite as I could be, just as my mum had instructed. 'My dad told me.'

She said nothing, and her little eyes rested on the ground.

'Did you know that the olive tree is a symbol of peace?'

She looked out across the orchard now, where hundreds of olive trees stood so still, so silently. There was no breeze that day; not a leaf moved.

'They're like statues,' I said, and she laughed. I spoke to her in Greek with a heavy British accent. I was proud to speak the language that my father had taught me; it made me feel closer to him.

'Yes, I suppose they are. But they are alive. I'll pick the olives later and smash them.' There was a twinkle in her eye.

It was the year that my father died, and my mother had sent me to Greece to my dad's old village, to stay with Ekaterini and her family for a few weeks, to take my mind off things. But everywhere I turned, I was reminded of him. I found him in the lemons on the trees, in purple figs freshly sliced, in the crumbly feta cheese, in slivers of onions, in the honey baklava, in the steaming coffee. I saw him in the sweet red earth and the vast blue sky. He was everywhere.

My father was a postman by day, walking the east London streets, and a bouzouki player by night. In the evenings, my father would take off his postman's cap, shave, comb his thick black hair into a ponytail with a styling brush, put on his black shirt and black trousers, slap his face with aftershave and head out with his bouzouki strapped to his back and a fisherman's hat worn to the side, casting a shadow over one eye. He would stand in the light of the doorway to blow us a kiss goodbye. My dad's father had been a fisherman; he caught fish in the freshwater lake and in the sea at the bottom of the mountain in the old village where I live now. So off he went, my father, three or four times a week, wearing his father's old hat, to play music in dark and smoky London clubs.

He would play in late-night Greek tavernas that were open till the early hours or weddings in pokey city halls and sometimes in posh hotels with huge chandeliers. There was a large Greek community gathered in London – lost and bewildered, my father said, after the war in Cyprus, desperate to hear the songs of their homeland.

I went with him once, to one of these weddings, when Mum was away visiting her dying aunt in Devon, and I sat behind the speakers, watching my father's fingers dancing on the strings, listening to the songs. My favourite was 'Zorba's Dance' – the way all the people in the grand hall rose from their seats, linked arms and danced faster and faster until I thought their legs would fly off. I clapped and clapped to my heart's content.

His band consisted of five members: my dad – the bouzouki player – the violinist, the keyboard player and the vocalist – a beautiful, tanned woman with the straightest, shiniest hair I had ever seen. She drank only water with lemon and always wore a silk scarf around her neck. They used to come over to ours sometimes for a barbecue in our tiny garden. She would sing to me and explain the lyrics of the songs. I loved the song about the eagle that died in the sky, free and strong, after its wings were burnt.

'What you doing up, baby *mou*?' my dad would say, when he returned home after a late night. 'Come on, up the apples and pears we go before the current bun begins to rise!'

He would tell me the story of how his beloved bouzouki had once travelled from Turkey to Greece in his grandfather's arms when he was just a young lad, during the population exchange of 1923. He told me these stories in Greek so that I would learn to speak the language. Each night, my dad would embellish the story, adding more detail, making it so that his grandfather – then a fourteen-year-old boy – was alive in my bedroom, sitting beside us, plucking the strings gently with his grubby travelling hands. Then my dad would go downstairs and fall sleep in his armchair with the fisherman's hat still on his head and a cup of milky tea on the floor by his feet.

One morning, a week after I had turned twelve, he just didn't wake up. I shook him and climbed on him. I opened his eyelids and looked deep into his eyes. I whispered in his ear that I loved him, but he didn't wake up. So I sat on his lap and put my head in the crook of his neck and said, 'But Pappa, what happened to the boy when he got to Greece? Won't you tell me the rest of the story?' and when his reply was silence, I began to cry.

I stayed there all day. My mother had got up at the crack of dawn to bake before the punters arrived, so it was only me and Dad in the house, and he was meant to take me to school. I stayed on his lap, with my head resting on his shoulder all day long, listening to the hum of traffic outside, watching the blossoms fall from the cherry tree by the window – because it was spring and such a beautiful day, with a big blue sky and a huge yellow sun.

'About the olive tree,' Ekaterini said. 'Not so long ago ...' She nudged my leg to bring my attention back to her – she always used that phrase even if she was talking about thousands of years past or unreal times. 'Not so long ago, Zeus held a contest between Poseidon and Athena. The city of Athens would be the prize for the winner. He asked them both to make an offering. Poseidon smashed his trident against a rock, shaking the earth. An underground sea was created, unleashing a saltwater spring. However, there were plenty of rivers in the city, which was close to the sea, and Zeus was not really impressed. Athena, however, knelt down and planted something in the ground. Within minutes, a tree rose from the earth, with soft, silver-green leaves and an abundance of fruit. Zeus declared Athena the winner. Now, in the heart of the acropolis stands an ancient olive tree. It has survived many fires, mutilations, invaders. A sprig was *always* saved to be planted later.'

I wished I had saved a part of my father – his fingers, maybe, that ran like water over the bouzouki strings, or maybe his smile, or his right eye on the brighter side of his face that was not obscured by the hat. I wanted to replant him so that he could grow from the earth, even stronger and smilier than before.

I remembered that he had given me a gift before he died. A sterling-silver evil-eye pendant that I wore around my neck. So, after Tasso had finished his painting, I took his hand and dragged him through the orchard.

It was a hot summer's day. His hand was oily with paint, and it sweated and squelched in my grip.

'What are we doing?' he said, running clumsily to keep up. He was tall and slender and gentle and beautiful, and I felt that I was pulling a deer along behind me.

'I'm going to bury a gift that my dad gave me.'

'Why?'

'Don't ask questions.'

And then I stopped, finding the perfect spot, there at the edge of the orchard grove, just at the point where the forest began. I knelt, my knees pressing into the soil. First, I wiped my palm on my trousers, and it made a forest-coloured rainbow on my jeans.

'Will you explain?'

'My dad gave me this.' I pointed at the pendant around my neck, and he looked intently at it. 'Just help me dig a hole.'

And so we clawed at the mud together until we made a nice round hole. I took off the pendant and put it in the centre of the hole, and from that moment on, he remained silent, and I loved him for it. I loved him so much for this. I felt that it was a gift. I thought he understood; he may have not known exactly what I was doing and why, but he knew where it came from. I may be wrong, because I have never asked him – I suppose I didn't feel that I needed to. But I remember how I loved him, there, on the edge, between the forest and the orchard.

I had just lost my father. The walls of my world had crumbled, like the images I'd seen of the blitz during my history class. One picture stayed in my mind even then, even before I lost my father – I guess we are all secretly preparing ourselves for loss – a picture of a young girl standing in front of a bombed-out building, and through the broken wall of the fallen house was a sky that seemed normal, the way it had always been. I could now relate to this girl even more, as I found myself looking up towards that slice of sky. And I think Tasso saw this. He knew about my fallen walls. It is something we had in common. Except, his walls were still standing; he was holding them up precariously with paintbrushes.

Together we buried the pendant, flattened the earth. Then he smiled in a way that made his black eyes shine.

Tasso's painting mesmerised me. Later that night, when everyone was asleep, I sneaked down to the cellar where he kept his work. It was a gentle painting – that's the only way I could think to describe it – as if a very soft voice was telling me something sad and true. He captured us so beautifully, not precisely – that was his style even then – but we were there, me and his mum, eternally talking about the olive tree while I was thinking about replanting my father and watching him grow.

The following year, when I returned, after Ekaterini had died, a tree had grown in that exact spot, and the olives were a beautiful blue, the colour of the dark part of the sea.

15

IN THE MORNING, CHARA'S VOICE wakes me up. She
is calling me. I stretch out to find Tasso but realise he
is missing from my side again, as he always is now.

Chara's voice is different; it is like it was before the fire.
There is life in it; there is excitement and panic.

I get out of bed and head downstairs.

'Mamma, Mamma, come and see!' she calls.

I go out to the porch and find her kneeling on the ground.
She is leaning over the body of a jackal. The animal is lying
on its side, its legs sprawled out in front of it.

'Mamma,' she whispers. 'Please come and see – please
come now.'

'I'm here,' I say and lean over and see that the jackal's eyes
are half open and that it is breathing heavily, as if there is
a huge weight on its chest.

'It's alive, Mamma,' she says, and I think she is going to
break down crying, but she doesn't.

Instead, she places her hand gently on the jackal's fur and strokes it with the lightest, most delicate touch, and I hear her catch her breath.

'He's just a baby,' she says.

'He's a boy?'

'Yes,' she says. 'I think so. A baby boy. Look at his feet.'

I notice that the pads of the animal's paws are red raw; there is no fur on his legs, and the golden fur on the rest of his body is matted. There are so many bald spots where it looks like he must have been burnt in the fire.

'What's wrong with him?' she says.

I look again at his feet, the way new blisters have developed over old scars and what looks like dead skin. 'Well,' I say, 'I'm no expert, but it seems as though he was injured in the fire and has never had the chance to heal properly.'

'It's been five months,' she says. 'Has he been in pain all this time?'

Her eyes are fearful and my heart breaks. 'I don't know, sweetie. The ground is also still hot in places. Perhaps he has been walking around trying to find food and has made his injuries worse. It looks like he has an infection.'

'He has managed to find us,' she says and looks up at me.

'Yes, he has.'

'What shall we do?' Even though her voice is a whisper, I hear panic.

'Let me get some water,' I say.

I bring out a bowl and a soup spoon. I give the spoon to Chara, and she scoops some water and gently drips it onto the jackal's mouth. The little jackal parts his lips, allowing more water to seep into his mouth. Chara repeats this about ten times, and then the jackal licks his mouth with his tongue, and his eyes open more. Without moving his head, he glances up to look at Chara.

'I think he's saying thank you,' she says. 'I think the jackal is pleased.'

I fetch some pillows and covers from the cupboard. I arrange them on the floor in the living room, where all Tasso's paintings of the forest hang. Then I go outside and gently lift the jackal up, with both my hands beneath his body, and transfer him, in that same position, onto the blankets.

Chara then sits down beside the jackal, stroking him as she did before.

I call up the vet and the receptionist tells me that she will call me back within the hour.

I sit in the living room with Chara and wait.

When all is quiet and the jackal is asleep, Chara puts her ear on the side of his chest to make sure he is breathing.

'He's OK,' she says, glancing up at me.

I nod and tell her she is doing a great job.

She doesn't smile. 'Grandad would have known what to do.'

'Yes, he would have,' I say.

She remains silent for a while, thinking. 'Will I have to go to school again?'

'Yes, of course. When you are feeling better.'

'I will never feel better.'

'Yes, you will.' I say this bluntly, in fact quite harshly, and her eyes darken. I cannot force this, I say to myself.

But I want her to be better. I want so much for her to be better. 'You will like your new school,' I say.

And she nods but says nothing.

Once more, she puts her ear to the baby jackal's chest. 'Who will look after him when I go back to school?'

'Let's just see what happens, OK?'

'OK,' she says and forces a smile. It is a smile that is so sad. It breaks my heart. 'Will Pappa be able to paint again?'

'I don't know. I have no idea. Honestly.'

'If he can, what will he paint now? There is nothing left.'

'Chara,' I say, 'don't speak like that.' I say these words, but there is a part of me that is pleased to see life in her again.

'Why not? There is nothing left. Nothing.'

'There is always something.'

'It is all burnt.'

'There is *always* something left.'

'There is nothing, Mamma. Nothing!'

She raises her voice at me; she scrunches her face, as if what she is feeling is physical pain. Then she remembers the jackal and observes him closely, perhaps making sure that she hasn't disturbed him.

'There is me and you and Pappa and Rosalie and now the jackal. There is this house.'

She stares directly at me, as if I'm the only person left on Earth. Then her face softens, and she quickly glances around, as if to remind herself that things still exist.

'Yes,' she says, 'and I will make sure that the jackal doesn't die.'

'I know you will.'

'But the forest – that is all gone. Pappa will not be able to paint it.' She says this resolutely.

'He can if he wants to,' I say. 'He can paint what exists now.'

'Mamma,' she says.

'Yes?'

'You are so argumentative. Why didn't you become a lawyer?'

I laugh and get up and kiss her hard on the cheek, and she laughs, too, and tells me to be less noisy – we don't want to wake the baby jackal; he needs his rest.

So we sit quietly. Chara's mention of her grandfather brings back memories.

Lazaros used to go to Maria's Kafeneon and get a ton of pastries. He was obsessed with them, because they were the exact same pastries that his late wife used to make – definitely not as good, though. He kept up this routine for more than twenty years. Time did not diminish his love for her; it did not make her memory fade. So, every Sunday we would sit in the garden if it was warm and in the living room on the colder days and eat baklava dripping with syrup, crumbly kourapiedes coated in icing sugar, honeyed loukoumadies.

It's not the same, though, as when the person you love makes them and the entire house smells of their sweetness. This is what he used to say, with tears in his eyes. Every single time without fail.

A few times when the Kafeneon was closed, Lazaros decided to make the pastries himself. He wore Ekaterini's old apron – the blue one with the daisies. He wouldn't let me help, so I would sit on the kitchen chair at the large wooden table and listen to him going on about trees. He would tell me how trees grow, about their vascular tissues.

On one occasion, when I was in the garden while he baked, Lazaros came to the door, oven gloves on and a tray in his hands.

'Bloody hell,' he said.

'What's up?'

'I burnt it all.'

'Really? I can't smell anything.'

'Hmmm.'

He returned to the kitchen, and I followed.

I went in and he was slouched at the table. Black lumps sat there on the baking tray.

'My god, Lazaros. What are they supposed to be?'

'Kadaifi,' he said.

We both stared at them.

'Ah. I see. I can kind of see the angel hair.'

'More like horsehair now.'

He picked up the tray, scraping all the pastries into the bin.

The kitchen looked like a bomb had hit it: flour everywhere and walnuts, pistachios, cinnamon, sheep butter, sugar, oranges, lemons.

'Gosh, Laz,' I said in English, because he liked it when I suddenly threw in some English; for some reason, it made him laugh. 'It's as if the kitchen's exploded,' I added in Greek again.

He laughed from his chest. He also loved it when I took the mick out of him.

'I'll try again another day,' he said, when he had stopped laughing, spitting phlegm into a hanky that he kept in his pocket. 'Next time, I won't forget I put them in.'

This memory leads to another. I see him again, sticking out his tongue as far as it would go, with his mouth wide open, lines of anger on his face. 'My tongue is growing hair, Irini! That is how long I have waited for someone to hear me!' Now, he is standing in the dappled shade of the trees, wearing his wicker baseball cap that he used to put on when he went out to work. 'The droughts are so intense, my girl. You know, in the eighties, there was a time when the forest fires were quite bad – then, a decade later, people started to put two and two together and realise what they were doing to this Earth, but it's all getting much worse.'

I remember him going out with a drip-torch and a yellow builder's cap to make a contained fire in order to get rid of the excess wood and dried leaves on the ground. It was a practice that people had been observing for thousands of years, he had told me, which decreased the likelihood of hotter, more serious fires and also helped to renew the forest. But he was afraid that this practice wasn't working so well anymore. It was too hard to contain the fires; it was becoming too dangerous, even for a master like him.

When he saw that I was listening to him seriously, he would suddenly stop talking and smile, as if he was scared of upsetting me at all, and I would see again that twinkle in his eye and force myself to believe that everything would be OK.

Why is this only coming back to me now? I suddenly become aware of the painted forest around me, of the animals

159

existing safely within them. I remember Mr Monk. I allow his face to come into my mind, the rope around his neck, and once again I feel the fire surrounding me.

I am not the same person I was before I found Mr Monk. I will never be the same again.

I focus on Chara sitting on the floor in front of me, stroking the little jackal.

My phone rings. I pick it up.

'Hello,' the vet says in a hurried tone. 'I hear that you have found an injured jackal?'

I force myself to be present.

'We have,' I say and give her a brief summary of the animal's condition.

'OK,' she says. 'Keep doing what you're doing, and I'll come by as soon as I can – it'll probably be this afternoon.'

'The jackal is asleep now,' Chara says when I get off the phone. 'Completely asleep. I wrapped the blanket around him. What time is the vet coming?'

'Not until later.'

Chara strokes the jackal.

We sit there for a while without speaking. This time I do not allow my mind to drift. I look at my daughter and remember the scar on her back, now hidden beneath her winter jumper.

'Should we feed him when he wakes up?' she says.

'Let's wait for the vet to arrive.'

'How long now?'

'A couple of hours.'

She nods and lies down, with her arm resting gently over the jackal's chest.

'Mamma, look!' she whispers. 'He is opening his eyes a bit more.'

I look at the jackal, his little face, and how hard he is trying to turn his head to see who is helping him. I am happy that Chara is preoccupied with something other than her father. It is as if this little jackal came into her life to remind her that the world still exists out there.

Every now and then, she puts more water to his lips using the spoon. Every now and then, the jackal shifts his eyes to look at her. Chara does not remove her hand from him, even for a second; she kneels over him as if she is praying. I stay where I am and listen to her muttering words of reassurance in his ear. And this all reminds me again of the year I met Tasso, when I was eleven, and he showed me the jackals in the woods and taught me not to be afraid. But hand in hand with the good memory, I feel anger for the fact that he is outside on his own, lost in his world. I want him to be right here with us now.

Chara lays down beside the jackal and, in a few moments, falls asleep with the spoon still in her hand and her other hand resting on the animal's side. I see his body rising gently. The jackal's breathing is laboured, but at least he is breathing.

I get another blanket and cover her with it, and in her sleep, she whispers that the baby boy is still alive.

16

JUST BEFORE 2 P.M., I hear the rumble of an engine and go to the window. The vet pulls up in a clean silver van. Two people get out, both wearing blue. The woman is holding a large medical bag, and the man walks up to the door ahead of her and rings the bell.

Chara is already at the door, and she opens it, glances at me fearfully but says nothing.

I greet them both. The woman shakes my hand and introduces herself as Dr Kostas and the man beside her as Andronikos, the practice nurse. I lead them into the living room, where the jackal is lying. His breathing seems less laboured now, and his eyes are fully open, but he is not moving.

The woman kneels down, and the man unzips the medical bag and hands her items from within it. First, she checks the jackal's heart and lungs with a stethoscope. Then she looks into his eyes with a torch, lifting his lids. Then she examines his paws closely, without touching them; she tilts her head this way and that.

'Poor thing,' she says. 'How has he managed to survive? He definitely has a bad infection. There are old burns beneath the blisters. Also, I believe he must have been walking around on the hot forest land for a while – we have seen many animals whose paws were continuously burnt so that the skin was so damaged it could not heal on its own. These wounds look like they've *never* had a chance to heal. I guess now that it's cold, his little immune system just packed in. I'm going to administer a dose of antibiotics and some painkillers.'

She signals to the man kneeling beside her, and he prepares two injections. She gently inserts one needle into the jackal's side by his thigh. The jackal whimpers, the first time we have heard him make a sound.

'All right, little guy,' the vet says. 'You are doing so well.'

I can feel Chara tense beside me.

The nurse gives the vet another injection, and she administers this one a little further up. She pauses now to stroke the baby jackal's fur. 'Don't worry,' she says. 'We will get you all better. You'll see.'

I notice Chara's shoulders soften at the vet's words.

The vet stands up. 'I have to take him with me,' she says, and Chara, his protector, stands up, too, to face her. 'He will need grafts,' the vet continues, addressing us both, 'on his feet and paws – they are too badly damaged. Once the infection has cleared with the antibiotics, I have a method of using fish-scales to heal the skin of an animal. I use the scales of a tilapia fish.'

'So he will be a jackal with fish-scales?' Chara says.

'Yes, on his paws and feet.' The vet smiles with her eyes.

'That's a funny thought,' Chara says. 'But it won't hurt him?'

'He will be asleep when I do it. Then, as soon as he wakes up, he will slowly begin to feel better. As soon as those open wounds are covered, they can begin to heal.'

'And will he be able to walk again?' Chara asks.

'I should hope so. If all goes well and the grafts take, then yes.'

'And will he be able to play again? Because baby jackals love to play – did you know that?'

The vet really smiles at her now. 'Yes. As a matter of fact, it is one of my most favourite things in the world, to see baby jackals playing.'

'He might be alone now, though.' Chara suddenly looks very sad; her determination to save the jackal has gone now that the responsibility for his welfare has been taken out of her hands, and so her sadness for him is over-whelming her.

'Well,' the vet says, 'he won't be all alone, because now he has you.'

She nods her head at Chara, and Chara smiles. It is a real smile.

'Can I come and see him?'

'Yes, of course. We will give you a call once he has woken up.'

'Thank you very much,' Chara says in an adult voice.

The nurse heads out to the van and retrieves a small stretcher, which he places on the ground. Chara and I stand back and watch as they gently lift the jackal onto the stretcher and carry him out to the van. I notice for the first time that there is a driver, a young man with long brown hair, who has fixed his gaze on the dead land. For a split second, I see the same deadness in his eyes, the kind that exists out there, as if he and the land are one. I look away when he catches my eye, and he starts the engine.

The vet and the nurse get into the back of the van with the jackal. They reassure Chara that they will be in contact soon and close the doors.

Then we stand in silence and watch them drive away through the dust.

I think of Mr Monk being transferred into the back of an ambulance, white sheet over him. There is no hope for Mr Monk. My heart aches. I feel that I have breathed in the deadness of the forest and that I will never be me again.

When the van is out of sight, Chara begins to cry.

'Now, come on,' I say, putting my arm around her and pulling her close to me. 'Come on now – you saved that little jackal. He will have a good life now, because of you. Do you know what that means?'

She nods into my chest without saying anything. We stand there together for a while. I stroke her hair and look out at the land beyond. There is no more snow and the land is barren. I wish I could protect her from all this, but I can't. I am powerless.

I walk alone down to the fish market in the next town and buy sea bream, potatoes and some bits and bobs for a salad.

Then I head home and prepare the dinner, lay the table, squeeze some oranges.

I try not to think about the police or Mr Monk or even the jackal. But when I am alone, I think of Lazaros again.

This time, he is wearing no hat. It is a hot summer's day. I am tuning my bouzouki at the kitchen table. He is sitting quietly opposite me, running his hand the wrong way through his hair – from the back of his neck all the way up to his forehead – something he used to do when he was deeply contemplating something.

'What's up, Laz?' I say in English.

'I have a problem,' he says. 'I can't stop this' – he taps his head – 'from whirring.'

'What's on your mind?' I say, still in English.

'Well,' he says, 'it's bloody hot.'

'Shall I make you a frappé?'

He nods and I get up to prepare it.

'Bloody, bloody hot,' he says again, first in English, then reverting back to Greek as he can't sustain it. 'This hot, dry air is like a sponge! It soaks up water from whatever it touches – the soil, the rivers and streams, the plants and trees.'

Then he stays quiet for a while. I finish making the frappé – black, no sugar – and place it in front of him.

He slurps at the drink for a while, then he says, as if he has been thinking the worst of things, 'You need three things to start a fire: the right weather, the right climate conditions – and a spark. And thanks to us, the climate conditions are always right.'

166

Before I can remember what my response was, he fades away. Trying to recall the rest of the conversation feels like trying to catch a dream. He disappears, vanishing into darkness like the forest.

The Book of Fire

The boat sailed away from the fire but remained parallel to the shore. When all was calm, the mother could see the pain on her daughter's face again. The girl was sitting with her shoulders and head hunched over. She had now been overtaken by the pain.

The mother grabbed her hand and held it tightly. 'I wish there was something I could do,' she whispered in her daughter's ear. 'We'll be at the hospital soon. It'll all be over soon.'

The girl leant back now and looked into her mother's eyes. 'Sometimes, I don't feel anything, Mamma,' she said. 'It's like my body forgets. Then it's bad, it hurts so much.'

'Just close your eyes. Close them and take long breaths.'

The girl leant forwards again and closed her eyes and breathed slowly. The mother held on to her hand and watched her shoulders gently rise and fall.

As the boat sailed further away from the fire, the mother sighed. She could see how far the fire had spread; they travelled for at least fifteen minutes before they could make out land that had not been consumed by flames. Now, their surroundings became softer and cooler. She looked at her daughter, who was still hunched over, taking long breaths. She squeezed her hand again, and the daughter sat up and looked at her. The water and fire had vanished from her face. The mother could see the darkness of the sky in the reflection of her eyes.

'Where is Pappa?' the girl asked.

'He will find us,' the mother said, sounding as confident as she could. But she was not sure – she was uncertain about everything – and the thought crossed her mind that she might never see him again. Her body turned cold. She tried to push the thought away.

The sky was black. It wasn't night-time; no, it must have been early afternoon by this time. The sky was covered in a thick layer of smoke, smoke that moved and undulated so that it appeared to her like a stormy sea. It stretched away and trailed off as it reached the horizon. The dog was lying down with its head on its paws and its eyes shut.

One of the men approached them. He knelt and looked into the girl's eyes.

'How are you doing?' he said.

She nodded. It seemed as though this was all she could find the energy to do.

'How about I get you both some water?' he said. 'And some for your dog, too?'

At this, the girl gave him a little smile, the tiniest smile, but it was clear from the way her eyes glittered that it came from her heart.

The man patted the dog on the head, and it lifted its eyelids ever so slightly. Then the man left and returned with three bottles of water. He gave one each to the girl and the mother, before kneeling down again, opening the third bottle, pouring some water into his palm and putting it to the dog's mouth.

'Come on, baby,' he said. 'Come on.'

The dog lifted its lids again and this time its chin, too, and started to lap up the water. When it drank all the water, the man poured more into his hand and offered it again to the dog, who lapped it up faster this time. He did this again and again.

The mother looked at this man, at his wet jeans and blackened T-shirt, at his eyes that seemed to be brimming with blood and his bright-red face. What little hair he had was stuck to his forehead. He filled his palm one more time. 'Oh, that's a good ...' He glanced at the daughter.

'Girl,' she said. 'She's a girl.'

'Well, what a good girl you are,' he said to the dog. 'I bet she worked hard in the water, am I right? I have a dog, an old mutt, and she's as loyal as ... well, as loyal as a dog!' He laughed. 'Dogs know when their humans need help, and they will do anything to help them.'

The girl nodded and smiled again and placed her hand on the dog's back.

Then the man stood up and looked out to sea, then in the direction of the land, and the mother saw the humour and the energy drain from him as he sighed loudly, then inhaled deeply, as if he was trying to revive himself. In the next

170

moment, he put on a strong voice again. 'We won't be long now,' he said. 'You hold on there. We're going to the town after this, where the nearest hospital is.'

On the other side of the deck, the man was still rocking the baby and the woman still leant upon his shoulder. She seemed to be asleep now that she was no longer frightened for her life and the lives of her family. Her face looked relaxed, and her hand rested gently upon the hand of her child while they slept.

The mother then spotted an old man on the deck whom she had not seen on the boat earlier. He was standing up, looking down at something in his hands so intently that even the rocking of the boat did not stir him. His white hair was bright even without the light of the sun, and he wore a checked shirt that was torn and black.

The mother stood up. It was the old man who had helped them! He had somehow managed to climb the gate! Her heart leapt. She wanted to embrace him, to thank him for what he had done for them, to tell him how glad she was that he had survived.

She approached him and placed her hand on his shoulder. He turned to face her, and she saw immediately that this man's face was different. This guy had large grey eyes and a round nose. Her heart sank. The old man, she remembered, had tiny blue eyes; she could see them as clearly as if she were once again looking at him through the gate.

'Yes?' the man said.

'I'm so sorry,' the mother replied. 'I thought ... for a moment, I thought you were somebody else.'

The mother looked around the boat now. There was the middle-aged man sitting on his own. He was still looking numbly out at the water. In fact, it seemed as if he had not moved an inch; he was so covered in soot that he could have been a statue there on the deck. The teenage girl had a blanket around her shoulders; she was looking down at what seemed to be a cracked screen on a blank phone. Then the mother noticed the boy again, the one who had been calling for his mamma. He was no longer crying. He was sleeping now on his father's lap, and the father was looking up at the sky.

Then the baby began to cry. The woman woke up and took the child from the man's arms and told him to get some rest, too, and she showered the baby's face with tiny kisses.

After a while, they drifted towards the shore, and when they arrived as close to the sand as possible, the man who had brought them water anchored the boat. There was no port here, so they all climbed out of the boat, one by one, into about a foot of water, and trudged to the shore. The mother held her daughter's arm. The girl was now finding it hard to walk because of the pain she was feeling.

'It's getting worse, Mamma,' the girl said as they walked on the sand. She bent her knees as if she was about to crouch to the ground, but her mother gently pulled her up from her armpits.

'I know, baby,' she said, 'but we have to keep going. We are nearly at the hospital. OK?'

The girl nodded, took a deep breath and straightened herself, walking again with her mother's help.

The two men carried the body of the old lady to a car that was waiting. 'Don't worry,' the man whispered to the mother and the girl. 'Her body will be taken to the morgue, and if you leave your name and number, we will contact you. My cousin owns the morgue, and I know that he is diligent and attentive to his work. He will make sure your loved one is safe, and he will call you as soon as he can.'

The man gave the mother a green leather notebook. There were a few pages torn out at the beginning and after this a list of ten names with numbers. Already in this notebook were the loved ones of so many people taken by the fire. And this is just the beginning, the mother thought.

The man perhaps saw the look on her face and said simply, 'What can we do?'

He handed her a pen, and she wrote down her name and her number. Somehow, she had become this old lady's next of kin and she didn't even know her name.

Everyone was silent as they walked along the sand. The mother thought that they were all numb. That was how she felt – a numbness that reached the core of her soul, if there is such a place – and even her daughter was silent. She didn't complain now of any pain. She did not cry; she didn't even speak.

Something pulled the mother out of her numb state. It was the rustling of leaves; it was the sound of the sea and the birds flying above their heads. It was the sight of the ferns so green and bright along a slope that led to a road. Here on the shore, there were three pine trees leaning down low on the sand, casting long shadows. The mother had been in the water for only a number of hours – god knew how many – but it felt like a hundred years. It was as if she had not heard the rustling of leaves for a hundred years. This sound now seemed to belong to a different world.

Maybe she was shaking, or perhaps she was crying and hadn't realised, because her daughter suddenly looked at her and said, 'Are you all right, Mamma?'

'Yes, yes,' the mother said. 'Oh yes, I'm OK. More importantly, how are you?'

'I don't know,' was all the girl said.

On the road ahead a bus was waiting for them. The man who had given them water told them to get on the bus, which would take them to the hospital. He wished them good luck and, just as he was about to turn away, the girl approached him and put her arms around him. As she did this, the mother saw again the deep lines of pain on her face.

'Now, there, that's OK,' the man said softly. 'You don't have to thank me.'

On the bus, the mother looked out of the window at this town that had not been touched by the fire. She looked at the trees and the wildflowers that lined the road. How quickly this all could vanish, she thought. How fragile it all seemed now. How huge destruction can be, how consuming, how final. In her mind flashed the enormity of the fire, an entire wall of flames reaching east to west and up to the sky. Only the water could stop it, and by the time it had reached the cliff, it had consumed so much.

She would never see her bungalow again; she was sure of this. And now, in this quiet space, with only the sound of the engine and the crying of a child in the back, another thought came to the forefront of her mind and grew and grew and grew: would she see her husband again? She was so afraid that this fear etched itself in her heart and in fact would never leave her.

Then she realised her daughter was crying beside her; she was rocking back and forth. The mother had never seen her do this before, and when she leant close to look into her eyes, she saw that she was far away.

She placed her hand over her daughter's. 'Speak to me,' she said.

'It hurts, Mamma – a lot.'

And the mother felt so helpless. 'We're nearly there,' she said, though she didn't even know where they were, let alone how far away the hospital was.

But it wasn't too long before they arrived. Outside the hospital, she saw how many others were in the same position; people arriving in vans and cars with red faces, burnt limbs, singed clothing. Some were on stretchers.

Eventually, the mother and the girl were ushered inside the hospital by a man who stood at the entrance, he seemed to be one of the many volunteers who had arrived to help out. He was short and stocky with thinning grey hair, wearing a pair of glasses that seemed to sit crooked on his nose and made his brown eyes seem slightly bigger than they were.

'We can't leave our dog,' the girl said.

'We will tie her by her leash to this post,' the man said.

'She doesn't have a leash.'

'Fair enough,' he said amiably. 'I will look after her. I will stay with her and give her water, and when you come out, I will be here. OK?'

The girl was apprehensive. 'But what if we do not come out today?'

The man took a rucksack off his shoulders, fumbled around and retrieved an old receipt and a stub of a pencil. He pressed the receipt onto the wall and wrote down his number. 'Get your mum to call me and let me know. I promise that I will look after your dog until you are out.'

'But why are you doing this for us?' the girl said, and the mother nudged her shoulder.

'It's OK,' the man said. 'It's a good question. I would like to help. I feel like I want to do something to help. I am lucky that my family are safe. I have a son about your age. He loves dogs. I promised him I would get him a dog for his next birthday. When I tell him that I looked after this beautiful greyhound, he will be so happy. And if you should stay in overnight, then I will take your dog home, and my son will give it lots of attention and love, I can assure you. He's a good boy, very conscientious – like you, I suspect. It will make him happy to help someone.'

The girl looked into the man's shimmering eyes and then nodded at the dog. 'You be good, young lady, OK?'

The dog barked, and she ruffled its fur.

Inside the hospital, they were told to take a seat in a corridor that was full of light. The girl sat down and put her head in her hands, and the mother stroked her hair.

'Where is Pappa?' she said quietly.

'I don't know,' the mother said.

The girl remained quiet, then after a while she said, 'And Grandad ... where are they both?'

The mother didn't know what to say, so she sang very quietly, close to her daughter's ear, a song that she used to sing to her when she was a baby, a song that her father used to sing. In fact, it was the oldest known complete musical composition, the Seikilos epitaph, which had been carved on a tombstone. This was the only song that came to mind in that sunlit corridor, and she heard her voice overlaid upon her father's and in the background the gentle strum of the bouzouki:

'*While you live, shine.*

Have no grief at all.

Life exists only for a short while.

And time demands its toll.'

And just as she was about to repeat the verse, someone called her name. A man's voice. Her husband's voice?

He said it again. It *was* her husband's voice – she was sure – but she was too frightened to look. The man said her voice once more, louder this time, and when she finally looked up, she saw his silhouette against the beaming rays of sun. Was it really him?

'Thank god,' the man said. 'Oh, thank you, god.'

And when she looked up, she saw that it was not her husband at all but a man whom she saw in the mornings drinking coffee at Maria's Kafeneon.

'I'm sorry,' he said. 'I didn't mean to startle you. It's just that I saw you both out in the water. I was waving – did you see me? I was further out along the port. I was worried about you and your daughter – I wanted to make sure you were OK. Then I was distracted by something, and when I looked back, you were gone.'

She stared at the man, unblinking.

'I am sorry I startled you. It's just that I see you every morning. I think mornings will be different from now on.'

It was a strange thing for the man to say, but in those words was so much truth. Everything would be different from now on, she wanted to say, not just mornings. But yes, they would no longer be having a coffee at the same time at separate tables with a smile for each other.

The man sat down next to them. 'My daughter is in the operating theatre,' he said. 'I'm waiting for her.'

The first thought the mother had was a dark one. She hoped that he wouldn't be waiting forever.

'I'll pray for her,' the mother said, and the man remained silent and looked over at the girl, before returning his attention to the mother.

'Do you believe in God?' he said.

'I don't know what I believe in. But I will pray, just in case it helps,' she said.

Then they did not speak again, and the man didn't move; he stayed right there beside them, occasionally checking his watch. Maybe they sat like this for an hour, maybe two. It was not clear how much time had passed when a nurse called them.

The girl was told to sit on a bed and lean forwards. The doctor, harried, obviously exhausted, was a short woman with dark hair. She checked the girl's pulse, her breathing and oxygen levels, and then examined her back. 'These look like second-degree burns,' the doctor said to the room and then, to the nurse, 'around eighteen per cent. Can you check her vitals again in half an hour? They're all within normal range now, apart from her heart rate, which is elevated. Numb the site. Remove the material. Clean and dress the wound. A thousand milligrams of paracetamol and a high dose of penicillin. Any allergies?' She was now addressing the mother, dark alert eyes looking straight into hers.

'No, none.'

The doctor seemed overwhelmed by the fire victims who were streaming into the hospital. At the moment when it seemed that she was about to leave the room and dash off to see another patient, she paused in front of the mother and said, 'Someone will come and speak to you tomorrow more thoroughly, when things have calmed down.' She smiled a sad but reassuring smile, and that was all the mother needed. She would hold on to this smile the entire night.

First, the nurse inserted a cannula into the girl's hand before administering the antibiotics and paracetamol. Then she inserted an injection directly into the wound on her back. The mother held her daughter's hand. She sang her the song her father used to sing to her. The girl flinched, scrunching up her face, but then her entire body began to soften.

The nurse, a middle-aged woman with thick curly hair, began peeling away the T-shirt that was stuck to the girl's back. Finally, the wound was exposed, and the mother looked at her daughter's back, how the fire had melted the skin from shoulder blade to shoulder blade and down her spine. Tears fell from the mother's eyes, but when the girl turned to look at her, she wiped them away quickly.

'I'm OK,' the daughter said. 'It doesn't hurt anymore.'

The mother nodded. 'I'm so glad, baby.'

'Does it look bad?'

'It's hard for me to say. Not too bad. Don't worry at all.'

'That means it's bad. Why do you never tell me the truth? Pappa would tell me the truth, you know.'

'It's hard because I love you so much.'

'Pappa loves me so much, too, but he always tells me the truth.'

The mother knew this was true. But she did not have the strength her husband had.

She wanted to be honest. But what could she do? Would she tell her that layers of her skin and nerves had burnt, that her body would never look the same again? Perhaps if she told her daughter some semblance of the truth, at least she would be prepared.

But once again, the mother lost her voice. She tried to speak, but the words would not leave her mouth. It felt as though all the words in her mind were burning in the fire, turning to ash.

Instead, she took her daughter's hand in hers, leant in close and whispered, 'I love you. I love you so much.'

17

THE FOLLOWING MORNING, TASSO HEADS out to the garden, and Chara follows him. Now that the jackal isn't here, her attention is fully on her father. It is quiet. There are no birds chirping in the tree today. I wonder where they have gone. Maybe they have found the half chestnut tree in the dead woods? Perhaps they have flown away to another place.

Although Tasso has had his bandages removed, he is sitting in exactly the same position as before, palms up, slightly open, as if he is holding two oranges. Then I realise that on the table in front of Chara is an artist's sketchbook. It is open to two blank pages and on top are pieces of charcoal and paintbrushes. She is holding a small pot of paint in her hand, and she is dipping a paintbrush in and out of it. It is the most beautiful blue. Like a sky in a dream.

'Won't you at least try and hold the paintbrush?' she says.

'Come on, my love. Leave me now.'

'Is it because the paintbrush is so small? Is it too hard to hold?'

'Yes, you are absolutely right. It would be too painful.'

She nods, but she looks heartbroken. 'Maybe you can exercise your hands? You can open and close them to make them feel free!'

'That's a great idea, my lovely girl,' he says and smiles at her, and for a moment she beams at him, just as she always did.

As I approach, I look at her as she continues to put the fine brush into the pot, watching the paint drip, and I feel that my eyes are filling with tears, because I remember the morning before the fire, when we all sat together in the garden to have breakfast.

'Hello, you two,' I say. 'Shall I make us all a lovely pot of tea?'

'No, thank you,' says Tasso.

'Yes, please, Mamma,' says Chara.

I go inside and prepare a tray with tea and toast. I make extra for Tasso, too, just in case. I have found lately that he has become so accustomed to saying no that it is almost a reflex. So I will put the steaming tea in front of him and see if he drinks it, see if maybe he attempts to pick up the cup himself. I, too, like Chara, am desperate to see him come alive again.

I put the tray down on the table beneath the fig tree. I place the teacups on the table and pour the tea.

'I didn't want one,' Tasso says.

'Don't drink it then,' I say.

He watches the steam rise from the cup but does not move, and then he turns his face away and looks out at the dead woods.

Chara holds the cup between her palms. The dream blue colour is dotted about on her fingers and wrists. I put a thick blanket around her shoulders. Rosalie is sitting on Chara's socked feet, warming them.

'Aren't we lucky to have Rosalie,' she says.

'We really are,' I say.

'Soon we will have the jackal, too.'

'Let's see,' I say.

'Why "let's see"?' Her voice rises almost immediately, like something has ignited within her, and I see her cheeks turning red. 'The vet said the little jackal will be OK!'

'I'm just keeping an open mind.'

She is desperate for certainty. So desperate in fact that she begins to cry, still holding the cup; the tea spills out onto the blanket.

'Chara,' I say. 'My sweet, beautiful girl, I didn't mean to hurt you with what I said.' I put my arm around her shoulders and kiss her gently on the cheek. I can taste her tears. I am worried about giving her false hope. I am so worried about this, because it terrifies me to see her heart break. I would rather let her down gently.

'You're mean,' she says.

'I'm not mean.'

'You think everything is going to go wrong all the time.'

'I know how much you want everything to be OK.'

She begins to cry even harder; her tears fall and fall, and she scrunches up her eyes. 'I can see the old world as it was before – it's all in my head.'

I look over at Tasso, hoping he will turn to me, help me with Chara, embrace her. But he stares out ahead as if we do not exist.

'I know,' I say to Chara. 'I really do understand.'

'I wish there was such a thing as magic. Then we could make it all come back. Then we could make the old lady live again so that she can go to the shops with her daughter.'

'You still think about her?'

'Every day. She was my friend.'

I squeeze her shoulder tighter and try to stop myself from crying.

Tasso is so lost that he still doesn't even turn to look at us, and this makes my heart sink even more.

'How about we visit her grave tomorrow, take her some flowers? They let us know where she was buried. Maybe it's time we go say hello.'

She nods. Her crying eases up a bit. 'I want the jackal to be OK.'

'I do, too.'

'And I don't want to go to a new school.'

'Well, that is something that cannot be negotiated. You have to go.'

She doesn't say anything now but blows on her tea and takes a sip.

I look at Tasso again, and Chara glances over at him, too. 'Pappa,' she says, 'your tea is getting cold.'

Tasso does not respond. He seems to be in a trance.

'Pappa!' Chara nudges him, and he looks over at her as if he has just woken up. 'Please can you drink your tea? Please?'

He glances at the tea. He looks as though he is about to say no, but he catches her eye, and something stops him in his tracks. Instead, he looks back at the cup. Very, very slowly, he takes the cup between his thumb and forefinger without moving them too much. He brings it up to his mouth, before tilting his head to sip the tea. He does this until it's finished, then returns the cup to the table.

We are all silent. The silence stretches out for a very long time. I am reminded that the fig tree is silent, that the dead woods are silent. Chara is holding a piece of charcoal in her hands, rubbing it between her fingers, then between her palms, making them go black.

She very suddenly stands up. It is so abrupt that Rosalie stands to attention, and I stand up, too, without knowing why.

For a second, she seems amused. Then she takes the sketchpad and some charcoal from the table.

'What are you doing?' I ask.

'Standing. You?'

'The same.'

She smiles at me. 'How are you going to let me go to school if I can't even stand up on my own without you freaking out?' she says.

'Fair point.' I sit down.

Then she begins to walk off towards the woods. Rosalie glances at me. I try to keep quiet, but I can't.

'But where are you going?'

'In there,' Chara says. 'I'm going in there.' She points at the woods, and my heart races; my mouth becomes dry.

'What for?'

'I just want to go and see. You've been. I want to go, too.'
Rosalie glances at me again.

'I'd rather you didn't go.'

'It's not dangerous,' she says.

I think of the barren, open land, of the tree-stumps jutting out of the earth. I think of all the memories that hover around like lost ghosts.

'It *is*,' I say.

'Why? What can happen?'

I pause. 'You could get hurt.'

'I don't think that's possible.'

Chara turns on her heel to leave, and I am about to stand up to call her back, but Tasso gently places his hand on my knee. So, he is with us after all.

'She's a sensible girl,' he says. 'She won't go far. I think it might be good for her.'

I turn and look at him and nod. I know that he is right, and I wish he would stay like this with me forever.

I look back at Chara, who is now close to the gate. 'Stay close by then!' I call out. 'And stay on the path!'

'OK, Mamma!' she replies, and her voice is carried to me by a wind that has suddenly picked up.

'Rosalie,' I say, 'go.'

And Rosalie dashes off after Chara.

When she's gone, I sit there, staring out at the motionless land. Tasso has shut himself away again, and there is nothing I can do. I glance down at his hands and see how translucent the skin looks in places; the veins beneath are visible, and in other places, the new skin is purple or red. I put my hand ever so gently over his and look to see if he is in pain, but he smiles a little with his eyes. It is as if I am touching the delicate wings of a dragonfly with their beautiful intricate honeycombed webs.

The image of Mr Monk leaning against the old chestnut suddenly comes into my mind, and I hear his sobs. I see the blue of his eyes. I remember the noose around his neck.

The people, he had said.

I do not want to think about Mr Monk.

Chara returns some hours later, holding the sketchpad. She puts it down on the kitchen counter. Her hands are even blacker, and I wonder if she has been using the charcoal or if she has run her hands along the tree-stumps.

I'm standing at the stove, stirring the soup I have made for dinner. She comes over to look into the pot and inhales. 'Smells so nice, Mamma.'

'Go wash your hands,' I say.

She washes her hands in the kitchen sink with plenty of soap so that all the black washes off, and then she helps me set the table. I glance at her to see if she will say anything about the woods, but she remains silent and slightly absent.

It is after dinner when the sun has already set that she mentions her time in the forest. She has put on her pyjamas and brushed her teeth, and she comes downstairs to collect the sketchpad.

'I did some drawings,' she says.

'Oh yeah?' I say, trying not to sound too enthusiastic.

'They are of that place in there.' She raises her eyebrows and glances in the direction of the dead woods.

I nod but say nothing.

'Would you like to see?'

'Of course I would.'

'Shall we go and sit on my bed?'

'That sounds good,' I say.

So we head up to her room, and she gets cosy under the duvet, and I sit down on the bed beside her. She hands me the sketchpad, and I put it down on the bedspread and open it.

It is the first time since she was very little that I have seen any of her drawings. In front of me is a beautiful and disturbing picture of the dead woods, just at the point where the barren land ends. Her childlike lines are crooked and free. Her shading is more delicate, more uncertain. The combination gives the drawing a raw quality. It is so vivid, so real, so dark, that it makes me want to cry. She has somehow managed to capture the forest in all its static desolation. I hold my tears. I hold them tight, because I don't want her to see me cry, not again.

'My god, Chara.'

Something seems to move and shift in the drawing; it is in the way that she has used the white of the paper to capture the light. There is a shimmering ghostliness to the softness of the sky and the debris upon the ground against the sharp tree-stumps. It is as though I have stepped into the drawing, as though I am surrounded by the fallen burnt forest and the afternoon mist.

'Chara,' I say, feeling as breathless as if I have been running. 'It's ...' And this time I have not lost my ability to speak as

I did before, as I did when we were in the water surrounded by flames. No, this time I simply cannot find the right word. There isn't a single word that feels right. And this makes me feel helpless.

'Thank you, Mamma,' she says.

I look at her and she lowers her eyes.

Then she closes the book and changes the subject.

'Can you tell me how my back is doing?'

I nod, and she pulls off her top and turns around so that I can look at her back. With my finger, I trace the rippled skin. I feel the scar that stretches from shoulder to shoulder, then weaves down the centre of her back like the twisted bark of an old tree.

'You know,' I say, 'it really does look like the chestnut tree.'

She turns to face me. 'It's gone, Mamma,' she says. 'That beautiful chestnut has gone.'

'No,' I say. 'It is still alive. Half of it is burnt, but the other half is alive, and its branches reach up to the sun.'

She smiles. I kiss her cheek.

She lies down and closes her eyes.

'I love you so much,' I say.

But before I have even finished the sentence, she is asleep.

18

THE FOLLOWING MORNING, I TAKE Chara to visit her friend Neo in the eucalyptus woods at the edge of a nearby town. Neo is the son of the family who helped us after the fire. It takes us more than an hour to get there, because there are no buses around here anymore, so we walk to the part of the harbour that survived the fire and get a bus from there.

When we get to the woods, the sun is sparkling through the trees, and I see Chara pause for a moment as we walk up the driveway to the house. She closes her eyes and takes a deep breath. Is she preparing herself to see Neo again? This is the first time she will be seeing him since we left their home to live in Lazaros's place. I am worried that the boy will remind her of the trauma, that seeing his face will bring it all back: those first terrible weeks after the fire, those days when we thought her father was dead, when the skin on her back was so blistered and so painful that she could not shower or lie on her back to sleep.

Neo's parents are out of town for the week to visit a dying relative, so I will not get a chance to see them this time, which saddens me. I still do not know how to thank them for what they did for us.

Neo opens the door before we even reach it. He stands with a massive smile on his face, and Chara walks ahead of me hastily, but before she reaches him, she turns back to look at me.

I nod, very gently. She turns back to Neo.

He sees me and waves. I cannot get closer to the house just yet. In a way, I am glad his parents are not here. What would I say to them? How could I repay them for their warmth and generosity? But another part of me wishes they were here so that I could embrace them and also maybe tell them how lonely I am — how Tasso is still as lost today as he was the day he was found.

Neo's auntie appears at the door. She is a short woman wearing a floral dress and a thick cardigan, which she wraps around her as she stands in the doorway. 'Come in!' she calls. 'Welcome!'

I suddenly become aware of how I am dressed, that my jumper has stains on it, which she probably cannot see from here, my hair has not been combed and the laces on my boots are untied.

I wave. A big smiley wave. 'Thank you, but I'm in a rush! Send my love to Neo's parents!'

'I will!' she calls back. 'I will drive Chara back tonight!'

When I return, as I walk into the hallway, I hear a car pulling up the drive. I look out of the window and see the lipstick-red

Beetle, the one that used to wind up the road to Mr Monk's house. This red Beetle usually made its appearance on Saturday morning, followed by a second visit on Sunday night. It's not that I was being a nosy neighbour; it was just so hard to miss, so red, rumbling past our house on the country path.

I shift away from the centre of the window, making myself less visible behind the open curtain. The car door opens and out steps an immaculately dressed woman, wearing a black suit and a floral shirt of pinks and oranges. She looks fresh from the office. Her hair is long and loose. Her mouth is set into a line, and her movements are functional.

She walks around to the other side of the car and opens the passenger door, and a young girl of about five or six steps out. Her hair is tied into a high bun; she is wearing a thick winter coat. She holds what looks like a tattered green dinosaur tightly to her chest. She slips her hand into the woman's hand, and they walk towards the house. I dash away from the window now, and when the doorbell rings I wait several seconds before opening.

They both look at me for what feels like an entire minute. Nobody speaks.

'Can I help you?' I say.

'Yes, yes, sorry,' the woman says, and her voice is much softer than I imagined, more uncertain. She glances down at her feet, as if to compose herself. Then she draws her shoulders back, stands straight and looks at me again with renewed conviction.

'I am Mr Trachonides's ex-wife. My name is Loulla. This is my daughter Zoe.'

'I see,' is all I manage to say.

The little girl gazes up at me silently.

'May we come in?' Loulla says. 'It's cold up here. Colder than I ever remember it being.'

'Yes, of course.' I open the door wider and step aside for them to enter. The woman takes off her daughter's jacket, pulling down the sleeves one by one, while the girl moves the dinosaur from one arm to the other.

I feel myself begin to shake again. I thought Mr Monk was always alone. This is how I imagined him, like a well-dressed robot in his beautiful villa.

I stuff my hands into the pockets of my cardigan, hoping they won't notice my nerves. Do they know something? Do they know what I did? But how could they?

Loulla bends down slightly, looks into her daughter's eyes and moves her hands into beautiful shapes, her lips forming words, and I realise that the little girl is deaf. I stand quietly and watch them, excluded from this intimate conversation. The girl begins to sign back, and they enter a sort of dance with their hands and faces, with occasional whispers of broken words.

In that moment, I remember the forest when it was alive, its gentle, beautiful whispering communication. I want to stand there and watch them forever and forget about the fire and everything else. But my moment of calm dissipates as I begin to wonder what they are saying. There is a flash in my mind again of Mr Monk leaning against the old chestnut. And now, inexplicably, standing in the hallway of this house is his ex-wife and his daughter.

'She was just asking who you are,' the woman says eventually. Her voice is louder now than it was before – firmer, more confident. 'I was just telling her that you knew her father.'

I smile anxiously at the girl, who glances at me, and I notice then that her eyes are the exact same colour as her father's: the blue of a clear open sky. I turn away from her and lead them into the living room. They sit down next to each other on the two-seater by the heater, and I sit in the armchair. The dinosaur is on the girl's lap, and it has been positioned to face me. The girl and the dinosaur stare at me. The woman glances around at the paintings on the walls.

'Can I get you a drink? Tea or coffee? Maybe a juice for Zoe?'

The woman signs to the girl, and she signs back. It is only a few words exchanged between them, but it reminds me of the movement and sound of feathers.

'Yes, thank you,' she says, and again her voice startles me. 'I'll have a coffee, and Zoe will have some juice.'

I leave them and head to the kitchen. I just wish they would go. Having a beverage means that the visit is going to be longer than I anticipated. Reluctantly, I put the coffee and juice on a tray with some slices of marble cake, because I can't help but be a good host.

They are not talking now but sitting in silence. When I place the tray on the table and glance up, I see that the girl is looking about at the paintings on the wall. Her eyes are wide and bright. The light is falling on her in such a way that it makes her eyes appear luminous. She seems to be absorbing everything. She does not focus for too long on any particular painting; instead, her attention drifts around the room, from right to left and up and down, and there is an expression of awe on her face, as if she has entered a magical world.

'Please,' I say to her mother, 'help yourselves to some marble cake. There are small plates on the tray.'

'I'm OK with the coffee,' she says and signs to Zoe before taking a slice for her and handing her the plate. The dinosaur takes a seat beside her while she eats. I see that she is extremely careful not to drop any crumbs.

'You're probably wondering why I am here,' Loulla says.

'Well, yes.' I laugh a little.

'I understand you were the last person to see Michael.'

'Michael,' I repeat, and for a moment his name hovers in the space between us. 'Yes, I was.'

The little girl signs to her mother.

'She wants me to thank you for the cake. She is asking if you made it yourself.'

'I did,' I say, looking at Zoe. 'I made it with my daughter, Chara. She loves it, too.'

I smile, and her mother translates for her. She smiles, too, and eats the last crumbs from her plate. Then she takes the orange juice and downs half of it. She places the cup on the tray, picks up the dinosaur and puts him back on her lap.

'Did he say anything?' the woman asks.

'No,' I say, and my voice comes out in a rasp. I cough and take a breath. I am lying to her, and it makes me feel sick to my stomach. I see the desperation in her eyes as she stares at me, wishing, hoping, longing to hear something from me that will ease her pain. But what can I possibly say to her?

195

I am sorry that the father of this girl has died. I might have been able to save him, but I left him there alone as he passed away.

'Nothing at all?' She is leaning forwards in her chair now, gripping one of her hands with another.

I glance over at the girl and see that she has her full attention on the painting of the chestnut tree. She seems to be completely mesmerised by it. She puts the dinosaur on the sofa and heads to the painting, staring up at it.

'I'm sorry,' I say, 'but when I found him, he had already passed away.'

The woman nods and looks at her daughter, then at the ground. 'I just thought maybe ... I don't know.'

I do not say anything. My heart is beating hard. I'm beginning to get that feeling again, like I am surrounded by the fire.

'I was talking to him just the night before he died. He called me late. We separated a few years ago, because – well, it doesn't matter why, but we have remained close, for Zoe's sake.' She pauses and glances over at her daughter now, who is standing beneath the painting like a statue. 'He couldn't sleep. The guilt was eating him alive. It was ... What can I say? ... It was *eating* him. He was fading away. Maybe it's only right, after what he did.'

She stares at me as if this is a question, but I say nothing.

'I told him to focus on Zoe. To not think about anything but her. He loves her, you know.' Then she catches herself. 'I meant to say, he loved her. I can't believe I'm saying that.'

I remain silent. The girl turns from the painting now and glances at me.

She stares at me with those big blue eyes. I remember her father. I remember his eyes clearly and the fire that I saw within them – how I saw the burning of the forest and the burning of the people, how I ran and left him there.

She now signs to her mother.

'She is asking who made these paintings.'

'My husband,' I say. 'He is an artist.'

The girl signs again.

'She says she loves this one of the really old tree the most.'

I smile at her, and my heart breaks completely. Thank god this little girl doesn't know that this is where I found her father, alive and struggling to tell me more. What was he going to say? If I had stayed there with him a little longer, maybe I would have overcome my need to run away.

'We split up some years ago, like I said,' Loulla says, drawing my attention back to her. 'But he would have Zoe every weekend. She adores him. But he was a greedy, selfish man. Not with Zoe – with Zoe, he was amazing – but with his work, with anything that had to do with work. I barely saw him when we were together – he was always working, always another project. This was his downfall, you see. He was greedy. So unsatisfied, always wanting more. Look what he did. He decided he wanted something. He wasn't granted planning permission, so he went ahead anyway. He desired that piece of land. He wanted to take it for his own, so he set the trees on fire.'

She pauses there and laughs, but it is not a happy laugh; it is fraught with anxiety, with darkness. The sunlight high-lights her cheekbones, her dark eyes. She stares at me intently; her cheeks are flushed. I think of Tasso, sitting out in the garden. Tasso used to be the kind of man who could quieten down the noise of the world, who could bring up an imageless memory from the depths of your heart, some extraordinary sadness or beauty or fear that you didn't know existed – draw it up, like a magician, and hold it there for you to see. *This is something you knew that has slipped away from you.* That is what his paintings whispered.

And now, look at the man who started the fire. He did not give the world anything good; he knew only how to take.

'But,' Loulla says more slowly, 'and I'm not saying this to excuse anything, but there are so many fires every year.' She is holding one of my napkins. 'Michael wasn't the first to start a fire, was he? It happens most years.' She is folding the napkin and unfolding it, with such careful precise movements, as if she is making origami. I imagine her fingers on the keys of a piano. She has good fingers for the piano, long and light and agile.

I remember my instruments and how they have all been lost. I wish that I could hold my father's old bouzouki in my arms, close my eyes and play. For a second, I feel the vibration of the instrument in my chest.

'How many wildfires are there every summer?' she says, and I stop looking at her hands and focus now on her dark, intense eyes. 'How many start on their own, and how many are started by morons like Michael?'

'I don't know,' I say, 'but there are many, yes.'

'Three years ago, in the next town … That guy started a forest fire – do you remember? It burnt so much of the land, but it didn't become …' And she pauses there. I stare at her shimmering eyes. Her daughter, too, looks away from the painting and at her mother, as if she has sensed something in her.

'Yes?' I ask.

'This fire was like a demon, the way it moved, the way it lit up across the land, the way it charged down the mountain, swallowing up whatever and whoever stood in its way. Why was it different this time?'

I don't know what to say. I simply shake my head, and it suddenly dawns on me that she is right. That this intense and desperate person, this woman who I wish would disappear, is saying something that feels true. The forest fires have always been worse during a drought, and as the years pass, the droughts have become longer and more frequent, the land drying out most summers, and the winds becoming stronger, too, the humidity lower. The conditions have progressively worsened. Tasso knew this – that was why he kept painting the forest. That was why he *could not stop* painting the forest.

These thoughts make my heart beat faster, my hands begin to sweat. I see Mr Monk again – this time, how he looked at me, how open and pleading his eyes were.

'He just thought it would be another contained forest fire – as if that isn't bad enough, but he thought he could control it. This is what he said to me over and over again.'

It is as if she is appealing to me, this stranger, because that is all I am. She is begging me to hear her – begging me to understand.

'Still,' I say. My word seems to cut like a small but very sharp knife.

And she grimaces and nods. She knows what I mean.

'I'm sorry,' I say, 'but I don't know why you are telling me this. I am just the woman who found him.'

'It is *because* you are the woman who found him.'

I truly do not know what she means by this.

'There is no one to talk to. No one who will listen. I thought maybe he might have said something to you, and then we would have something – something to talk about, something to understand.'

I feel this woman's desperation. Somehow, I have become a possibility for her, some tiny opportunity for a resolution. And perhaps she sees my face soften, for she drops her shoulders and takes a sip of coffee.

'He came from a poor background, you see. His mum was from Cyprus – she worked in the corn fields, in that heat, in all that heat. He has a picture of her in his pocket wearing her headscarf bent over the corn. He carries it around with him everywhere, to remind him – to remind him to stay on top of things, to live a different life, to be as successful as he can. It came from watching his mother bent double and struggling.'

I imagine Mr Monk now, sitting beneath the tree as he was that morning, but now with the picture of his mother tucked away in his pocket.

'And,' she adds, as if it is connected to what she previously said about his mother, 'he handed himself in to the police.'

'I heard that a neighbour saw him and turned him in,' I said. 'The old farmer who lived by the stream on the upper side of town – apparently he was out walking his dog.'

'No,' she says, sitting up straight and creasing her brow. 'What you heard is not true. He handed himself in. I know he handed himself in because I went with him.' She taps her delicate fingers on her chest. 'The police had no clue who started the fire, or how in fact it even started, until we arrived at the station and he explained to them what he had done.'

She takes a sharp breath and looks over at her daughter, who is inspecting the other paintings. The girl's blue dress matches the sky in some of the landscapes, and she seems for a moment to belong to their world.

Loulla shifts in her chair, drawing my attention back to her. She has drawn in her shoulders, her knees firmly together, her hands clutched in front of her, as if she has pulled herself together, and she says, very calmly and resolutely, 'I don't believe he killed himself. In spite of everything, I don't believe he did.'

'Maybe not,' I say, meaning it.

Perhaps seeing this doubt in me, she leans forwards and adds, 'There wasn't even a suicide note. He was the sort of person who would tie up all loose ends.'

I nod but say nothing.

'You didn't see anything, did you?' she asks.

I see his blue eyes. I see the fire in them. I see myself walking away.

'Anything at all,' she continues, 'that would suggest——?'

'I have given all the information to the police,' I interrupt her, 'and I'm sure they will conduct a thorough investigation.' I can hear the coldness in my voice and imagine how she must see me now: this hard, unsympathetic woman sitting here before her. Inside, however, I feel that a part of me has died. It is the part that saw myself as a decent person: the girl my father loved; the woman my husband loved.

'Yes. Yes, of course.' The delicate uncertainty in her voice returns.

She stands up and goes to her daughter, touching her shoulder to get her attention. The girl turns to her mother, and the mother signs to her. They sign to each other for a minute or so, and my heart drops, and I feel my eyes fill with tears – so many tears that are threatening to fall.

'She wants to know how you knew her father,' Loulla says, turning to look at me. 'I just told her that you and he were childhood friends. She suspects something else – she's very sharp. I don't like to lie to her, but she is too young to know the whole truth.'

The girl signs to her mother again; while she does so, her eyes fill with tears.

'She wants you to know that she misses him, that he gave her the dinosaur.'

The girl signs again.

'She is saying that she loves him, because he tells funny jokes, and he takes her to the beach. He also tells her what all the sounds in the world are so that she can imagine them.'

I stare at the little girl, and she stares back at me. I feel an incredible sadness. 'Thank you for telling me,' I say to her. 'Your daddy sounds great.'

The mother translates, and the girl nods and smiles.

Loulla is about to turn towards the door when the small painting of the bouzouki catches her eye. She goes up close to it and stares for a while.

'God,' she says. 'My dad used to play the bouzouki. The way your husband has captured something so alive ... I can't even explain it. It is like the opposite of what is happening now, of what our life is now.' Then she looks at me. 'My dad wasn't a professional player or anything – he just played for the family. He has Alzheimer's now. But the other week, I took his old bouzouki to him, and he ... he remembered one of the songs. It was like he was back, you know? Like he wasn't completely lost. My father was there again. I could see him.'

Instinctively, it seems, the girl looks up at her, pauses to absorb what is happening on her mother's face, then wraps her arms around her waist.

'You're a kind girl,' the mother says to the girl, though she cannot hear her. Loulla places a hand on her daughter's head, then she leans down and kisses her with so much love that it almost makes me cry.

Then the mother and the little girl with the blue eyes like the sky walk out of my house. We say nothing more to each other. I stand at the door as they get into the car, and she looks at me one last time before the red Beetle rumbles away – not up the hill towards Michael's house as before, but down towards the sea and away from this burnt and lifeless land.

The Book of Fire

The mother and the girl were ready to leave the hospital the following day. The mother was desperate to find her husband. Using some coins that she found in her pocket, she dialled his number at the hospital phone booth. The phone didn't even ring; it went straight to voicemail. She frantically tried another five or six times, hoping that there was a bad signal and that it would begin to ring, but it did not happen. Then she tried her father-in-law's house number, as he didn't have a mobile, but the phone rang and rang. She imagined it ringing out in the silence of an empty house. Although she was frantic with worry, she held on to the fact that the phone was ringing which meant that the house had not been completely destroyed.

The mother and the girl waited in the queue to speak to the receptionist. 'Please,' the mother said, when they got to the front of the queue, 'please can you see if my husband has been brought in?'

'Name?' the woman said, without glancing up. Her eyes were fixed on the screen.

The mother told the receptionist her husband's name and she checked, clicking the keys, her eyes lit up by the light of the screen.

She shook her head. 'No,' she said slowly. 'I do not believe he is here.'

'You don't believe? So he might be?'

'Well, he is not on the system.'

'But what if he's here and he's unconscious? What if he is lying in one of these beds and the doctors and nurses don't know who he is?'

'They would have checked his pockets for any identification. Does your husband normally carry his wallet with him?' the receptionist asked, still with her eyes fixed on the screen.

The mother nodded. 'But ... in the fire, who knows if he still had it ...'

The receptionist looked up for the first time and caught her eye, and something seemed to soften in her. Her shoulders dropped, and she placed a hand on the desk. 'I'm sorry,' she said. 'I wish I could help you more, but I can't.'

'We have to find my father.' The girl stood straight and looked firmly at the receptionist.

But the receptionist glanced at the long queue forming. Then she looked into the girl's eyes. 'I know, sweetie,' she said. 'I really do wish I could help.'

'We could go and check all the rooms?' the girl suggested.

'I'm afraid you can't do that – the hospital is big.' Then she looked again at the mother. 'What I would advise you to do is wait – that is all you can do. Go somewhere safe, get yourselves cleaned up and wait. I know it's easy for me to say, but what else can you do?'

The mother and the girl walked away, the girl slowly but steadily, holding on to her mother's arm. The pain she'd experienced the day before made her weak. But her back had been bandaged now and they had all the medication she would require for the following weeks in a white plastic bag. They had been instructed to return immediately to the hospital if the pain worsened or if there was any bleeding.

The man from the day before was at the entrance, exactly where he had promised he would be. He had someone else with him, too: a boy of about twelve, holding the dog's lead. He looked fresh and clean, not covered in ash and soot and grime like the girl and her mother. Perhaps this made him feel bad, for he caught the girl's eye as she walked towards him, and he shifted his eyes to the ground. Later, the girl would learn how frightened he had been of the fire, how he had watched the smoke consume the sky in the distance from his bedroom window.

When the dog spotted the mother and the girl, it pulled on the lead so hard that it stood for a moment on its hind legs.

'Sit,' the mother said to the dog. She didn't want it to jump on the girl and unintentionally hurt her.

The dog did exactly as it was told, and the mother leant forwards and kissed its face. The girl patted the dog's head, and it panted happily.

'How can I ever thank you?' the mother said to the man.

'Oh, no need for that,' the man replied. 'This is my son. He has been looking forward to meeting you both.'

The boy smiled at the girl and the woman. They smiled back. 'Where are you going from here?' the man said.

'They told us to wait for the coach that will arrive here in an hour to take us to a hostel. But I don't know where my husband is. We lost him in the fire – he turned back to find his father, and we haven't seen him since. I want to wait here in case he turns up, but Chara needs to rest. I have asked at the hospital, and as far as they know, he is not here.'

'I'm so sorry to hear that,' the man said. 'If it helps, me and my wife would like to invite you both to stay with us instead of going to the hostel. I have heard the hostels are packed. I'm not sure how comfortable it will be there for you. This way you will not be too far from the hospital, so you can return here each day to wait for your husband.'

'Oh god,' the mother said. 'We can't possibly accept that!'

But she liked this man, and she liked his optimism. *Return here each day*, he had said, *to wait for your husband*. Her husband would return – yes, he would; she was certain. She loved this man for giving her hope.

She turned her head and watched as people streamed out of the hospital, heading to where the coach was due to arrive. There were already fifty people waiting, maybe more.

The man followed her gaze. 'Well,' he said, 'the offer is there for you. If you choose to go to the hostel, you have my number and you can call me any time. My wife and son and I are the lucky ones. We would like to help as much as we can. This could have happened to anybody, any one of us.'

The girl squeezed the mother's hand, and the mother took it as a sign to accept.

'Under normal circumstances, I wouldn't want to impose on you and your family. But thank you – we will accept your very kind offer.'

The drive to the house was not too long at all. The man took the road along the seafront and then headed up into a forest of eucalyptus trees. Normally the girl would have opened the window to take in their scent, but she kept her head down. It seemed as though she did not want to look at anything. It was as if the whole world had died.

'We are going further from Pappa,' the girl whispered as they sat together at the back of the car. The mother squeezed her daughter's hand and swallowed down her fear and her tears.

The house was a beautiful wooden bungalow nestled among the trees. The mother wanted to cry when she saw it, how the light rested on the misty grey eucalyptus trees and how they were so tall, their silver barks shooting up to the sky.

'Well, welcome to our home,' the man said, and for the first time the mother realised how empty she felt. She held nothing in her hands: just a plastic bag with her daughter's medication and an empty carton of juice that someone had given them. But more than that – a hole had opened up inside her, huge and dark and stark.

The front door opened, and the man's wife came out to greet them. She hugged the mother and lightly touched the girl's arm and led them into the house. The hallway was dotted with vases filled with wildflowers from the forest. There was an old Turkish rug that paved the way to a lovely, low-ceilinged living room. It was welcoming and warm, and the woman had prepared pastries and tea on a large wooden table.

'They have just come out of the oven, and the tea is hot. Now, please,' she said, 'sit down, eat and drink – we will deal with the formalities and introductions later. The first thing is to get you watered and fed.'

The mother and the girl sat down, and for the first time the mother felt a heavy exhaustion, as if her heart was struggling to keep beating, and she sunk deep into the chair. She closed her eyes. She listened to the tea being poured, to the slicing of a knife through pastry. She heard the stirring of a spoon and the sound of sea-birds flying over the forest. She listened to her daughter's gentle breathing beside her and to the dog's pants and to the tinkle of cutlery. But it was something the man's wife said that split open her heart.

'Sugar?'

Just a tiny word. A word that meant the world was still spinning and time was still moving. *Sugar, sugar, sugar, sugar.* Tasso took half a sugar in his coffee. She did not take sugar in her tea.

'No, thank you,' she said.

'How about some galatoboureko?' the woman said, picking up a tray of milk pies and offering them to her.

The mother looked at the flaky filo pastry, the creamy custard inside and the syrup that dripped over the top. It reminded her of the pastries her father-in-law used to try to make and how they would all sit together around the table in the garden to eat them – though they were always slightly burnt. But she loved them. She loved that charred taste.

Now, instead of taking one from the plate, she began to cry. Without opening her eyes, she cried with all of her body and all of her mind, and she felt the warm hand of this woman on her back.

'It's OK,' she said. 'But what a silly thing for me to say – it's not really OK, is it? I know. But you are safe now at least. At least there is that.'

The mother felt her daughter's hand on her knee, and she tried to stop crying, but the more she tried the more she sobbed. And they simply stayed like that: the wife of the man rubbing her back while she cried; the daughter resting her hand on the mother's thigh while she cried; the man and the boy and the dog sitting silently, not daring to move while she cried. They all stayed like that, and all that could be heard were the woman's sobs and the song of the birds.

Her crying slowly abated, then subsided entirely, until they could hear the rustle of branches upon a window. The wind was strong, just as it had been the day before. The mother opened her eyes and looked out of the window and saw that it was a lemon tree, with beautiful yellow-sunshine lemons hanging jewel-like on the branches.

'My god,' was the first thing the mother said, 'what a beautiful tree.'

And they all looked in that direction.

'Would you like a drop in your tea?' the woman asked.

'Yes.' The mother smiled through her tears. 'That would be nice.'

The woman went outside and returned with a few lemons in her arms. She put them in a bowl on the table and took one, slicing it in half. Then she squeezed a few drops into the woman's tea and asked the girl if she would like some, too.

'I'm not really keen on lemon in tea,' the girl said, 'but thank you very much.'

For a while, everyone ate without conversation. Gradually, the tablecloth became covered in pastry crumbs. More tea was poured. The man's wife put some food down for the dog, who lapped it up in almost a single gulp.

'She's a lovely dog,' the woman said. 'So attentive and caring. My son would like a dog. Maybe we will consider a greyhound.'

The boy said nothing but gulped his tea and looked at the girl over the brim of the cup. She didn't notice. Her eyes were distant and her shoulders hunched, and the mother saw the huge clock on the wall and noted it was time for her medication. She asked for a glass of water. But by the time the man went into the kitchen to fetch a jug of water and returned, she realised that the hands of the clock had not moved.

'What is the time?' the mother asked, and the man looked down at his watch. In fact, as he was not wearing his glasses, he brought his wrist right up to his face and looked closely at it.

'My god!' his wife said. 'How many times have I told you to keep your glasses on you! Where are they now?' She slipped her hand into a bag by her side and retrieved her phone. 'It is 12 p.m.,' she said. 'Exactly midday.'

'So it *is* time for her medication after all,' the mother said. 'Four hours precisely have passed since her last dose.'

And it seemed that the girl's body knew well the passing of time. The woman thought of how differently time passed for the trees, how softly and slowly time passed only for them, while the creatures around them – the creatures on their branches and in the soil – they were bound by the movement of a different clock. She remembered this, and once again tears filled her eyes.

'I have no idea what has happened to my husband or my father-in-law.'

'I will take you back to the hospital this evening,' the man said.

'Thank you.'

She handed the girl the tablets, one by one. As well as paracetamol and penicillin, the doctor had prescribed another strong medication.

'I suppose it would be a good idea for you to take a bath or shower,' the woman said. 'I have laid out some clothes and blankets for you on the bed. Would you like me to show you to your room now?'

The mother and the girl and the dog were taken to a converted loft room in the roof of the house. The mother held on to her daughter's hand as they climbed the staircase; even with the strong medication, she could see her daughter grimace when she made too many movements. The dog was close by, diligently watching the girl's feet as she took each step.

In the middle of the room was a large double bed with towels laid out, and there was an unlit lamp on a bedside table. The woman had also laid out some thick blankets on the ground near the bed for the dog. The floor and the slanted ceiling were all made of wood the colour of the golden resin that used to drip from the trees. There was a rocking chair in the corner just below the window, which was inlaid within the slant of the roof and looked out upon the tops of the eucalyptus trees where they met the sky.

The girl sighed. The mother was pleased to hear this sigh. It meant her daughter felt safe. But there was something that made her uneasy – she had a notion that this house, this beautiful warm house, was part of a different time and a different world.

The man's wife brought a flannel and a bowl of soapy water. Although the girl had been washed by the nurse when her wounds were being attended to, her arms and neck and lower back were still caked in black soot. Together, they gently took off the girl's jumper and vest and they cleaned her arms and the skin around the bandage and her neck and face and hands with the soapy, warm flannel.

The girl sat there and said nothing at first. Then she whispered, 'Mamma, where is Pappa? I want to see him. Will we see him again? Do you think he has found Grandad?' Her eyes were wide and fearful as she looked at her mother intently.

The woman beside them wrung the dark water out of the cloth.

'It will all be OK,' the mother said gently. 'You'll see. Just close your eyes now and try to rest.'

The girl closed her eyes. Perhaps she was listening to the afternoon birds. The mother hoped that this was what the girl was doing. She hoped that she was not wondering whether she would ever see her father again or remembering the fire.

Then she looked at the man's wife, who knelt on the floor and washed the cloth in the soapy water, wringing it out and handing it back to her. She caught her eyes for a moment. They shimmered with sadness. The man's wife smiled gently at the mother but said nothing.

They worked like this in silence, the woman cleaning the cloth in water to remove the black of the burnt forest from the girl's skin. It was so thick that it turned the water dark.

The man's wife took the bowl and poured it into a basin in the en-suite bathroom, which the woman had just noticed. She came back with fresh soapy water and a new flannel, and they fell into their dance again.

The black soot swirled upon the girl's arms and shoulders like thick clouds. The more soap and water the woman applied, the more those dark clouds lightened, and finally they could see the rich olive hue of her skin.

The girl still had her eyes closed, her head against the pillow.

'She seems to have dozed off,' the man's wife said.

'I hope so,' the mother said, and together they dried the girl with a warm towel from the heater and lifted her feet onto the bed and allowed her head to fall back onto the pillow. The man's wife brought a multicoloured knitted blanket and laid it over her.

'It's beautiful,' the mother whispered.

'My grandmother made it. She lived her whole life in the part of the forest that has burnt.'

'But how much of the forest has burnt? Have you been watching the news?'

Perhaps the man's wife saw the fear in the mother's eyes, for she said, 'Come on, now – you go and have a shower, and I will sit right here next to your daughter until you come out. Don't worry about a thing.'

There was another tiny window in the bathroom, which looked out upon the barks of the tall trees. She turned on the hot water, and as she washed herself in the shower, she watched the outside world through the stream. She saw the silvery barks, the silvery leaves, the golden sunlight streaming down from above. The leaves and branches swayed in the wind. The warm water drenched her skin. The burnt forest ran off her body and down the drain.

It was like being covered in blood, she thought – the blood of the land, the blood of the animals and the trees.

19

After Mr Monk's ex-wife and daughter leave, I sit alone in the kitchen and look at Tasso as he sits beneath the tree. We are so close yet so far from each other. I miss him. I miss Lazaros. I think of Mrs Gataki, who doesn't have the privilege of being able to go out into the garden to sit next to her husband if she wants to. And this is all due to Mr Monk. Mr Trachonides. Michael.

But what about the parched land? What about the drought, the wind? What about the changes that Lazaros warned me about for so many years?

The little girl's eyes, her bright-blue eyes, hover in my mind. Then I see her mother, sitting before me, folding the napkin like origami. *How many wildfires are there every summer? How many start on their own, and how many are started by morons like Michael? Why was it different this time?*

I want to go outside to speak to Tasso; I want to feel his hand in mine. I think of Mr Monk, leaning on the old chestnut tree – the beautiful chestnut, half dead and charred black, half with its bark twisting up into branches and tiny buds, reaching towards the sun. I remember kneeling down and speaking to Mr Monk.

Can you tell me what happened? Can you tell me your name?

The people.

The people?

Then he tried to say something more but couldn't. Yes, I remember. I wish I could forget. I wish he had been able to tell me what he meant.

I remember how he began to cry. What was he thinking about when those tears fell from his eyes? He cried so quietly.

I remember his blue eyes. Just like his daughter's, just like her dress and the sky in the landscapes on the living-room wall. Fire blazed within them. Within them, I saw Lazaros standing in the old forest – the pine trees and fir trees and poplars and plane trees; the weasels and minks, the wildcats and the badgers, the beautiful red deer that roamed the lowlands, the birds and the rabbits and the hares and the moles and rats, the lizards and the beetles, the tiny insects, the ladybirds and butterflies. I saw the wildflowers in his eyes. I saw the colours of the forest. I cried with all my heart, like that woman who stood on the rock and cried into the fire. I cried for the fifteen people who had died holding on to each other. I cried for all the others who were still missing. I cried for Lazaros, for Mrs Gataki's husband, for the old lady in the sea. I saw my husband's face and my daughter's. I saw the fire blaze down the mountain and reach the edge of the cliff.

And then I ran. That's what I did. I ran, and I ran. I ran away from the man who had started the fire, and I left him there to die. This little girl, this beautiful girl whose name means life, has lost her father because of something I did. I remember Loulla's words and the little girl sitting on my sofa with the dinosaur on her lap.

I remember Lazaros holding the soil of the forest in his palm, frightened for the future. I see him wearing his wicker baseball cap, sticking his tongue out, all the worry lines on his face stretching around his mouth. *What if one day this forest becomes a desert?* he once said, during another glass of frappé, as he slurped the coffee through a straw.

Well, it won't be in our lifetime, I replied, and he had raised his eyebrows and remained silent.

Outside now is a black desert.

The phone rings. When I pick it up, Lieutenant Makris greets me warmly.

'Hello, Irini,' he says. 'I am wondering if you could come down to the station this afternoon. We have the results of your DNA test and fingerprints, and we have a few more questions we would like to ask you.'

'Yes, of course, Lieutenant,' I say.

'I will send a car to collect you. Shall we say 5 p.m.?'

I cannot sit still waiting for 5 p.m. to arrive. I head out to Maria's Kafeneon.

Everywhere I turn, eyes dart in my direction. The professor is playing backgammon, this time with a woman I have never seen before. They look alike; they have the same long nose and wide-set eyes, and they play as if they have known each other forever. They laugh like that, too. I have always thought that you can tell how close two people are by how they laugh together, whether they set each other off easily. However, as they chat and laugh and play, the professor's eyes flick towards me. I am not imagining it. Even when I look down into my coffee, I can feel his eyes on me, and when I look up, he is staring at me. I wave a small, shy wave, and he nods and returns to the conversation he is having with his probably-sister.

The men from the garage aren't here today. Only the main guy is here – the one who is always egging the others on, the one who threw the milk pie at the prime minister on the TV. He is sitting on the sofa beneath the vines, vaping. The smell of doughnuts wafts towards me. He, too, glances at me. Whenever I look up, I see that he is watching me.

They must all know by now that I found Mr Monk in the woods. But why are they looking at me? Are they curious or anxious?

Mrs Gataki arrives. We didn't contact each other, but she is always here. She comes straight to my table and takes a seat.

'How is Chara?' she asks, fanning herself with another crime thriller.

'We found an injured jackal a couple of days ago – she is waiting for him to come home.'

'Where is he now?'

'At the vet – he needs an operation on his paws. They're going to sew fish-scales onto them.'

'He will be a magical jackal.' She smiles, and the green on her eyelids glitters. 'With golden fur and silver paws.'

'I think you read way too many novels,' I say.

'I read crime novels, Irini – they are the opposite of magic. Plus, there is no such thing as reading too much. It broadens the mind, even if they're the sort of books that are displayed between the beach-balls and the tampons at the local shop.'

Then her attention is drawn to someone across the room. When I follow her gaze, I see that it is the professor's probably-sister. The woman comes over, and they immediately hug each other, kisses on both cheeks.

'How is Julia, my darling?' Mrs Gataki inquires.

'Oh, she's marvellous.'

'And Georgios? And Christiano?'

'All good, all good – they are all doing well.' She proceeds to tell us lots of random facts about each person, how many children they now have, in which part of Greece they now live, their jobs and even how well or poorly their careers are going. I am about to yawn, but I try to control it.

'Oh, I'm so pleased to hear that!' Mrs Gataki says.

Then Mrs Gataki remembers me, places her manicured hand on my shoulder and introduces us.

'This is Fifi,' she says. 'Fifi, this is my good friend, Irini, from the neighbourhood. Fifi was born here on this mountain. She lived here for many years, but I think she left just before you arrived.'

Fifi greets me warmly, and they spend a few more minutes asking each other about various family members. She is a very attractive woman, in her fifties, with thick, silver bobbed hair that she has half pulled back from her face. I notice, as she talks and Mrs Gataki shakes her head and replies with oohs and aahs, that Mrs Gataki is still missing an earring.

Fifi is telling us about her son's PhD in environmental sciences; she is talking on and on about his BA and MA at a London university and how he did so well that his supervisor, a Dr Something-or-other, convinced him to continue with his research studies. 'He's so good at what he does, but I don't understand a single thing he says!'

The earring bothers me, because I realise that I have never seen Mrs Gataki without these earrings. They are such a bright gold that they always catch my eye as she talks or moves her head.

Then Fifi is telling us something about coming back here after all these years to see what has happened to her old home. 'I went into the forest, my love,' she says, 'and I nearly died an early death, seeing what this place has become.'

I allow myself to drift off. Mr Monk is constantly on my mind. I imagine him climbing the tree with the rope in his hand, tying it to the branch and placing the noose around his neck. But I cannot imagine this for too long. Something feels wrong about it.

Then I imagine the men from the garage, knocking at his door, dragging him down to the forest where the chestnut tree stands, one of the men climbing the tree to tie the rope on the thick branch. Here, Mr Monk will die looking at what he has done, at the devastation that his fire has left behind.

I begin to feel sick. I imagine the little girl sitting on my sofa, looking at the painting of the chestnut tree.

'So, anyway, I must get back to my game! It was so lovely to meet you ... ?'

'Irini.'

'Ah, yes, Irini. Absolutely lovely to meet you.' And then she is off.

'What's wrong with you?' Mrs Gataki says. 'You're constantly miserable these days.'

'Well, thanks.'

She grins and raises her purple eyebrows. 'Apart from the obvious, of course, is there anything troubling you?'

'Well,' I begin tentatively, 'it's this thing with Mr Monk.'

'The fact that you found him?'

'Yes. And also, not knowing what happened to him.'

I glance around again; nobody is looking at me. Another man from the garage has joined the leader guy.

'Does it really matter? I've told you before, and I'll say it again: you think way too much. The guy deserved to die, one way or another.'

'Yes, I suppose.'

'Irini, what do you mean *you suppose?* He was released on bail. The man killed so many people, and he was wandering free as a bird.'

'Perhaps he didn't mean to cause such a huge fire. Not that it makes it better, but maybe there's more to it than what *this* person did.'

'Such as what?' She doesn't give me a chance to reply. 'Do you mean the way the police and fire services handled it? Yes, that was dreadful, and that is being dealt with, too. I have already told you that we are taking the police and fire department to court for negligence.'

'Mrs Gataki,' I say, 'I don't think you understand.'

222

'What do I not understand?'

I look at her dark eyes and bright eyebrows. I glance again at the people around me. I remember the leader guy throwing the pie at the prime minister.

'Nothing,' I say. 'Absolutely nothing at all. Now, let's order some coffees, because I'm going to need to head off soon. And ...' I add. 'You seem to have lost your earring.'

'Oh yes,' she said. 'I know, my love. I lost it a few days ago. It's my fault – I knew the screw was a little loose. I keep thinking it'll turn up. I have had these earrings since I was a little girl. In fact, I've never really taken them off. Only once, in fact, on my wedding day. My grandmother gave me some beautiful pearls to wear, and I took these off and put them right back on after. If I take this one off, it'll be like admitting defeat. I will keep going until I find it. That's all we can do, eh?'

When I get home, the house is empty; I find a note from Chara on the kitchen table.

Mamma, Neo's auntie just brought me home in her car, and I am going to the forest with my sketchpad! Love you!

I cannot focus on anything except for her whereabouts and the conversation with Lieutenant Makris. Sometimes, I imagine her walking among the black tree-stumps. Other times, I see myself sitting in that cell of a room at the station. What other questions will they ask me? Maybe they think I am involved in his death. I don't have a chance to think too much before the phone rings again. This time it is the vet.

'The operation was successful!' the vet says, with a smile in her voice, and I snap out of the state of mind I am in to speak to her.

'Chara will be so pleased! I am, too.'

'I'll bring him over tomorrow, and I'll run through some things about how to keep him, how to ensure that he gets both the care and the freedom he requires.'

When I put down the phone, I wish now more than ever that I had never gone for a walk that day, that Rosalie and I had not been the ones to find Mr Monk dying in the woods. I just want to focus on my daughter and this little jackal, without having to carry the burden of Mr Monk's death.

I head outside and sit next to Tasso for a while, with a blanket around my shoulders.

'She's out there again,' I say.

I look at him and he nods ever so slightly. I glance down at his hands; they are still on his lap, palms facing upwards. The skin is still raw, red in places and purplish in others. Tasso must have heard the car earlier when Loulla and Zoe arrived, but he is so lost in his own world that he does not mention it, and doesn't bother to ask who visited.

'Do your hands hurt?' I ask.

'They look like they should. But the pain isn't that bad. Paracetamol is enough.'

'Do you think you will be able to paint again?'

'No,' he says simply.

224

'But why not? When your hands get better, you can begin again.'

'No, Irini. I won't be able to.'

I want to argue with him, but I remain quiet. 'Chara has been drawing,' I say.

'I know.'

'Have you seen what she's done?'

'No. She didn't show me.'

'You should at least ask to look at her drawings.'

He doesn't respond.

'It won't kill you, you know.'

Again, he says nothing and out of frustration, I get up to leave.

'I'm really sorry,' he whispers as I turn away.

I want to keep walking, but I can't. His soft voice draws me back, and I turn to face him again.

'I will ask to see her drawings.'

'Thank you,' I say and smile. What I really want is to put my arms around him, feel him close to me, plant a thousand kisses on his cheeks. I hold back. I don't want to scare him, overwhelm him, make him draw into himself again.

'I'm going down to the police station again soon,' I say.

'Oh, how come?'

'They have the DNA results, and they want to ask me more questions.'

He nods and stares back at the dead forest. 'Don't worry,' he says. 'It'll be fine. It's not like you've done anything wrong.'

*

The police car arrives just after 5 p.m. I am taken to the old, shabby building overlooking the shore by a junior officer. I sit in the back of the car. She is friendly enough, but my hands shake throughout the entire journey.

Like last time, I am left alone in the same small room that feels like a cell. This time, nobody asks me if I want tea or coffee, and I am pleased as I do not feel like interacting with anyone at all. I stare at the concrete walls and halogen lights and the metallic bin in the corner. Then I notice the window again, the one that looks out at the sea. This time clouds cover the sun, and the water is dark.

Lieutenant Makris comes in. 'Hello, Irini. I'm so sorry to keep you waiting again. There's always one thing or another in this place.'

I glance at my phone and realise that I have been here waiting for half an hour already. Just as before, the detective enters the room a few moments later. She seems to be wearing the same dark-navy suit but this time with a light-green shirt.

'Detective Lamprides is joining us again,' says Lieutenant Makris, and I nod.

Detective Daphne Lamprides – I remember her first name. She opens a rucksack by her feet and takes out a notepad and pen, which she places on the table.

'Are you ready?' she says.

I nod.

'Can we start the recording please?'

Lieutenant Makris presses the button of the recording device, then says the date, the time of the interview and the names of the people present.

'Irini,' Lieutenant Makris says, 'we have the results of your fingerprints and DNA. What we discovered is consistent with your description of events.'

I try hard not to exhale too strongly.

'Your fingerprints and DNA were on Mr Trachonides's left wrist, on his left arm and on the right side of his neck, where the main artery runs. We found your DNA on his rucksack, on the pencil case and the cardboard folder inside the rucksack. What was rather strange, however, is that your fingerprints were also on the paperwork inside the folder. You were very clear that you looked inside his rucksack in search of a phone. Can you explain to us why you looked inside the file when you had just discovered a dead body?'

For a few moments, I am at a complete loss. I stare at them both. Lieutenant Makris's green eyes glow beneath the halogen lights. Detective Lamprides's eyes are clear and sharp. She hardly blinks.

I take a deep breath. 'After I realised, he was dead,' I say, 'I sat there for a while.'

I pause and the window and the sea catch my attention again. I wish I could go outside and stand by the shore, out of this awful room.

'That doesn't explain why you opened the file,' he says.

'Because as I sat there and watched this man who had destroyed so much, who had stolen so much from us. I wanted to know who he was. That's all.'

Lieutenant Makris nods. 'Do you remember the details of the paperwork?'

'It was the termination of some sort of development contract.'

'Did you learn anything by finding it, then?'

'Not really. Only that perhaps there might have been a link between the termination of this contract and the fire.'

'How so?'

'It didn't occur to me then, but I wonder now if it was an indication that he might have felt guilty, that he didn't want to keep building things after what had happened here.'

Lieutenant Makris nods again.

Detective Lamprides jots something in her notepad. I wonder why she even needs that notepad if everything is being recorded.

'I also think,' I say, 'it seems strange that he would have killed himself if he was heading off to a meeting.'

At this point, the detective quickly glances up at me, but she says nothing.

'What makes you so sure he was heading to a meeting?' Lieutenant Makris says.

'Well,' I say, 'I assumed so because of the paperwork.'

'And if you are correct, what are you suggesting? Can you make your thoughts clear for the sake of the interview?' he says.

'Perhaps he didn't kill himself,' I say clearly into the device and pause. 'Maybe somebody else did it.'

'Was anyone with you?' Detective Lamprides says.

'No. Why?'

'You were completely on your own – you saw nobody else around?'

'No, I was alone the entire time. Why do you ask?'

'Well, there are two reasons.' She takes something out of her rucksack – a plastic A4-sized wallet – and slides out a photograph, which she places on the table, facing me. 'The minute we arrived on the scene, before any of the other officers entered the cordoned-off area, the first detective at the scene found a pair of footprints in the dry soil. They do not match your footprints. They are very faint, but we have had them analysed. They are trainers, size 39. There is an indication that there may have been more footprints around the area, but they are so faint that we cannot establish whether they are in fact footprints at all. But we do have this.' She taps the photograph with her index finger, drawing my attention to the footprint.

'Well,' I say, 'I didn't see anyone. I was alone. With my dog.'

Then, from a file on the table, Lieutenant Makris retrieves a gold earring. It is a stud in the shape of a heart. 'We found this by the body. Is it yours?' he says, laying it in the palm of his hand. I freeze.

'No.'

He places it on the table in front of me, and I watch it twinkle, this tiny gold heart that catches the light. Mrs Gataki's missing earring. I cannot believe what I am seeing. Then an unfathomable thought: was Mrs Gataki involved in Mrs Monk's death? She couldn't possibly be!

'Could someone have dropped it before the fire?' I ask.

'No, it couldn't have been dropped at any time,' Detective Lamprides says, lowering her chin and looking up at me. 'A jeweller has confirmed that the earring is eighteen-carat gold, which has a melting point of 926 degrees Celsius. The temperature of the fire was over 1,000 degrees Celsius. If it had been dropped before the fire, the gold would have melted, which means that this earring was dropped there after the fire. We believe it was dropped recently because it was not dirty, and we found it on top of some fallen leaves. Also, very few people go into the woods these days and the earring was found right next to Mr Monk so we have to consider it as a clue.' She pauses. 'Why, do you know who the earring belongs to?'

'No, not at all,' I say quickly. I cannot possibly say what is on my mind; I cannot incriminate my good friend without knowing anything for sure.

Lieutenant Makris clasps his hands together on the table in front of him. His eyes look up to the ceiling for a second and then back at me.

'It could be completely innocent,' he says to me, as if he suspects that I'm holding something back and is gently trying to coax it out of me. 'Someone could have gone for a walk in the dead woods and dropped it. It doesn't mean the person who was wearing it has any connection to Mr Trachonides's death. In theory, this would also explain the footprints. It could have happened that very morning or even the evening before. These are all possibilities. They may have simply paused to see the magnificent tree, or for some other reason.'

I stare at the earring on the table. I can feel their eyes on me. I wonder, for a split second, whether I should tell him who the earring belongs to. But something tells me to keep my mouth shut. I will speak to Mrs Gataki myself; she doesn't need to go through all this questioning, not after everything she has suffered since losing her husband. If I speak to her, I am sure she will tell me that she went out for a walk before Mr Monk died beneath the tree.

But what if she *was* involved in his death? It would be impossible for Mrs Gataki to lynch Mr Monk alone. Someone else would have been with her. In any case, this would mean that she is not the person I thought she was. I have always loved how her name matches her character. Gataki. Small cat. Superior, cool, aloof, playful, neurotic, curious to the point of obsession.

A chill goes through me. I feel that the world has changed colour around me.

The truth is, *I* am not the person I thought I was.

The fire has burnt our souls, our hearts. It has turned to ashes the people we once were.

The Book of Fire

The girl slept safely in the roof of an old house. Her mother wished she dreamt sweet dreams and did not remember the fire that had burnt her.

The mother sat downstairs in the living room with the kind man and his kind wife. The man's wife had opened the window to let in some fresh air from the forest, and the man handed them each a cup of Greek coffee.

'Drink up,' he said. 'It'll warm you and then wake you up, so we can go back to the hospital.'

The mother nodded but found she could not speak. She felt that she was now a different person to the one she had been yesterday morning.

'They don't know yet how the fire started,' the man said, 'but what I do know is that somebody called up to report the fire but nobody suspected it would get so bad, so the fire brigade didn't jump like they should have. They responded like they normally would – they sent one helicopter to spray down the area. At that stage, the fire hadn't yet garnered speed. The wind was still relatively calm, calmer than it is now.'

The lemon tree rattled against the window.

'How do you know all this?' the wife asked.

'Well, you remember my old school friend, the one who became a firefighter?'

'The one who cheated on his wife and then came here in his uniform to drink ouzo and tell you his sob story?'

'That's him.'

'Hmm. I never liked that man.'

'Anyway, he is senior now, works in the offices, and he told me everything this morning. I rang him to see what was happening.'

'You stick your nose into everything,' the wife said.

'And why shouldn't I?'

'It's not your business.'

'It's all of our business,' he said and placed his mug on the table, undrunk. 'Come on, if you have finished your coffee,' he said to the mother. 'Let's go – this might take a while.'

The mother got up and put on her coat, which was hanging on the back of a chair.

'Did she stay with him?' the woman said. 'His wife?'

'No, she left him. She took everything, including the cats, and went to stay with a friend up north, apparently.'

'Well, good for her,' the man's wife said. 'Sometimes, things do go the way they should.'

It was late afternoon and the sun streaked through the trees and the leaves whispered around them. The wind had settled down. They wound down the mountain to the sea. When they arrived at the hospital, it was quieter than it had been the night before. But there were people still being rescued, found alive or close to death. There were also people like her, desperately searching for lost loved ones.

'My son,' she heard a man say to the woman behind the desk. 'Please have a look to see if anyone has brought him in. He is all I have now. He is *all* I have.'

The receptionist, the same woman they spoke to that morning, looked exhausted. There seemed to be darker shadows beneath her eyes, and her lips were even more dry and cracked.

The mother couldn't bear all this. She wished she could leave, but it was her only chance of finding her husband.

She remembered him sitting at the table in the garden yesterday morning, drinking coffee and talking about roller-skating. She remembered the moves he had made, attempting to show their daughter how to brake.

'I miss him,' the mother said to the man who had helped her, the man who was still by her side.

'I know,' he said. 'I can only imagine.'

There were twenty people ahead of them in the queue to the front desk. Each time, another name was added to the missing persons' list.

'We will take down the name of your loved one and your contact details. We will get in touch as soon as we have any news. Please go home and try to rest in the meantime.'

Or:

'Yes, we have the name you have given. Your loved one is on the system. They are here. Please take a seat in the waiting room and a doctor will come and see you when they can.'

One by one. One by one. So many people sent away, so few waiting.

Then it was the mother's turn. The man placed his hand on her shoulder and said, 'If he is not here, we will come again tomorrow. Do not lose hope, OK?'

She took a deep breath, approached the desk and said her husband's name clearly.

The receptionist searched on the computer; her eyes flicked over the screen.

'Yes,' she said finally. 'He is here – in room 321. Please take a seat and a nurse or doctor will come and collect you.'

'Oh, thank god,' the mother said. 'Oh, thank you, thank you.' Her legs were suddenly shaking, and the man, who was sensitive and observant, said, 'Come on, let's go and sit down.' He led her to the waiting area.

They sat in silence. In that bright corridor, they watched people come and go.

Twenty minutes passed before a nurse came to get them. He was a very tall, slim man, who reminded the mother a little of her husband. She smiled at this nurse, who smiled back gently and warmly and said, 'Come on then, let's get you to your loved one.'

He led them down three very bright corridors and up one flight of stairs before they reached room 321. They walked along a ward where every bed was cordoned off by blue curtains. From time to time, a curtain had been left open, but the mother made sure not to look. She did not want to see a single other person suffering or in pain. Then the nurse slowed down and paused, ready to open the curtain.

At this point, the kind man said, 'I will leave you here. Call me when you want me to come and get you.'

'Please let my daughter know, as soon as you get home, that her father is in the hospital,' the mother said.

'Of course,' the man said. 'I will break the news to her.'

She felt his hand squeeze her shoulder before he left.

The nurse drew back the curtain.

There he was, lying peacefully on the bed. Her husband. The man she loved so much. There he was. He was alive, and she was looking right at him; she couldn't believe that this was not a dream. He was wired up and plugged in with drips coming out of his arms on both sides.

'He has third degree burns on both hands. We believe he attempted to climb a metal fence. He inhaled a lot of smoke. A man found him unconscious by the shore. He collapsed and fell into a coma. He is stable now and breathing on his own. The doctor will come to see you shortly.'

The nurse drew the curtain and left. She was alone with her husband. His hands were bandaged and resting on top of the covers. The heart monitor beeped steadily. His face looked red and bloated. She touched his shoulder first, ever so gently, feeling the warmth of him, his alive body. Then she leant over him and kissed his cheek.

'It's me,' she whispered. 'Please wake up.' But he did not move.

She studied his face closely, holding her breath. Not even his eyelids flickered. She felt as though she would start sobbing, but she swallowed hard and stopped herself. There was a chair by the bed, and she sat down, sliding it as close to him as possible. She placed a hand on the covers, feeling the slow soft rise and fall of his chest.

She watched him for a long time. Her mind was empty now. All she could do was look at him, remind herself that he was real, that he was here. As she focused on his face, she saw his eyelids flicker. She got up. She kissed his lips, but he did not move.

'It's me,' she said again. 'I love you so much. Please wake up.'

But he remained completely still and silent.

She sat down again and took a deep breath, placing a hand once more on his chest.

'Your daughter is waiting for you,' she said. 'We're staying with a family. They're lovely – they've really helped us. You will love them when you meet them.'

She sighed again and looked out of the window. Now, the clouds had cleared and the sun had begun to set. The moon was already visible in the darkening sky. It looked ghostly and she longed for night so that she could see it glow like the white sails of the boat that had rescued them.

Isn't it strange how memories come back to us again and again? Like fairy tales we hear a million times until something is resolved and our heart is safe.

She remembered once more being a little girl, waking up at 2 a.m. to laughter and police sirens and the music from Charlie Chan's. She remembered looking at the moon from her bedroom window after her dad's death. And years later, when she walked with her husband in the forest, he would point up at the moon because he knew what it meant for her. The moon had stopped her heart from breaking completely.

'I love you,' she said again. 'Please wake up.'

But her husband made no movement, aside from the rise and fall of his chest.

'You never listen to what I say. Can you not just hear me this once?'

Of course I listen, he would have said. *Of course I do. I always listen to you.*

'Good evening.' The greeting came from a young nurse with a sparkling diamond stud in her nose.

'Good evening,' the mother managed. But it was not a good evening.

The nurse fussed around the woman's husband, checking the drip, the heart monitor. 'The doctor will be here shortly. I'll tend to his dressings after I've taken his blood.'

The mother did not answer. There was nothing to say. She watched the nurse flit about the room in the light of the sunset.

'Why don't you get yourself a cup of tea?' the nurse said. 'There's a vending machine along the corridor.'

Then she was gone, and there was such silence, such stillness.

The mother wanted to tell her husband that she loved him, once more. She felt that she needed to keep repeating it, hoping one utterance might reach him. But, just like before when she was in the water, she could not speak. There was something about this nurse that had startled her into silence.

Why don't you get yourself a cup of tea? She heard the nurse's sweet voice as if she were still in the cubicle. Sweet like sugar. Tea. All the normal stuff of life, reminding her that life was now anything but normal.

It is the simple things we miss the most.

I love you. Please wake up.

She heard the words in her mind. They were there, like gleaming fish beneath the sea. But she could not catch them; she could not bring them to her mouth. They slipped and slid away. They were lost beneath a sea that glistened with flames.

'Did you have a good nap?' She could hear the nurse talking in the next cubicle.

'Not really,' a man replied. He sounded like an older man. 'I think I need something to help me.'

'The people we're staying with – they live inside the eucalyptus forest,' she told her husband. Her voice was back, and it resonated in the quiet cubicle. 'I know how much you love the smell of eucalyptus. We can go and walk there when you wake up.'

Again, he did not move at all. Again, she felt like sobbing. She thought that maybe if she cried like a child, if she allowed herself to drop to the ground and cry, that all this would go away, that she would wake up in her bed yesterday morning and none of this would have happened. She took a deep breath. And another. And another. She allowed her body to rest in the chair, with her hand on his chest, and she stared at the barely visible moon and imagined standing up there all alone, staring down at the Earth.

'Dear Earth,' she whispered. 'Heavenly Earth, I thank you for the forest. I thank you for allowing me to walk in the cool shade of the trees for so many years. I fell in love in the forest, had my first kiss there and watched my child play and laugh and grow. Dear Earth, beautiful Earth, I ask you to protect my husband, to bring him back to me. Please protect my daughter and my husband. Please make sure that they never again feel the pain they feel now.'

The mother sighed again. 'Do you remember the man with the pea in his beard?' she said to her husband.

Only the heart monitor responded with a steady beep.

'Do you remember? Well, of course you remember! It was after all those years. We didn't see each other for years – do you remember? And then, out of the blue, I bumped into you on the train. In England. I mean, what are the chances?! But life has a way of doing that, doesn't it?'

She stopped talking and looked at him: his mouth and his eyelids, the mole on the side of his cheek, the soft hairs on his earlobes, his thick brown hair with fine silver threads appearing here and there.

'It was at the end of August, wasn't it? I was leaving the village by the sea – on the train back to the city. Everything around there was full of the sea. I chose a seat by the window with a table. I wasn't reading. Instead, I looked out at the landscape. You know I love doing that, don't you? Sitting on a train or in a car and watching the world pass by? You know that about me just like you know how I like my tea – milk and honey with two cloves and a stick of cinnamon. I'd been visiting my mum's brother who lived by the sea. I told you

240

about him. I loved that man. I spent most summers with him and his family after we stopped coming to Greece. I was never really sure why my mum stopped coming to Greece. I think it broke her heart – reminded her of my dad too much. But she never spoke about it, my mum – just kept kneading the bread. She must have made a million loaves of bread, you know. He was once an English professor, my uncle. I'm not sure if I ever told you that. He died shortly after our meeting on the train. That man taught me a lot. It's probably because of him that I became a music teacher.'

Once again, the woman stopped talking. This time, there was a very long silence. The heart monitor beeped steadily, consistently, reassuringly.

'Then, at the next stop, I looked up and saw you standing there. Later, all the possibilities frightened me! I could have stepped onto another carriage – I could have been on a different train! I could have booked the 3 p.m. or the one after! Aren't you frightened, too, sometimes? Of how life could have taken a different turn?'

She looked out of the window at the moon again. It was hovering above the sea and becoming clearer as the sky darkened.

'I'll never forget that day, when I saw you all grown up, standing there, smiling at me. You were as shocked as I was. Then you sat down and said, "Where are you heading to?"

'"I'm going home," I said.

'There was so much I wanted to tell you about my life, about how my mother had died and left me the house in the city where I still lived. I wanted to tell you how I studied music at university and had never really fallen in love with anyone because I had always been in love with you. I wanted to tell you how on Sundays I went for long walks in the forest and thought about the forest in Greece where you lived.

'But what I said was, "Where have you been?"

'I remember it so well, like it was yesterday. You took my question literally and told me you'd been visiting friends on the coast, that they were fishermen. You said something about the sea, how you'd felt in touch with the elements. And I laughed, because I could see that you hadn't changed one bit. Then you told me how these friends had given you some fresh fish to take home with you, that you were staying in London with a friend for a month for an exhibition, where you were showing your paintings for the first time.

'"The fish is in a box in the luggage section," you said, and you looked in that direction – you were so anxious. "Can you smell anything?" you said.

'And I said, "No ... why?"

'"I'm worried the container might break." Your features contorted and changed into expressions I couldn't understand. Now, I know those expressions so well! You got up to have a look and came back relieved.

'"Once they gave me live crabs," you said, "and they escaped in the carriage. I looked down, and there were four crabs walking around, going up and down the aisle. This man even screamed and stood up on his seat! They were just scuttling around as if they were looking for the sea!"

'It was so funny, and I could just imagine you getting all stressed out, and I couldn't stop laughing.'

Laughter suddenly escaped from the woman's mouth, as if she were really on that train and he was really sitting opposite her in the morning light as they whizzed through the countryside. She laughed out loud. But then a terrible sadness came over her.

She leant over him again and gently kissed his eyelids. *Please wake up, please wake up, please wake up.*

'How is my daughter?' she heard a woman say in a cubicle not too far away. 'Can I go and see her?'

She could not hear the nurse's response, just a mumble of words and a shuffling of feet. Then again: quiet, such quiet, apart from the machinery.

She could not stand that the only sound was the beeping of the heart monitor.

'We sped on,' she continued, taking herself back. 'I looked out of the window for a while, at the open sky and miles of green hills and slopes, at the grazing cows and sheep, the cottages dotted here and there. Next to me sat a woman with hair the colour of bluebells. Do you remember her hair? Next to you sat that man in the three-piece pin-striped suit and a beard so long it touched the table. And then – then I got a pen and a piece of paper from my bag, and I wrote *He has a pea in his beard. One o'clock.*

'I slid the paper towards you.

'Then you signalled for me to give you the pen and you wrote *There it is, waiting to be eaten. I can't stop staring at it. Make me stop.*

'You pushed the paper back to me and I wrote *I've missed you.*

243

'And you wrote: *Me too.*

'And I wrote: *Shall we tell him he has a pea in his beard?*'

Then a nurse came in to tell the woman that visiting hours were over.

'But the doctor hasn't seen me yet.'

'We're sorry,' the nurse said. 'We have been inundated. These are very trying times. Will you come back tomorrow morning? The doctor will be in again and can see you then.'

The woman stood up and put on her coat. She didn't say anything, but she did as she was told. She gave her husband another kiss on the cheek. 'I'll see you tomorrow,' she said, 'first thing.'

It was so hard to leave him there. She texted the kind man and asked for his address so that she could get a taxi.

I will come and get you, he replied. *Wait right there!*

20

THE VET ARRIVES IN THE van just after noon the next day. I am in the living room with Chara and Rosalie, having a mug of hot chocolate, when we hear the engine.

Chara jumps up immediately, her eyes wide. She says, 'The baby jackal is here, Mamma – he's actually here!'

'Yes, baby girl.'

We go out to meet them. The vet does not have the nurse with her this time, and the driver steps out to open the back doors. The vet picks up the jackal in a blanket. I hear Chara gasp, for he is the most beautiful little thing, the most unusual creature I have ever seen. He has been washed so that his fur is a deep dark gold, with areas of soft grey around his snout and ears and along his neck. His ears are alert, his eyes like black marbles.

We lead the vet into the living room, where Chara has created a little home for the jackal beneath the painting of the chestnut tree. It is comfy and warm with bedding and cushions and a sheepskin rug. She has placed some of her soft toys on the cushions and a bowl of fresh water nearby.

The vet unwraps the jackal from his blanket and puts him down onto the rug, and we all watch him. He stands tentatively, tail down, and looks around. Now that we see him clearly, he is astonishing. The jackal's front and back legs are wrapped in fish-scales. They are silver and shimmer purple and pink in the light. The dark-grey outline of the scale-pattern is so clear that it looks like he is half fish, half mammal.

Chara is silent. She stares at this creature with tears in her eyes. I look at her instead of the jackal. I absorb her happiness and awe.

Rosalie comes closer, very slowly, and sniffs around the area where the jackal sits.

'Be very, very gentle, Rosalie,' Chara says quietly, and Rosalie looks up at her with questioning eyes.

The jackal pushes one of the teddy bears with his nose; then he sits down and rests his head on one of his silver-scaled paws.

'I think he likes it here,' Chara whispers.

'I think you are right,' the vet says.

'Is he in pain? Do his paws hurt?' she asks.

'He doesn't hurt so much now, but here are some pain-killers for you to crush into his food three times a day for the next ten days. In a few days' time, he should be able to go out and wander around and even begin to play.'

Chara stares at him. 'I will look after him well,' she says. 'But when he is fully better, I won't be able to release him into the forest to live his best life, because there is no forest. If I take him to another part of the forest, he won't know it.'

The vet nods now, and I can see a darkness filling her eyes. 'You're right,' she says. 'I think the only thing you can do is to wait to see how things go. If you think he is happy and settled here, then he can stay with you – if he is restless for the wild, then we can think about rehoming him. We will stay in touch, and I'll come and visit again in a few weeks. But for now, he is yours to take care of.'

Chara nods at the vet with confidence and determination on her face, and the vet gives her a warm and trusting smile.

Chara does not leave the jackal's side all day. Rosalie stays close to them, too. Chara sits on the ground next to the little animal, occasionally stroking him or scratching behind his ears. Sometimes, she reminds him to drink water, and later I cook him some chicken, and she cuts it up into tiny pieces and places the bowl beside him, first offering him a piece from her fingers. The jackal licks the morsel off her hand and then goes to the bowl of food. He takes a piece, chews it, looking into Chara's eyes; then he takes another and another and at some point, he begins to simply lap it up. Then Chara pushes the water bowl close, and he has plenty, before settling back onto the sheepskin rug.

By the afternoon, she has fallen asleep on the floor beside him, and I cover her with a blanket. Rosalie has not moved either; she is observing the jackal diligently and with a certain maternal air.

I sit in the armchair and watch them, but I am not relaxed. I keep thinking about the earring that the detective and

Lieutenant Makris showed me, the tiny gold heart-shaped stud that belongs to Mrs Gataki. What should I do? Should I tell the police that I know who owns that earring and that she lost it at the same time as Mr Monk's death and let them carry out their investigation? But what if Mrs Gataki *is* involved, and what if I am then getting her into trouble for being involved in the murder of a man who deserved to be murdered? But *did* he deserve to die? *I* left him to die.

The lessons that Lazaros taught me drift through my mind, and I see him again, as if he is standing in front of me, wearing his wicker baseball cap, scratching his chin, looking out at the forest with apprehension at its changing state.

But even if I *had* called the ambulance straightaway, would they have made it in time?

In any case, it was me who decided that he did not deserve to be helped. Who will right my wrong? Who will decide whether it is in fact right or wrong?

It may be left to the little girl with eyes like the sky in the paintings to live in a world that is increasingly breaking. All this will be her inheritance. Why is it so important that wrongs are righted?

Harmony. It is something to do with harmony.

And where is the beginning and where is the end?

The people of this town built their villas along the shore and blocked the way to the water. The people of this town did not collect the wood from the forest, did not care for it and tend to it and nurture it. And yet here we stand like warriors against the man who started the fire, against the police and the fire service.

The land was dry. It was drier than it had ever been. Who is responsible for that?

We will turn this forest into a desert, Lazaros had said.

One day. Some day. Now. Once upon a time. Once upon a time, there was an ancient forest.

Was it Aristotle or Plato, or both, who thought that the principles embodying the law were believed to be perfect and permanent and therefore not subject to change at the will of the people? Law was the same for all, and therefore it meant freedom. Obedience to law led to liberty. Within these ancient scaffoldings and structures was a land of potential harmony.

I remember all these lessons in the old, tattered books my father bought me. *Learn about your heritage*, he had said – yes, albeit with a hint of irony. *You're not Greek until you can make coffee and read Plato. Learn to read Plato and learn to make coffee. They're both good for the soul and are essential.*

After he died, I read those books at night before falling asleep, and my dreams became vivid – dreams about kings and warriors and broken lands.

The baby jackal moves, and Chara stirs in response. She is attuned to him even in her sleep. Her internal world is consumed by him. In her sleep, she moves her hand and places it on his little chest. His eyes open for a second and gleam in the sunlight; then he falls asleep once more. Half mammal, half fish – half of this world, half of a world of dreams and thoughts, where all the other hybrid creatures live and breathe. Like the centaur, thought up when the Minoan people first met tribes of horse riders and were so impressed that they wrote stories of horse-humans. Echidna:

249

half woman, half snake. The Gorgon: a woman with hissing snakes for hair. The Minotaur: part bull, part man. The satyr: part goat, part man. The siren: a woman with the legs and tail of a bird. These creatures from my childhood move and flitter and fly through the landscape of my mind.

But I remember the blue of Mr Monk's eyes. The anger I felt as I looked into his eyes. The fury. The fury that consumed me.

Mr Monk lit the fire.

I look at the paintings that surround me.

Yes. This is a fact: Mr Monk lit the fire.

I look at the painting of the chestnut tree.

Mr Monk lit the fire.

I look at the leaves and the animals around me, at the flowers and the pine needles. The world of the past.

Mr Monk lit the fire.

Yes. That is true.

But there is another truth:

The fire was lit long ago, long before Mr Monk lit the fire.

Lazaros knew this, he understood what was coming and he carried it. I remember him with his baseball cap and the fierce look on his face: *We will turn this forest into a desert.*

Tasso had heard his father. The fire was already ignited in the present of Tasso's paintings. It was lit before the paintings even existed, before the colour and the light and this quiet truth were even captured within them.

It was captured by the pure fact that Tasso was obsessed with painting the forest. He had painted it in the way that he had painted his slowly dying mother.

The fire had already been lit before Mr Monk lit the fire.

I think of Tasso's silence, of his inability to imagine himself painting ever again.

I stand by the window and watch him in the garden beneath the fig tree, unmoving. He has become like one of his paintings. His light and soul have been captured and frozen in sadness, for all that has been lost.

The Book of Fire

When she returned to the house in the eucalyptus woods, the mother found that her daughter was sleeping soundly. The girl couldn't lie on her back, so she was sleeping on her side with soft pillows tucked gently behind her. She wanted to tell her about her pappa, how he was, but she didn't want to wake her. There was an open book by her side. The mother picked it up – a collection of tales from Greek mythology – and saw that the pages were open on the story of the harpies: women with the wings and tails of birds, the spirits of storm winds.

Outside, the wind blew hard again. Branches scraped against the window. The birds were silent now. The mother kissed her daughter's cheek and went downstairs to join the kind couple.

They were sitting at the table, eating vegetable soup, a late supper. The man stood up and filled a bowl for her. He offered her some bread, which she accepted and spread with copious amounts of butter.

'Thank you for everything,' she said, in between mouthfuls of soup. She was suddenly so hungry that she could not stop eating to speak. 'Thank you for caring for my daughter and putting her to bed. I mean, what I want to say is: thank you for all you have done to help us.'

She dipped the bread in the soup and crammed it into her mouth. Now that she knew her husband was alive, her appetite had come back.

'Oh, come on now!' the man said. 'Look, I would say the same to you, had it been the other way around. Listen: *your* forest has burnt, and it could have been *ours*.'

'But how is your husband?' the man's wife asked, handing the mother a napkin and pouring water.

'The main thing is that he is alive. Both his hands are burnt. He inhaled loads of smoke. He hasn't woken up.' Her voice cracked at the last two words, but she swallowed down her tears with the soup. 'The main thing is that he is alive. I thought he was dead. He is alive.' She wanted to repeat these words again and again, to make sure that they were real.

'Of course,' the man's wife said, placing a hand upon her arm.

'The doctor is going to speak to me tomorrow,' the mother said. 'They were too busy today.'

'I will take you again first thing,' the man said.

'I don't know how to ever repay you,' the mother said.

'Honestly – you have to believe me, when I say this – you don't need to repay us for anything.'

The mother soaked the bread into the last bit of soup. Then she gulped down the water.

253

The man's wife got up and dimmed the lights. The mother felt warm and sleepy.

'The police know who started the fire now,' the kind man said.

'Oh yes?' his wife replied.

The woman sat up straight. 'Who was it?'

'I can't remember his name, but he was a property developer, lived up on the mountain. Someone saw him do it. Then he confessed, apparently. A few people went after him,' the man said.

'How do you know this?' his wife asked, raising her eyebrows.

'My friend told me.'

'The cheating fireman?'

'Yes, him,' the man said, shaking his head in exasperation. 'He told me that a few men from the village – they worked in the garage there apparently – got together and went looking for him. Luckily for him – the man who started the fire – he was still being held in the police cell. But these men, they would have murdered him, I tell you.'

'It would have done no good for them or their own families to get themselves into trouble. Leave it to the law, I say,' the man's wife said.

'Well, try telling them that. He'll probably be out on bail soon. They'll be after him again, no doubt.'

'Stupid men,' the man's wife said.

'You can understand it, though.'

'No,' she said. 'No, I cannot. Now, why don't you go and get us a nice drink to wash down the food?'

The man got up and went to a cupboard in the corner of the room and retrieved a ruby red bottle of Xinomavro. He placed glasses on the table and poured the wine.

The mother gulped it down. 'Look what he's done to us,' she said, 'the man who started the fire.'

And the man's wife said something in response, but she did not hear it, because all she could think about now was her husband lying alone in the bed, with tubes coming out of him and lungs full of smoke and bandaged hands. And then she remembered her daughter's burnt back.

The man poured her another glass of wine. She drank it, feeling its warmth, feeling her body relax, her mind beginning to swim. She remembered the old lady who had died beside them in the water.

'Are you OK?' the man's wife asked. 'You don't seem yourself right now. I mean, not that I know you well, but you seem distant and scared.'

The mother looked at the man's wife, forced herself to focus on her. 'I keep remembering the fire,' she said.

'If it helps to talk, I'm all ears.'

'But I don't know what to say.'

'Come, then,' the man's wife said, taking the wine from her hands. 'I will make you some aniseed tea. Go and get ready for bed.'

As the mother walked up the stairs, she could hear her daughter speaking to the couple's son on the landing outside the loft room.

'No way!' he said. 'That sounds amazing.'

'I can never show you now, though.'

And then, there was silence. The mother reached the top of the stairs and saw them sitting cross-legged, facing each other, the dog right beside the girl with its head on her knee. The girl jumped up as soon as she saw her mother.

'Did you see Pappa?' she asked, her eyes open and clear as the sky.

'Yes, I did.'

The girl wrapped her arms around her mother and cried silently for a while. Then she wiped her tears on the back of her hands, and she turned to the boy and said, 'Thank you for helping me to not lose my mind.' Then to her mother, 'How is Pappa?'

'He is still sleeping.'

The girl nodded and looked down. 'Can I see him?'

'Very soon,' the mother said. 'And anyway, what are you two doing up?' She forced a smile, trying to appear as positive and light as she could.

'I had a bad dream,' the girl said. 'I got up because I didn't want to be by myself. I was too scared. I started to think about stuff.'

'I saw her standing at the bottom of the stairs like she was completely lost!' the boy said. 'So I came here to keep her company until she got sleepy.'

'I couldn't stop thinking, Mamma. I had nightmares of—'

'It's OK, baby, don't repeat it – let's not think about it all again.'

The girl's face dropped, for it was her father who was good at listening to the deepest, darkest parts of her heart, to her greatest fears and worries. These things made the mother too scared; she always tried to change the subject, and it broke the girl's heart a little each time. The mother knew this, but she just couldn't help it.

'But the main thing is that your pappa is alive,' she said.

'Yes.' The girl nodded, and for a second her eyes beamed. 'I think it's time I got some sleep,' she said.

'I'll see you in the morning,' the boy said, standing up, smiling at the girl and patting the dog on the head. 'I'm so glad your dad is OK. I'll make you some pancakes tomorrow – how's that?'

'With strawberries?'

'Of course!'

The girl smiled a real smile.

The mother suddenly loved this boy, for the kindness in his eyes that she could also see in his parents. She stood there for a moment and held on to her daughter's smile. She closed her eyes and envisioned this smile like a gem. It *was* a gem, the most beautiful and the most precious thing on Earth – to see that her daughter was not completely broken, in spite of her wounds and her pain, in spite of the losses that haunted them all.

In the morning, the kind man took the mother to the hospital. She convinced her daughter to stay at home. She wanted to protect her until she had more information about her husband's state; she didn't want her daughter to feel any pain, to hear any bad news. They drove through the eucalyptus forest. Now

257

that she wasn't so fearful about her husband's whereabouts, she remembered that she had been here before – once, many years ago when she was a young girl, before her father died.

They were out on a trip visiting one of her dad's school friends. They had driven along this same road, she was sure. It had been summer then too, and just like now, the eucalyptus trees were in flower. The woman looks around at the forest, full of fluffy bursts of colour, like dandelions gone to seed. White. Red. Orange. Pink. Green. How beautiful! She remembered being a young girl in the car and when she had told her dad how much she loved these flowers, he'd said, 'So, which is your favourite?'

She was in the back, her mother sitting quietly in the passenger seat, window rolled down, breathing in the forest. She could see her mother's face in the mirror, and she focused on it for a moment, because she had never seen her so calm, so much at peace, her eyes closed, facing the soft breeze, wearing a fine silk scarf that flapped about her face.

'Well,' she had said, 'my favourite are the lime-green ones.'

Her father had stopped the car abruptly, as if he had taken a wrong turn. He stepped outside, leaving the car door open so the scent of eucalyptus poured into the car, overriding the smell of the bubblegum tree that hung from the rear-view mirror. She got out, too, and looked up to where the tall trees met the sky.

'Oh, tomtit!' her dad exclaimed, using cockney in his ridiculous way again, jumping without reaching the flower. He jumped again and again, until finally he grabbed hold of a branch and plucked one of the lime-green flowers. Then he came up to his daughter, beaming, and placed it in her palm. It was breathtaking. The flower was made of hundreds of spike-like stamens, emerging from a central cone-like bud. It reminded her of a flower that you might find in another world, or perhaps in shallow parts of a turquoise sea.

'Wow,' she had whispered. 'Just wow.'

She had thanked her dad and kissed him on the cheek, and they had got back into the car to continue their journey, while she held this flower in her palms.

Now, this forest was just as beautiful, on the surface at least, nothing much had changed. She wished she could stay right here forever with her memories and not have to face the present, let alone the future.

But the car rumbled on towards the hospital. The mother and the kind man sat in silence. She wanted to tell him what she had remembered, but who was this man? She knew nothing about him, nor he about her, and she had imposed upon his good nature enough. They reached the shore and continued for a few more minutes until they arrived at the hospital.

The kind man parked the car and walked with her to the entrance. 'Now, I hope you're OK,' he said. 'I know this is difficult, but hold on there, will you?'

She nodded.

'I hope you find him well.'

Then he was gone, and she braced herself to enter the brightly lit corridors and all the noise and commotion and uncertainty that hospitals bring.

She was taken to the ward by a different nurse this time – a young petite woman, probably just out of nursing

259

school, with wide alert eyes, who walked fast and with an air of efficiency. She pulled back the curtain.

To her astonishment, the mother saw that her husband was awake. He was lying down, as he had been the day before, but when she entered, he turned his head ever so slightly towards her.

He said her name, though it was merely a whisper. But he spoke. There was never, *ever* a time when she had been happier to hear the sound of her name.

'Yes,' she said. 'I'm here. It's me.' She went to him and looked down into his eyes, and she saw that they were filled with tears.

'You kept telling me to wake up,' he said.

'Yesterday?'

'Yes.'

'You heard me?'

'Every word.'

She kissed him gently on the lips.

But then she suddenly felt that she had lost him again, that he had slipped away from her. His eyes became distant, and when she asked him how he felt, he did not reply but turned his face to the window through which the moon had shone the night before.

She sat down and placed her hand on his chest, just as she had before. 'I love you,' she said, and once again the only response was the steady beeping of the heart monitor.

But this was a beautiful thing. This was the sound of her husband's living, beating heart. She held on to this thought: that the man she loved, the man she had forever loved, was alive.

'How are you feeling?' she said.

But once again he did not reply.

So, she sat like that, in silence at his bedside, while he stared out of the window. The hospital was louder during the day. She could hear conversations from the other cubicles, various beeping noises, the rickety wheels of the breakfast cart, the woman greeting the patients with a merry, 'Good morning! We have some warm cheese pastries today ...'

There was a comfort in all these sounds, in life continuing around them. Cheese pastries. Tea. Sugar.

She focused on her husband's bandaged hands, which lay unmoving on the bedsheets. Then something else filled her mind: her father-in-law. Where was he? Did her husband find him? Was he in this hospital, too?

But looking at her husband's face, at his dark eyes, she felt a sense of dread. She didn't dare to ask him. They would just sit quietly like this for as long as possible, and whatever was true could remain unknown.

Where is your father?

Part of her wanted to say these words out loud, but she pursed her lips and shut her eyes. When was the last time she had seen her father-in-law? He had come around on Friday – or was it Thursday? He'd arrived early in the morning and tended to the garden – he would never let anyone else tend to their garden. He had planted all sorts of flowers and herbs. His favourite was the peonies, which would bloom in the winter, frozen red flowers, native to Mount Parnassus. *These flowers will cure your nightmares when the days get cold and dark*, he had said.

He would always tell her the history of the plants, their journey. 'See,' he would say, 'they began their existence up there, looming over the ancient site of Delphi, and ended up in your back garden! When the winter comes, if you have bad dreams, get up and have a stroll about and breathe in their lovely smell.' But the winter was here and the land on which the seeds had been planted was completely burnt. *Your entire garden will be filled with the scent of peonies, like sweet roses. A winter garden filled with red flowers.* His eyes always beamed when he talked about these things, and he would make sure to teach his granddaughter as much as he could. He would have her following him around the garden, holding the spade or clippers or seeds or watering can. Then, when they had finished all the work, he would make them a nice refreshing aniseed tea, and he would lean across the table and pretend to steal her nose with the knuckles of his forefinger and middle finger.

'Grandad! Oh my god, Grandad – I'm not five anymore!'

He would then get up and give her a big bear hug.

Again, she wanted to cry, but she looked at her husband lying there so helplessly and held it in.

She sat up straight and took a deep breath. 'Where is your father?' she asked.

This time, he turned his face towards her, but his eyes remained distant. 'I didn't find him.'

'What happened? Was he not at home? Was he in the forest? Do you think he made it to the water? I called the landline but there was no answer, but it did ring which means the house is not all burnt down.'

'So many questions,' he said with a dead voice.

'What does that even mean? Do you think I can sit here and not ask and not care about where he is?'

'Please,' he said gently, and he scrunched up his face, and she saw that he was full of pain. 'Just, please.'

She exhaled. She placed her hand on his forehead; she gently stroked his hair. 'I'm sorry.' The words were barely audible, but he nodded very slightly.

Then he opened his dark eyes, and they were as black as the night sky, the type of sky where the moon and the stars are hidden.

'I went to his house,' he said. 'That's what I did after I left you. I went straight there, but he wasn't in. The fire was moving through the forest so fast – I have never seen a fire move so fast. It was coming further east, and I wished he had been at home because he would have been safe there, at least until I arrived. But the house was empty. So, I ran as far into the forest as I could. But the smoke was too much. It was like I was drowning. I can't even tell you. It was so bad. I called him – I searched for him – I went as far as I could ...'

She placed her hand on his chest again and felt the beating of his heart. The beeping of the monitor was faster.

'So, then I couldn't take it anymore. I ran down – I left him. I ran down to the sea.'

'You didn't *leave* him,' the mother said. 'What else could you do? You didn't *leave* him – you just didn't find him.'

But he didn't seem to hear what she was saying; his eyes moved as if in a dream.

'I ran down towards the sea, but it was all blocked off, and the fire was so close – I could feel the heat all over

263

me and inside me. I grabbed hold of a metal fence to get up over it, and my hands – this searing pain, this pain I can't explain ...'

'It's all right,' she said. 'You're safe now. We're all safe now.'

There were too many moments of silence now, and her last words drifted through her mind as if she could hear their echo. *We're all safe now.*

'You know I had no choice.' His voice broke the quiet. 'I grabbed hold of that burning metal, and I pulled myself over that fence. If I hadn't, I wouldn't be here. I ran through someone's back garden, and then everything went black.'

He continued to look into her eyes; their darkness seared into her, and she did not know that this would be the last time he gazed at her for a long time.

'I let him go,' he said.

'You can't think like that.'

'I should have kept going.'

'You would have died.'

'But where is my father?' With these words, he turned his face away and looked out of the window again, and she did, too. The sky was bright blue today. Not a single cloud.

The following day, he had to leave the hospital. They needed the beds for more serious cases. The hospital was inundated. He was out of harm's way now.

The mother and the kind man came to collect him. She held on to his arm as they walked outside into the warm summer morning. He was wobbly on his feet. He didn't speak much, apart from saying a quiet hello to his wife and thanking the man for his kindness.

'You will see your daughter,' the mother said quietly to him, as they approached the kind man's car. 'She is so excited to see you.'

Her husband nodded, but he did not smile, and this broke her heart and made her anxious. He used to beam at the mere mention of his daughter; she was so precious to him. She was the most precious thing in the whole world. This is what he always said. Now, he was quiet. But perhaps the mother was expecting too much. She just wanted to hear her husband speak in the way he used to, so she could feel that things would be OK. In this moment, she felt like a child. She held on to his arm to stop him from falling, but really it was she who was holding on for dear life.

They got into the car and drove away from the sea and into the eucalyptus forest. Her husband glanced out of the window momentarily and then looked down at his bandaged hands, and that's where his eyes became stuck. The mother put her hand on her husband's thigh, but he did not acknowledge it. She had sat in the back with him to make sure that he was OK, but she felt his darkness engulfing her, and she wished she could get out to smell the invigorating scent of the trees.

When they arrived at the house in the woods, her husband kept his head down. His daughter ran outside, ready to embrace him, but when she saw her father's face, she stopped in her tracks and then looked at his hands.

'Pappa,' she said and took a step closer.

'It's OK, my lovely,' he said. 'Don't be alarmed, but ...'
He didn't finish his sentence, and she didn't attempt to
embrace him again. She was a very thoughtful and sensitive
girl, and she saw something in him that stopped her.

Then the husband looked up. The girl and the mother
followed his gaze. There was a raven in the sky, circling
the house. They could see its black wings above the eucalyptus trees.

Inside, the man's wife had prepared soup, and they sat
together at the table to eat. The mother fed her husband the
soup, a spoonful at a time. She tore off small chunks of bread
from a bun, soaked each piece in the soup and placed them
into his mouth, one by one. He did not look at anyone during
the meal; he kept his eyes down.

Then the kind man finished his soup, put his spoon down
and said, 'We are all so glad you are here – we were worried
there for a while. You are welcome to stay as long as you
want or need.'

The husband looked up now and smiled and said, 'Thank
you. Thank you with all my heart.'

The boy and the girl collected the bowls and spoons and
used napkins and took them to the kitchen. The mother
could hear the running water of the sink and the clinking
of cutlery and now and then a giggle or a burst of laughter.
It made her happy that her daughter was still able to
feel joy.

When the kitchen was tidy, the children left to go for a
walk in the woods with the dog. When they had gone, the
atmosphere became heavier.

'The heatwave was even worse this year,' the man said.

'Yes,' his wife agreed. 'I heard them discussing it on the news.'

'The surrounding villages have been evacuated,' the man continued. 'People have become refugees in their own country.'

Her husband's eyes moved from one speaker to the other; they were dark and brooding and frightened, but he said nothing.

'Everything is changing,' the kind man's wife said.

The mother heard all this, but her mind was drifting. She was imagining her daughter walking in the eucalyptus woods, just as she had walked with her husband in the forest where he had lived, all those years ago – in the years when his mother was still alive, and he had painted her, trying so hard to capture her beauty, her inner vivacity and her gradual fading into death.

Later that night, the mother and the girl and the man's wife went to the room in the loft. The girl took her painkillers and sat down gently on the bed.

'Where will Pappa sleep?' the girl asked.

And the man's wife replied, 'I'll set him up downstairs in the living room – it'll be easier for him. Don't you worry now.'

'And what about Grandad? Is he in the hospital? Can we go and see him?'

The mother could not look into her daughter's pleading eyes; it was as if she was begging her mother to give her some good news about her beloved grandfather.

'Your father didn't find him,' she said clearly and simply. There was nothing else she could say.

The girl nodded and remained quiet.

The man's wife brought a flannel and a bowl of soapy water like she did last time. Together, they gently took off the girl's jumper and vest, and they cleaned her arms and the skin around the bandage and her neck and face and hands with the warm flannel. Just as before, the girl sat there and said nothing, except this time her eyes were wide and alert and full of thoughts. The man's wife knelt there on the floor and washed the cloth in the soapy water, wringing it out and handing it back to the mother.

Then the girl said, 'Will Pappa be OK?'

'Yes, of course,' the mother said.

'But I have never seen him so sad.'

The woman patted the girl's arm, and then she took the bowl to the bathroom and poured the water into the basin.

'Now, get under the covers and get warm and have sweet dreams,' the mother said.

The kind man's wife wished the girl goodnight and went downstairs.

'Can you tell me the end of the story?' the girl asked her mother.

'The one about my great-great-grandfather?'

She nodded.

'But that is a sad story. I don't even know why I chose to tell you that one in the sea.'

'But it held our attention,' she said, 'and it was a good story for my friend, the old lady, to hear. It helped her to not think about other sad things. I could tell, because she was really concentrating while you were speaking.'

The mother tapped the girl's arm a few times. 'Fair enough,' she said.

'So, will you tell me the end? We have never ever managed to get to the end of this story. Sometimes, one of your students arrived or I fell asleep, and the last time ...' She paused. 'The last time, my friend ...' The girl's eyes widened with sadness and shimmered with tears, but she did not finish her sentence.

The mother paused for a moment to look up at the ceiling. 'You see, it becomes so sad, this story. If you remember, Vassilios worked as an assistant for his father, and together they made string instruments of all kinds. Their little shop was located on the Pontic port of Samsun on the southern coast of the Black Sea. One hot day in September, as he sat outside drinking coffee, he saw a tower of smoke rising from the next village. Then he heard a loud rumbling sound, and a herd of buffalo stormed past in a cloud of dust, driven through the streets by soldiers. The neighbouring village had been looted, and the Greek minority in all the surrounding villages were in danger.

'Then a young girl, close to his age, approached him. It was obvious that she had come from the burning village. She was completely covered in dust. Vassilios asked if she wanted to stay. He wanted to help her.'

'That's where we got to,' the girl said.

'Yes,' the mother replied. 'But then, something terrible happened. Vassilios's father and grandmother were taken away – someone broke into the house and dragged them out of their beds in the middle of the night, and Vassilios was left alone. But the little girl was still with him. He was so sad that he could barely eat – he found it hard to get himself out of bed in the morning. He stood for hours at the window, waiting for his father to return, but he never came.

'So Vassilios continued to make the instruments, and the girl watched and tried to learn. He had a companion to see him through, and this is where he found his strength. And she was a funny little thing. Despite the circumstances, she would tell jokes and do great impressions of the neighbours. They became good friends and laughed together a great deal.

'In the distance, however, they would see pillars of smoke rising from the other villages. He missed his father so much. Every day, with each instrument he made, he remembered him sitting beside him – he could almost see him sipping coffee or carving a piece of wood. Sometimes, he could hear his voice in the quiet of the shop: *Have you finished yet, Vassilios? But listen, I shouldn't ask you that, because I don't want you to rush. Remember to take your time. Do not jump to conclusions and do not carve wood too fast. Time and patience.*

'But Vassilios hated the Turks for taking his father. He didn't know if his father was dead or alive. He didn't know if he would ever see him again. So he hated these people who had once been his friends. At night, he lay awake, imagining what he would do to a Turk if only he had the courage or the strength. He had forgotten the words of his father.

'Then one day, the Turkish soldiers came for them. It was early in the morning, and they were dragged out of the shop and told to walk. They were going to be banished from their home, banished from their land. They would have to walk all the way from Turkey to Greece. That is what everyone kept saying. That is what happened to other people – there had been rumours, whispers, fears, and now it was happening to them.

'The boy and the girl stuck together. They held hands. They didn't say much to each other, but they stayed close. Sometimes, she would tell a little joke, but most of the time, she was too frightened and tired, and she held on to his hand so tight, as if he or she might blow away like a kite if she let go even for a second. He had taken one of the instruments with him – the first bouzouki that he had ever made on his own – and he held it just as tightly in his other hand. He wouldn't dare to play it, though, even when they stopped for a few hours in the night to rest. There was too much hatred in his heart.

'They walked for days and weeks, this long trail of lost people. Like a slow train, they weaved through the land, and it seemed endless. They slept on the ground. They ate whatever they found. Some people lived, but the weak collapsed, and they were left behind like fallen leaves.

'Then one day, one warm day, when the sun was high and they walked across an open field – god knows where – he suddenly saw in the distance what looked like the reflection of themselves. Appearing over the hill was a long trail of thousands of people. As they came close, they walked in opposite directions, parallel to each other. Vassilios saw something that would never leave him: the people were as tired as he was, heads bent to their chests – but when they glanced up, they looked fearful and confused and close to death.

271

There was one boy who caught his eye, similar in age to himself, tattered clothes and forlorn eyes, and in his hands, he held a bouzouki. For a split second, the boy thought he was seeing himself, that he was in fact looking into a mirror that stretched across the land. But then he realised that the instrument in the boy's hands was not the same as his: it was a baglama, a long-necked lute.

'"They are Turkish," a man behind him said. "They are being led away from their homes by the Greeks. They are heading the way we came."

'And with these words, the boy understood what his father had meant. *They demonise each other*, he had said. *The "other" is always to blame and it fuels people and groups and governments with fire. This never leads to any good on this earth.* And right here Vassilios could see that they were all their own enemies, that they were all human, all in pain, all hurting each other from hatred and fear. From that day forth, he plucked the strings of his bouzouki, but he did not play until they reached Greece. Every time he played a note from the instrument he felt that he could hear the sound of his father's voice. A word here. A word there. *Vassilios. Listen.* He could not take it. When he made it to the old chestnut tree and sat beneath to rest, it was then that he finally picked out a tune.'

The mother looked across at her daughter and saw that she was fast asleep. She saw from the slanted window the glistening black wings of the raven as it sat upon the branches of a tree, and night fell upon them all.

*

272

Later, she went downstairs to the living room to find her husband asleep on the sofa-bed. She sat down on the edge of it for a moment, then she lay down next to him and placed her hand on his chest.

He was not asleep. 'Hey,' he said.

'I couldn't sleep. I wanted to see you.'

He remained silent, and the lemon tree scraped against the window.

'I was thinking,' he said. 'Once we're able to return, we can stay in my father's house. If it is still standing, though it was when I went to find him.'

The mother sensed that this was such a hard thing for her husband to say, for he drew a sharp breath after the last word, as if someone had plunged him into freezing water.

'OK,' she said. 'You know I love you so much.'

And they stayed like that in the dark. He fell asleep, but she stayed awake all night and thought about her father-in-law and watched the sky change colour as the sun rose over the woods.

21

CHARA STAYS BY THE JACKAL'S side. He is asleep most of the time, but she watches over him as if she is his parent. I think about Mrs Gataki's earring. Should I call her? Should I tell the police that I know who it belongs to? These questions never leave me. When night falls, I dim the main lights and turn on a soft lamp. The jackal's paws glisten – a soft shimmer that catches the light whenever he shifts from one position to another. Chara watches him. Time ticks by slowly.

She leaves him for a while to go outside to sit by her dad. She takes the sketchpad with her and opens the pages to show him. She taps him on the shoulder, but he does not turn towards her; it is as if he is in a trance. He is looking out again towards the burnt land.

I watch them through the window. Chara tries one more time to get his attention; she puts the book on his lap and turns the pages. He glances at her for a moment, before gently placing his hand on hers. He says something to her, then he takes his hand back, places it on his lap and is lost again. Whatever he said, she sits quietly now, unmoving. She closes the book. She stays by his side for another couple of minutes, and then she comes inside.

'Are you OK, baby?' I say.

'Yes, Mamma. It's really cold outside.'

'I can imagine.'

'Pappa doesn't really talk to me.'

I nod.

'Tomorrow is never going to come.'

I see that her eyes are brimming with tears, but she will not allow herself to cry.

'It will come. You just need to be patient. Give him time.'

But these words do not seem to reassure her. If anything, they push her further away. She drops her head as if I, too, have let her down.

'Have you thought of a name for the jackal?' I ask.

'Neo,' she says.

'After the boy from the kind family who helped us?'

She nods now, blushing slightly, averting her eyes from me.

'And also,' she says, 'because it means "new".'

'That is perfect for him,' I say.

'I will call him Neo from now on. Look at him, Mamma – he is so cute and so little. When he's older, if he's still here and he doesn't mind, then I will always look after him and play with him. But I always remember that I will probably lose him one day. I have to remember it every second of knowing him.'

'Why is that?'

'Well, the vet might rehome him, which I hope she will so that he can run freely through the fields and play with other jackals.'

I go to her and hug her tightly.

'Come on,' I say, 'off to bed. Go and have sweet dreams, and you can see him again in the morning.'

'You know, Mamma,' she says, 'you can't force yourself to have a sweet dream. It comes or it doesn't come. A dream does what it wants.'

'You are very right and very cheeky.'

She smiles, but her eyes are suddenly full of her father's darkness.

'If I have a nightmare, don't be scared,' she says.

'Shouldn't I be telling you not to be scared?'

She glances at me quickly but says nothing.

Then she leans over the jackal to make sure that he is sound asleep and gives him a very gentle kiss on his head. 'Goodnight, little Neo,' she whispers, then she pauses for a moment at the window and looks out at her father. She glances back at me, as if she is going to say something. Her lips part ever so slightly, but then she turns back to the window. 'I'm so tired, Mamma,' she says.

'Well, there's a lot going on, I'm not surprised. Go and get a good rest.'

She gives me a kiss on the cheek and heads upstairs.

It is only after she is gone that I feel the weight of her words, the pain in her voice. *I'm so tired, Mamma.* There is such sadness, such resignation, a devastation that seems deep and dark and everlasting, and it sends a chill through my body.

276

An entire day has passed and I have not heard anything more from the police and I have not mustered the courage to speak to Mrs Gataki.

The following morning, I find Chara eating a bowl of cereal cross-legged on the floor beside Neo. His eyes are wide open, and he is resting his head on Chara's thigh.

'He is starting to feel better,' she says. 'I gave him some more water and also a little bit of milk, and he lapped it all up.'

'That's excellent, baby,' I say.

'Shall we make him some more chicken later?'

'Yes, of course.'

Then I see that she is distracted; she looks around the room as if she is searching for something, and she says, 'He is already outside.'

'Your father?'

'Who else, Mamma? Will he ever be with us again?'

'He will. I'm sure of it.'

'Mamma, can you watch Neo for a little while? He is very easy to look after because he is still so sleepy.'

'I will. But where will you be?'

'I want to go and do another drawing.'

'In the forest?'

'Yes, if that's what you like to call it.'

'Do you have to go in there again? It makes me so scared. Is it necessary?'

'Completely necessary. I have to go.'

She glances up at me seriously and with determination, holding the spoon in her hand. I want to kiss her for being alive, for being passionate. But I remember her words last night and the tone in her voice. *I'm so tired, Mamma.*

'Be careful,' I say, 'and don't go far.'

She tilts the bowl and drinks all the milk, before getting up and washing it in the sink. Then she puts on her thick coat and woollen hat and grabs her sketchpad and charcoals.

'Rosalie!' I call, and she replies with a little grunt, and I see that she is already at the door, waiting. 'Rosalie, stay with Chara. Make sure you don't get lost.'

Rosalie looks me in the eyes and barks, lifting her snout to the ceiling. And then I am less anxious. I am always less anxious when Rosalie is around.

I remember her paddling beside us in the water, licking Chara's face, staying close, never giving up, and it breaks my heart to think that she is so innocent and so full of love, having to live in this world that we have made for her.

'Thank you for watching Neo, Mamma,' Chara says.

Before I can respond, she and Rosalie are outside, and the door closes gently behind them.

I sit in the living room surrounded by the paintings of the forest while I watch Neo. Chara is right; he sleeps most of the time, and when he gets up to drink water, I kneel down beside him and stroke his back. Then he returns to his sheepskin rug and falls asleep.

I boil some chicken in the pan. The steam fills the kitchen and the living room, too. It is yet another thing that reminds me of normal life. It is a sunny day. There are no clouds again, and the living room is soaked in sunshine. The little jackal lies on his back with his paws dangling over his chest. It is the first time I have seen him so content. Around him are the painted leaves, the painted wildflowers, the painted trees and other creatures of the woods.

I sit beside him and stroke his belly.

Now, in the quiet, without Chara around, the chestnut tree grabs my attention. It is so green in the painting. I think about how it looks now and of Mr Monk leaning upon it, the noose around his neck. I imagine Mrs Gataki's earring sparkling in the soil beside him.

I empty my mind.

I do not want to think about these things right now. I watch the sky through the window. I sit there for hours and watch the movement of the sun. I only get up to make a cup of tea and toast, and then I return to the same spot with the view of the real sky.

I fall asleep beside the baby jackal for a long time, and when I wake up, it is dark and cold.

I jump up. 'Chara!' I call to the house. 'Chara, are you here?'

But there is only silence.

I venture into every room upstairs and down, but she is nowhere to be found. Her winter coat is not on the coat stand.

'Rosalie!' I call. 'Are you here?' I listen for the scuffle of her feet on the wooden boards, but there is nothing.

I go out to the garden, where Tasso is sitting. 'Tasso,' I say loudly and abruptly, 'have you seen Chara?'

He turns to me immediately. 'No. Not for some time. Why?'

'How long?'

'Not since this morning.'

'You haven't seen her since this morning?'

He shakes his head. 'What's going on?'

'She went out to do some drawings this morning. I fell asleep – she hasn't come back yet.'

'Where's Rosalie?'

'She's with Chara.'

Tasso stands up. He doesn't look at me but turns to face the dead woods. A cold wind blows.

'Go and get the torch,' he says.

I rush to the kitchen and grab the torch from the cupboard. Then I hastily scribble down a note for Chara in case she returns.

Tasso rushes out of the crumbling gate, and I follow, running behind him with the torch in my hand. We enter the dead woods, plunging into the darkness as if we are entering black water. For some reason, he stops in his tracks and looks back at me. His eyes shine with fear. They tremor with horrible possibilities. This darkness gets inside me, and I cover my face with my hands, my entire body tightening with an anguish that might be heading our way from the near future. I have lost my ability to move, to unfreeze myself. I have become a statue.

'Irini,' Tasso says, with such firmness, such urgency that I look up and see something different in his face now – along with the terror, an unwavering determination. *I am here*, his eyes seem to say. *I am here and I'm not going anywhere.*

Without a further word, we plunge deeper into the darkness. When we reach the tree-stumps, he stops and scans the area. He is panting, and his breath rips out in shreds.

He leans his arm upon a broken tree.

280

'Chara!' he calls.

Her name fills the silence around us.

'Rosalie!'

We move across the open plane. We pass the ruins of the house.

'I will die if something has happened to her,' I say aloud without meaning to. I'm glad that Tasso does not turn to face me.

'Chara!' he calls again, and his voice fills up the darkness. He spins around and calls her name again, this time to the south, in the direction of the sea, with all his might, with all his breath, like a howling wolf. He turns the other way now, to the north, up towards the mountain, and calls again.

I remember the fire, trees up in flames, rushing down the mountain towards us. I remember Chara beside me, her hand in mine, jumping from the cliff, down into the water. I see her face glistening with water, alight with fire. Her skin, her cheeks, her gasping mouth. I see her with the sketchpad beneath her arm, heading away from me into the dead woods.

'I will never let you go,' I say out loud.

In the light of the torch, I see that Tasso has frozen to the spot and is trembling.

Then suddenly, he breaks. It takes only a second. I see his body crumbling downwards, and he crouches with his torso between his knees, his hands limp in front of him, and he begins to sob. He cries in a way that I have never heard or seen him cry before; it is raw and wild and full of pain.

I cannot get myself to move an inch to go to him. The wind blows around us. It brings with it the smell of burnt things. There is a scuttling sound somewhere. I look at his shadowy figure crouched down.

Please, I say to myself. *Please – you must move. You must keep going.*

I force myself to go to Tasso. I place my hand on his shoulder and feel him shaking through my palm. I get close to him.

'Tasso,' I say, 'please get up.'

'It's my fault,' he says. 'I should have been there for her. She wanted to show me her drawings, and I ...' He cries more now, from his chest.

I attempt to lift him from under his armpits, and he unfolds.

'Look up,' I say. 'Look ahead. We have to find her. She is here – I know it.'

I clutch his arm. I hold on to him so tightly. For a moment, we stand there together, lost, in the middle of all the darkness and silence.

Then a sound emerges from the distance. I hold my breath. Is it the wind? No. It is a single note. A single mournful note, rising like a tower of smoke into the air.

'Tasso,' I say, 'can you hear that?'

He twitches his head. 'No,' he says. 'I hear nothing.'

Still holding his arm, I try to figure out the direction from which the sound is coming, and I lead him that way. After several yards, I pause again to figure out if I can still hear it, if I am going the right way.

There it is again. A howl. Louder this time.

'Tasso,' I whisper.

He lifts his chin and listens.

The sound rises up into the night. Up towards the stars.

'Rosalie?' Tasso says.

We head towards the howl. We trip over broken branches, bump into tree-stumps, fall over black things: a car tyre, a metal sheet, a fallen electricity post. We run along, the wind against us. But we will not stop. I am scared to grab hold of his hand, so I clutch his arm as tight as I can. I will never let him go.

The howl gets louder. It fills up my heart with both hope and fear. It is Rosalie for sure, because in between the howling I hear her barking. Maybe she has heard us.

We keep going. What has happened to Chara? What will we find when we get there? I almost cannot take it. I feel like I'm going to collapse, but Tasso is slightly ahead of me now, looking back whenever he hears me waver. We are weaving through blackened tree-stumps now, hundreds of them, thousands of them, and then we reach an opening, and I see the old chestnut, and beneath it is Rosalie, barking, not daring to leaving the spot where she sits. Next to her, on the ground, is Chara, crying.

We both run to her. Tasso rushes ahead of me and drops down to his knees and exhales. He is about to wrap himself around her but pauses, stopping himself, as if she is fragile. He approaches gently, placing his hand on her back. I kneel down beside them and put my hand on her shoulder.

She is still crying, but I hear her whisper, 'Mamma, Pappa,' through her tears.

Tasso moves the hair from her wet face. '*Agabi mou*,' he says. '*Agabi mou*, my beautiful girl.'

Then we both notice that she is clutching at her leg. Blood has soaked through her trousers.

'What happened to you?' Tasso says, his voice shaking.

'I fell from the tree,' she replies, through sobs.

Tasso gets his mobile from his pocket, attempting to call an ambulance.

'There is no signal,' he says.

Tasso holds his hands out in front of him for a moment and stares at them. He takes a deep breath as if he is bracing himself, and then he puts his hands under her back and thighs and lifts her up into his arms. She puts her arms around his neck and leans her head on his chest and cries quietly.

We head over the burnt land, back the way we came, with Rosalie leading the way. We do not enter the house. I call the ambulance as soon as we arrive, and we stand there waiting, Tasso holding Chara tightly in his arms.

It is dawn by the time we leave the hospital to go home, with Chara's leg stitched up and bandaged. There was a deep gash along her calf, and the X-rays showed that she had fractured her ankle. Considering the height from which she fell, she was lucky that she did not hurt herself even more. This is what the doctor said. Chara tells us that she climbed the chestnut tree because she wanted to draw the forest from its perspective.

She falls asleep in the taxi on the way home, and Tasso carries her upstairs and tucks her into bed, kissing her face, whispering in her ear that he loves her more than the *oooniverse*.

I sit beside her for a while, stroking her hair, until I am sure she is in a deep sleep. Then I go downstairs to find Tasso in the kitchen, leaning over Chara's sketchpad, his tall figure bent over the worktop. He takes a deep breath and turns the page. I see that his hands are shaking.

I stand beside him without saying anything. He is looking at one of the drawings.

'Look at this,' he says, more to himself than to me.

Nonetheless, I focus intently and a heavy sadness enters my heart. There is her drawing, and through it, I see the grief of the land. Chara has captured a part of the dead forest, a bit of unrecognisable open land with four tree-stumps of varying sizes.

'I thought we'd lost her,' he says suddenly, breaking the silence, not looking at me, staring still at the drawing. 'For a while, I was terrified that I would never see her again.' His voice breaks, and I hear him swallow hard.

What he is saying makes my chest shake. I inhale sharply. He turns for a moment to glance at me, and I reach out, gently touch his arm.

'My father,' he says. 'If he'd stayed right here in this house, he would have been fine. I was running towards the fire, but I couldn't *breathe*. And it's not just that. I left you and Chara. What if I had lost you both? I wasn't with you when I should have been.'

I don't say anything, but I lead him to the kitchen chairs, and we both sit down. I gently place my hand close to where his hand is resting on the table. Our little fingers are almost touching, but not quite. Not yet.

We stay there, unmoving, for a long time without saying anything to each other. I feel now that he is not lost forever, that the man I love is once again sitting beside me. I look out of the window as the sun rises over the land. The sky glows orange and blue.

'You've not been OK either, have you?' he says. He has been staring at the table, but his dark eyes slide towards me now.

'No.'

'Is it the memories?'

I nod.

'Is it only that?'

'I left Mr Monk to die.' I say this so quietly that I'm not sure if he has even heard me. 'He wasn't dead when I found him, the first time.'

Tasso remains silent again. I cannot stand the quiet, so I say, 'His ex-wife and lovely little daughter came to visit the other day. I keep seeing the girl sitting on the sofa, looking at your paintings. Her name is Zoe. These children – Zoe, Chara – they have been through so much. I don't know how to make things better.'

Tasso doesn't speak for a long time. I wonder what he thinks of me, if he understands. The sky brightens, and the room fills with light. Birds fly overhead. I hear their song. They seem to have settled in the fig tree.

'When it comes to Mr Monk,' he says, 'you should tell the police. It's the only way to make things right. Go and tell them what you saw and why you did what you did. As for everything else ...' His voice trails off; he does not finish his sentence. I wait, but he does not say anything else.

We sit in silence as the sun rises in the sky.

286

The Book of Fire

'They're called riverbed gums,' the kind man said. 'That is their real name.'

'There were a few along the dried riverbed in my village,' the mother replied, and immediately felt her eyes become hot with tears. She swallowed hard. But the man noticed and looked down at the ground.

They were standing outside in the garden of the house in the eucalyptus forest. The kind man had suggested that they get a breath of fresh air. The girl and the boy had gone off with the dog for another walk. The man's wife was preparing lunch. The sky was clear again today, and the birds flew high above the trees. Her husband stood beside her, so quietly she barely remembered that he was there. Sometimes, she would forget and think that he was still lost in the burning forest, but then she would see him, in her peripheral vision, like a ghost.

'My job is to collect the leaves,' the kind man continued, 'during the summer months, then I distil them. Distillation takes several hours in order to obtain a rich and balanced oil. My distillery is in the forest, about five hundred yards from here. My wife then packages the oil, in either large containers or bottles depending on who we are selling to. They're extremely flammable,' he said very suddenly and seriously, as if a dark thought had just entered his mind and taken it over. His eyes were wide. 'These trees – they are very flammable.' And then he glanced quickly at the couple beside him and perhaps, realising what he had just said, perked up and changed the subject.

'So! You say you're a musician!'

'Yes. I play the bouzouki mainly, but all sorts of instruments really, and I teach music,' the mother replied, trying to ignore the fearful look that still lingered in the man's eyes.

He nodded and said, 'Well, that is lovely. I always wanted to be a teacher, but I took over my father's profession here, and I guess I just kept going with it. Plus, I love being outside.'

She didn't reply; she just looked out at the forest before her, how quiet it was, how silvery and hushed and peaceful.

'Hey, so you say you play the bouzouki?' the man said.

She nodded, drawing her eyes away from the trees now and focusing on the man, who was smiling.

'I have my father's old instrument. It might need some tuning, but you can play for us later if you want?'

The mother smiled and said nothing. She thought about how her great-grandfather's old bouzouki, the one he had played all those years ago during his hundred-day journey from Turkey to Greece, had probably turned to ash in the fire. It was the very bouzouki that he had crafted himself from wood with his own two hands in his father's old shop on the Pontic port of Samsun on the southern coast of the Black Sea.

She felt such sadness as they went back inside the house to have lunch – such a deep and hopeless sadness. Although it was so warm in the house and the man's wife served them a hot spinach and feta pastry from the oven, the mother felt cold to the bone.

At the dinner table, the mother fed her husband, and he sat quietly and ate small morsels of food, not very much. Then she ate herself, and once again she ate well, because she was happy that her husband was there by her side. It was during this time, when she had eaten well and was not full of anxiety, that she was able to notice things in the living room that she had not registered before. There were photographs on the mantlepiece over the fire, many of their son in the forest or in the garden or holding a trophy of some sort.

The man's wife left the room, going into the kitchen with a handful of crockery. The man turned on the TV. The mother settled for a moment into the rhythms of normal life. But there was footage of the fire, flashing images of flames and burnt cars and houses, of people in the water waiting so desperately to be rescued.

Then the reporter was standing in front of the burnt land. 'The flames have died down now,' she said, 'and people are returning to the devastation to see what has happened to their homes.'

The husband did not look at the screen but stared instead out of the window.

The kind man turned off the TV. 'Maybe we shouldn't watch this now.'

'It's OK,' the husband said, realising that the room had gone quiet. 'We will need to return soon, to see if my father's house is OK. If it is, we will be able to stay there.'

'That sounds like a solid plan,' the man's wife said, returning from the kitchen, 'but keep in mind that you don't have to go soon – you can stay here for as long as you need.'

'I can't sit here not knowing,' the husband said. His face seemed flushed, and his forehead glistened now, as if a fire burnt within him. 'I want to go tomorrow. I want to see what's happening. I want to go to my father's house.' Then he turned to his wife. 'Is that OK with you?'

'I'm scared,' she said.

'But the fire is out,' he replied.

'That's not the point.' And in that moment, she saw that her husband's hands were resting on his trembling knees.

'We can try. We can go if that's what you want, but you know, it's not going to be easy.'

'I know,' he said. 'Thank you.'

He returned his gaze to the window.

'I tell you what,' the kind man said, standing up and leaving the room. They could hear him opening what sounded like the cupboard beneath the stairs, and then he returned with the bouzouki he had mentioned earlier in his arms. 'I thought you might want to take a look at it,' he said to the mother and placed it gently in her open arms.

She looked at her husband's bandaged hands and hesitated.

The man must have seen the uncertainty in her, for he said, very gently, as if he understood, 'Go on – just this once. It might do us all some good.'

She looked up at him and smiled. She remembered her father. She took the bouzouki from his hands. *Just this once*, she said to herself. She would play it one more time. Then she would stop. This world was no longer a place for music.

The kind man and his wife cleared the table, and the mother and her husband sat in the living room. The children had not returned, they had sent a text message to the kind man to say that they had bought some sandwiches at the kiosk at the edge of the forest and would be back after lunch. While the couple pottered around in the kitchen, she tuned the bouzouki, plucking at the strings and adjusting the tuning pegs. It required quite a bit of tuning. It had clearly not been touched for years, and she sat there with the instrument in her hands. The woods outside were still and silent. There was no wind today.

As she plucked, she thought about her daughter and the boy walking together, and once again she remembered her husband taking her into the woods all those years ago and painting her as she sat beneath the chestnut tree with their daughter in her arms. She stopped tuning for a moment, and she placed her hand upon her husband's leg, which was still now. She hoped that the sound of the notes finding their place had helped him to calm down. And he did seem calmer now; he was leaning back in the armchair beside her and staring out of the window.

The couple returned with cups of tea on a tray, which the man placed on the coffee table. 'How did it go?' he said with beaming eyes. 'Is it working then, that old thing?'

The mother did not speak; instead, she responded by playing a song – the same song that her father used to sing to her, the song that she had sung to her own daughter as they waited in the hospital after they had escaped the fire.

'*While you live, shine.*
Have no grief at all.
Life exists only for a short while.
And time demands its toll.'

22

I CALL THE LIEUTENANT AND ASK if I can come and see him. He says he has news for me, too. He offers me a ride again. He's been doing this to help me, I know, because buses do not come up here anymore and the walk down is difficult through the burnt land, but I thank him and tell him I will get there by myself.

I feel the anxiety mounting up in me. What will I tell Lieutenant Makris? Will I even be able to bring myself to say anything at all? Will I tell him about Mrs Gataki's earring, or will I just tell him what I did?

Then I see the little girl's blue eyes in my mind. I remember her sitting on the sofa and getting up to look at the painting of the chestnut tree, staring up at the place where her father died. These thoughts are swimming in my mind when someone knocks at the door.

The doctor is here, wearing his black-rimmed glasses, with nothing in his hands.

'How has he been?' he asks as we stand in the hallway and he removes his coat, placing it on the stand by the door.

'Things have changed,' I say, and he doesn't ask anything more. 'He is outside.'

When I take the doctor out to the garden, I see that Tasso is not sitting beneath the fig tree as usual but standing in the middle of the garden, looking out at the dead forest. And there *is* something different about him: he is standing straighter and is more alert, for he turns to look at us as soon as he hears our footsteps on the gravel.

I leave them to it and sit in the kitchen as usual. I make myself a cup of tea with milk, a stick of cinnamon and a couple of cloves. I see Chara's sketchbook on the counter, and I open it. I sit quietly, turning the pages, taking it all in: the way she has used the charcoal to depict the darkness, the shadows, the sharp lines of the tree-stumps, of a corrugated metal sheet on the ground, of a fallen telephone pole, the remains of a car, an oven, a bedframe, the starkness of the open field; the way the white of the paper gleams through the dark smudges and dark lines to depict the light.

The final page is taken up by the ancient chestnut tree. She has captured its divided state, half burnt and half alive, with the branches on one side reaching up to the sky, the tiny buds illuminated by the sun. It is beautiful in black and white.

But what I was not expecting was that beneath this tree sits a man – a boy, in fact, leaning upon the bark of the tree and playing a bouzouki. I almost hear the notes coming out of the page.

I'm not sure why, but without thinking I lean over and kiss the picture. I kiss it as if I am kissing an icon.

Then the doctor knocks on the kitchen door. I stand up and open it. Tasso is where he was before, but he turns back to look at me; I see that his eyes are alive. I smile at him, and he offers a small smile back. A gift.

'He told me about your daughter in the woods,' the doctor says, and I nod. 'He told me about the fire, leaving the forest to come and find you, terrified that you had come to harm. He told me about his paintings and about your daughter's sketches. He told me about you and your music.'

I look down, not knowing what to say.

'Normally, I wouldn't tell you these things, but I want you to know, for your sake, that there are stars in his dark sky.'

When the doctor leaves, I hear laughter from upstairs. Such light, beautiful laughter, like laughter before the fire. Laughter before Mr Monk lit the fire.

But the fire was lit before Mr Monk lit the fire.

I go outside, take Tasso's hand and head upstairs with him to find Chara playing with Neo and Rosalie. We watch them from the doorway. Chara is standing, holding on to her crutches. Rosalie is holding a soft toy in her jaw, shaking it about. The jackal watches intently and then jumps about, trying to pull the toy from Rosalie's mouth, but she resolutely clutches it. Then Rosalie lifts her head higher, so that Neo cannot reach the toy, and he runs around, nipping at her feet. Chara is laughing and laughing, and this laughter ripples around the room.

I feel Tasso tighten his grip on my hand. Then I feel him shaking. For a moment, I am worried that something has frightened him, but I realise that he has caught the laughter, that it has got inside him and filled him with light, and he has begun to laugh. It escapes him; it bursts from his mouth, and he scrunches his eyes. The more he laughs, the more Chara laughs, and then I catch it, too.

Chara takes gasps, trying to speak. 'Look. Mamma, he's playing!'

'I know – it's amazing!'

Then all the laughter settles, and the morning sun rests upon the flowers at the window and on the bedspread.

'He's even jumping around,' she says. 'I think the pain is going. But in a bit, he'll get tired.'

'He'll be right as rain in no time,' Tasso says, catching his breath.

Chara smiles, and when the jackal sits down with his big, beautiful ears twitching this way and that, she goes to him and pats him on the head, and he lifts his face and licks her hand.

'I love you, little guy,' she says.

Rosalie and Neo lie down now, basking in the sunshine. Tasso sits on the floor cross-legged and tickles the jackal behind the ears.

I turn to leave.

'Where are you going, Mamma?' Chara says, sitting down on the bed with her injured leg out in front of her and the crutches by her side.

'I'll be heading out for a bit, OK?'

'Where are you going?' she asks again.

Tasso glances up at me.

'I just need to speak to the police about the injured man I told you about.'

'Is he OK?' She looks at me with wide eyes.

'No, baby, he's not. He passed away.'

'Oh,' she says and looks down, and I'm not sure what she is thinking or remembering, but her face drops and is full of sadness. 'Who was the man who died?'

'You don't know him, baby.'

'But what was he doing out there? How did he die out there if there's no fire now?'

'I don't know.'

'I know that you know things you're not saying.'

'And how do you know that?'

'Because it's like your mind is far away. You are normally a very attentive person, and lately you have been in your own world.'

I look at her. She is serious. Her lips are pursed, and she waits for an answer. I wish she would laugh again, but the laughter cannot last forever.

'The man who died out there is the man who started the fire. Does it really matter how he died?' I feel my face heating up, and I regret immediately that these words left my mouth.

She looks into my eyes.

Tasso shifts his position but says nothing.

'I suppose people are glad that he is dead,' she says.

I don't say anything.

'Was he an old man?'

'No, fairly young. Like me and your father.'

'Why did he start the fire?'

'He wanted to build a small hotel.'

'That's very irresponsible,' she says.

'Absolutely. And very dangerous.'

'What a stupid man.'

Then she looks around, thinking.

'You said a *small* hotel – are you saying he didn't mean to burn so much land?'

'Yes.'

'Then why did it get so big?'

'There was such a strong wind, remember?'

She nods.

'And the land was so, so dry. We had that terrible drought.'

She nods again and looks down. 'Yes, the river dried up, and the fish died, and they lay there dead in the soil. The grass had turned to straw, so the insects and moles and hedgehogs, they had no food, and they began to die, too.' She pauses. 'I remember last year, another stupid person started a fire, and the fire-plane flew over and put out the flames and a few weeks later, another fire started on its own and another, and Grandad said, "we are not clearing the forest".' Then she stops abruptly and looks at me and says, 'His family must be sad.'

Her words pierce my heart. The image of the little girl flashes in my mind again.

When I leave them to go to the station, she is sitting in Tasso's lap, like she used to when she was a little girl, her arms around his neck, her head resting on his shoulder. Neo is now curled up by her feet. Rosalie sits right beside Chara, with her face on her thigh, opening her eyes to look up at her now and then.

I walk slowly to get down to the shore, and on the way, I notice something that has only just hit me: the silence. The immense silence of the dead forest. There are no birds singing, no leaves rustling gently, no animals moving around, no running water from the rivers and brooks. My footsteps make no sound. I used to love the soft crunch of the conifer needles.

After what feels like a long time walking across this dead land, the hill slopes downwards, and I catch sight of the sea in the distance and focus on that. It glimmers, and I remember the sea through the window of the office at the station. I imagine sitting there once more, and my stomach turns.

Soon, I feel the fresh sea air, but I must keep going to reach the next town. Here, the place is quiet and still.

Eventually, I arrive and see people walking along the promenade; others sit within the warm glow of a café. There are a few boats out at sea: a speed boat and a fishing boat. But in the distance, there is one boat with a white sail, and I wonder for a moment if it is the same one that rescued us.

I arrive at the old, shabby police station overlooking the shore. Lieutenant Makris is at the reception desk waiting for me. I have arrived right on time. It is exactly 12 p.m., and he is not caught up with something else this time. He greets me and leads me to the small room that looks like a cell. Once again, just like the first time, a junior officer fetches me a cup of tea and two biscuits, and Lieutenant Makris and I spend a couple of minutes talking about the cold weather.

He asks me about my family. 'How is your husband?' he says. 'And your daughter?'

I don't want to say anything about Tasso at all, so I tell him that Chara is looking after a baby jackal. He smiles warmly, and I notice again the heart pendant hanging over his uniform. I turn my face away and focus on the small window. It is filled with the morning sea and the bright-blue sky. The water ripples and sparkles.

'So, before your call today, I was planning on contacting you. I wanted to update you about the case concerning Michael Trachonides.'

I nod and hold my breath.

'We would like to thank you for the information you provided, and I would like to inform you now that the case regarding Mr Trachonides will be closed. We have recorded the death as suicide.'

I swallow hard. 'How come?' I say.

'Well, there was no evidence that anything sinister took place. Apart from the earring we found, there was nothing else to go by – nothing solid. We did try. We also found some scuff marks going up the tree. We examined these and found that they had been made by Mr Trachonides's shoes, which had evidently recently been polished. There were no other marks on the tree: no fingerprints, no DNA. Also, there were no other fingerprints at the scene at all. Only yours and his.'

I nod and say nothing. I feel my hands shaking, and I place them on my lap under the table.

'It appears that Mr Trachonides climbed up the tree, tied the rope onto the branch and ... well, I do not need to repeat it.'

I stare at him without speaking.

'Are you OK?' he says. 'You seem to have become very pale. Is there something I can get for you?'

'The thing is,' I say, and my voice comes out croaky and strained. I cough. 'The thing is, I have done something terrible.'

'Oh?' he says and sits up.

'I lied to you. I believe Mr Trachonides might still be alive if it wasn't for me.'

He creases his brow, urging me to go on.

'When I found him, he was still alive. He began crying, you see. He was sobbing. There was no reception on my phone, like I said, but he was alive. I was going to help him, I was – I mean, I really was, but then I looked into his eyes, and I saw—'

'Irini,' Lieutenant Makris says, 'I'm going to stop you there.'

'Please, Lieutenant, you don't understand. I ran off. I ran away from him and left him there, and I didn't return for a number of hours. I felt so guilty for leaving him like that, and I went back, but by that time it was too late. That's when I called the police.'

'I see,' Lieutenant Makris says and looks down at his hands resting on the table, his fingers laced together. He stays like that for a few moments, and just then the room suddenly darkens, and I look up to the window and see that a bird with pure black wings is sitting on the outer ledge, its dark figure obscuring the light.

'Irini,' he says finally and looks into my eyes. In the darkened room, the green of his eyes are muted. 'The autopsy revealed extensive damage to his windpipe. He would have died anyway. You couldn't have saved him.'

I nod, and his gaze is fixed on me.

'Try to remember that, when you found him, he was taking his last breaths. Think of it like that. Go home to your husband and daughter and don't allow this to bother you anymore. We've all got to learn to live again.'

He smiles a little now, probably hoping that I will smile back, but I feel that my body is cold.

'I can't drop it,' I say. 'Are you completely sure he committed suicide? You've closed the case so quickly. What if some other evidence comes to light?'

Lieutenant Makris leans back in his chair now and breathes out gently. 'Irini,' he says, 'if he did not do this to himself and somebody else did it instead, then all I can say on the matter is that it could have been any one of us. Any one of us. It could have been the professor, the mayor, the priest.' He pauses and stares at me intently. 'It could have been me or you. Don't tell me that you don't feel it ... the anger?' He touches the gold pendant around his neck, and I notice that his hand is shaking. 'I sleep better knowing that the man is dead,' he says.

I open my mouth to speak, but he cuts in. 'And I'm sure that every single one of us would have run just like you had if we had found him there like you did. I don't know one person who would have helped him to live. Let's leave it at that, shall we?'

I feel like I am in a cell. He has told me unequivocally not to insist. He has warned me. I can feel it in his gaze, in the set of his mouth and shoulders. He sits motionless, resolute.

I do not nod, and I do not speak. I understand what he is saying, and right there in that room on this day, I know that there is nothing more I can do.

Then the room brightens again, and his eyes sparkle green, and when I look up at the small window, I see that the bird has flown away.

Then I see a raven soaring through in the open sky, and my body is cold, and I remember the raven flying above the eucalyptus woods.

The Book of Fire

The kind man dropped them off at the edge of the dead forest.

'Now, call me if you need anything. I'll be here again in an hour.'

They thanked him, and he drove away, and they were left with the unbearable silence of the land that lay before them.

The girl stood in between her mother and father, and she held tightly on to her mother's hand. Her father's bandaged hands hung by his sides. He seemed so helpless and hopeless. The dog had already taken a few steps onto the ash and was sniffing the air, its tail down. The woman even thought she could hear the dog whimper.

The woman looked behind her. It was strange, because normally you would not be able to see the sea from here, far below – it was usually obscured by the fir and pine trees. But there, in the distance, it sparkled.

'I know where we are, but it's like a different place,' the woman said.

'How will we find our home?' the girl asked.

The dog barked.

'I think our dog might be able to help us,' the man said.

Right here was where the wildflowers grew, where the edges of the trees left shadows at the borders of the sloping field and the birds from the sea flew up the mountain, beating their wings and landing for a while upon the grassland, and somewhere in the distance would have been the gentle hum of the river. They would have walked across this land and into the softness of the forest. And how soft it had been, how gentle, how mysterious, with its own songs and whispers.

They followed the dog across this open land and into a place of tree-stumps. There was a car here, a carcass, its wheels melted into the ground. Further along, there were four more cars, in a similar condition, one behind the other. Around these vehicles was emptiness. Here, the earth would have been soft with conifer needles and the dappled sun would have touched them as they went about their business. Here would have been the pine trees where the woman's father-in-law spent most of his days, tapping the trees, collecting its golden resin.

They continued, following the dog further to the west, and the land dipped, ever so slightly. This was where there had been an old windmill surrounded by heather and a stream that zigzagged through the grass and an orchard of olive trees. Beyond was their home. But there existed nothing but the dips and grooves of empty land.

And when they finally climbed the small hill where they would have expected to see their bungalow on the other side, instead they found just two walls still standing, crumbling at the edges, and a mountain of bricks and gravel. In one of the walls – which would have belonged to the girl's bedroom, they realised – there was a window without glass, and it looked out at what should have been the fir trees climbing the hillside. The girl stood at this window and looked out like she used to. She said nothing. She did not cry. Her mother wished she would say something, but she just stood there, still and silent.

'I think we should leave straightaway,' the mother said. 'There is nothing to see here.' She didn't realise then that she had planted the word 'nothing' into her daughter's mind and that it would grow and grow and take over distant lights of hope. It would haunt her, and she would at times remember only this word and repeat it as if it were the truth of the entire world.

'OK, Mamma. Let's go,' the girl said through the open mouth of the window, as she faced the invisible firs of the past. 'There's nothing here anymore.'

The man said nothing. Even the dog was completely silent, and they walked back the way they had come.

Now, to the east, they would find her father-in-law's house.

The landscape was black. The tree-stumps seemed to be taller here. As they walked, they came across the bare walls of people's homes. The dog once more led the way, but the woman could see that it would often become confused. It would stop and sniff the ground and then the air before continuing. But then they reached the dried-up stream. This stream used to run past a café and trickle down the hill, then veer to the east. If you followed this stream and turned left at the crooked olive tree, you would eventually get to her father-in-law's house. She had taken this route many times.

Now that the dog had figured out where they were, it walked faster and stopped now and then to make sure that the family were following. The man walked with his head down. He looked at nothing.

They walked and walked, and eventually they saw a spot of colour in the distance, and they headed towards that place. The world in the near distance seemed like a dream.

'Mamma,' the girl whispered tentatively, as if the colour was a veneer of smoke that would vanish before their eyes. 'Look, Mamma,' she said so quietly. 'I can see Grandad's yellow door! And the green tree!'

'I need to tell you something, baby ...' the mother began, but the girl did not wait to hear the end of her sentence.

Instead, she ran ahead. Why had she not spoken to her daughter earlier? The woman chided herself. She did not want one more thing to hurt her. But they could not hide from this reality.

The girl was so happy, and she ran towards the house full of excitement. The woman's heart broke. She knew that the girl would not find her beloved grandfather there. She knew that already.

They finally reached the place where the fire had obviously died out. Beyond a certain point, things were still alive. The fire seemed to have stopped just before the fence. Some of the fence was burnt and most of it was black, but beyond that, it was as if God had drawn an invisible line: the garden was alive, and the fig tree stood glorious and fresh. The yellow front door was wide open.

Now, the man looked up for the first time and set his eyes upon his father's house.

'My god,' he said.

The woman saw that his bandaged hands shook at his sides. She put one hand on his shoulder and held her daughter's arm with the other. Like this, they walked through the gate and along the garden path that led to the house. It was so quiet.

In the kitchen, a slice of bread had been left on a plate with a knife. Next to it, butter had melted in the butter dish. There was a mug on the counter saying *Best Grandad*, which had a spoon in it and a powdery instant coffee. The kettle was full of water. A marmalade jar was open; the lid had dropped to the ground. The woman noticed all these tiny things. It was her way of imagining her father-in-law's last movements in his house. And there he was: wearing his wife's old apron, fetching a plate and a knife from the cabinet, the butter and milk from the fridge, taking the bread out of the bread bin, cutting a thick slice, opening the marmalade jar, humming, like he always did. Then, before he had managed to put the bread in the toaster, something had stopped him in his tracks. Perhaps the sounds had begun: birds screeching, wolves howling – the forest cracking and popping.

'Mamma?' the girl said, and the woman snapped awake and looked at her daughter, who seemed frightened. 'I want to see Grandad,' she said. 'How will we find him?' The girl went to the window and stood there looking out, past the garden towards the burnt land.

The woman did not know what to say.

'We should go and find him, Mamma.'

'There are search parties out there, baby. There's so many people searching for survivors – there's so many volunteers helping, too.'

'How do you know?'

'I saw it on the news.'

'Will they find Grandad?'

She wanted to tell her the truth, she really did – that there was very little chance her grandfather, as old as he was, would have survived the fire – but the girl looked at her with pleading eyes.

'I don't know,' was what she said.

The father left the kitchen and went into the living room. The girl and the mother followed him. He sat in the armchair where his father used to sit next to the fireplace. In the evenings, in the winter, when the woods were dark and frosty and the old man had more time to contemplate, he would often sit by the fire with a meze laid out before him: olives from the trees outside, soaked in lemon, garlic and crushed oregano; haloumi, fresh from the neighbour's goats, toasted on the flames; a plate of pickled octopus that he'd bought from the seaside town; and anything else that took his fancy – spicy sausage or aubergine dip or crumbly feta cheese. Winter was a time for rest, contemplation and plenty of food. That's what he would say. He was a gentle man, full of thoughts and observations. He felt his way through life with his hands along the barks of the trees and his knowledge of the natural world.

The woman was full of sadness. She turned to the window and looked out at the blackened land.

Long, long ago, the forest was alive. You should have seen it! From the soil grew wildflowers and herbs. It was beautiful and good. And birds flew above the woodland, and creatures moved among the shadows of the ancient trees, and waters trickled from the top of the mountain down to the sea. But after the great fire, the forest was without form.

Once, there were pine trees and fir trees and poplars and plane trees and oaks. Here, there lived weasels and minks and wildcats and badgers, rabbits and hares and hedgehogs and moles and rats and lizards and beetles. Beautiful red deer roamed the lowlands.

Now, there was a void.

Where once existed all the colours of the forest, darkness was upon the face of the land.

Once upon a Harry Lime. Yes, this is how her father started every story, even if the story was happening right in front of his face. Once upon a time, there was a lovely and lonely woman who made bread. She was always lost in her own world. But she loved her daughter very much, you know. Once, there was a man who wore a fisherman's hat and played his father's old bouzouki in a city that was not his own, and he had a lemon tree in his garden because it reminded him of home. Once, there was a woman who did not want to lose her husband, so she watched him sitting in the chair in the living room of his father's house and made

310

a wish. All she wanted was for him to look at her with the old love in his eyes, so that she could know for sure that his heart was still alive.

For a few minutes, her husband rested his bandaged hands on his lap and looked around at his own paintings on the wall. He allowed his eyes to settle for a split second on each, and once his eyes had travelled around the entire room, he focused on a black-and-white photograph above the mantlepiece, of his mother and father on their wedding day.

He dropped his gaze to the ground and stayed like that, as if he were frozen.

23

I PUT DOWN MY PEN AND flick through the journal. I see my handwriting flashing before me as I turn the pages, spiralling memories like vines – words and sentences, paragraphs and pages appearing one after the other, one after the other, like footsteps.

What does it mean that I have written it all down? Is it that I have unwound the chaos, like tangled-up yarn, untangled it and placed it down coherently before me? Is it that I have made it tangible, not just ghostly images whirring around in my mind? Is it that I have brought it from the recent past to the present and stood right beside it, not allowing it to fade down into my soul, existing like a volatile current beneath the surface?

I take a deep breath and run my finger along the words: *Once upon a Harry Lime.*

I stand up and leave the journal open on this page. I always keep it open on the last written page.

Long, long, ago the forest was alive.

I head to Maria's Kafeneon to see Mrs Gataki. I texted her as soon as I got back from the police station and asked her if she could be there at 3 p.m., and she replied, *Well, of course, daughter, anything for you. See you soonish.*

I arrive before her and take a seat right at the back in the library area, next to the globe. It is called a Da Vinci Globe Bar. Maria told me this, quite proudly. It is based on a hand-drawn eighteenth-century map, and it opens up to hold four bottles and nine glasses. It seems ridiculous to me, this globe bar.

I sit there, watching Maria dash about; she holds a plate of something steaming in each hand. But a sadness takes over as I turn away from the gentle hustle and bustle of the café and allow my eyes to rest upon the world. At this moment, the countries facing me are Latvia, Estonia, Russia. I shift my position and run my finger over Argentina and Chile. I have never visited any of these places. I wonder about the heat and the snow, the sun and the rain, the day and the night in these foreign lands. I move again; this time my eyes land upon the western coast of the United States of America. Right then, something grabs me by my throat. I feel the heat of the flames again, and into my mind flash images: breaking news, wildfires in California – first the flames, then the ravaged homes, the burnt forest, the destroyed wildlife, the lost people.

I don't have a chance to sink further into despair, because a voice says, 'Daughter, you're away with the fairies yet again.' I look up, and Mrs Gataki is grinning from ear to ear. 'Going to drop music and become a geographer? Is that even a word?'

I smile at her, and she takes a seat on the sofa next to me.

'So, are we eating or just having coffee?'

'I'll just have a coffee,' I say.

'Great! I'll have a coffee and an omelette.' She shuts the menu and places it on the table and lifts her hand in the air to grab Maria's attention.

Maria nods at her, goes into the kitchen and returns a few seconds later with her pad.

'It's a beautiful day today,' Maria says.

I haven't really noticed. My mind is elsewhere. The conversation I had with Lieutenant Makris has been repeating itself in my mind. I can't let it go. I can't put anything to rest.

I have come here to speak with Mrs Gataki. I would like to understand what her earring was doing by the chestnut tree. However, I don't want to begin talking about Mr Monk just yet. I don't want the conversation to be interrupted or in fact overheard by Maria bringing us the food and drinks.

I wonder now whether coming here was such a great idea. I should have asked to meet elsewhere, but Mrs Gataki, for sure, would have found that strange. I have never met her anywhere else, not even in our own homes before the fire. I only know Mrs Gataki in the context of this very café.

The professor is at a nearby table, without his sister this time. In fact, he is sitting on his own, just staring out into space and sipping his coffee. One of the garage guys is here – a young man in his twenties who moved to this town with his parents about a year ago.

In the meantime, I tell Mrs Gataki about Chara and the jackal. I also tell her about the sketches Chara has made of the burnt forest. Her eyes sparkle as she listens to me.

'Well,' she says, 'I always knew that girl of yours was special. She's a sensitive one. The sensitive ones always have secrets in their hearts, and if they are talented, they will find the means to reveal those secrets. Because they are secrets that *must be told.*'

'Well,' I say, 'you are sounding very profound today.'

'Daughter,' she says, and her lilac eyeshadow glimmers ever so slightly beneath her purple brows, 'I am always profound. Don't you know that already? And plus, I have been doing some thinking.'

'What about?' I ask.

'Well, that there are certain things in life that are essential to living, to recovering, to moving on. After all, what would the dead think if we remained stuck and ceased to live ourselves?'

'I'm not sure what they would think,' I say, 'but I'm also not sure I catch your drift.'

'To move on we must – *must* – put certain things to rest.'

Just then, Maria arrives with a tray. The Kafeneon starts to fill up. Two or three people enter: the shopkeeper, another one of the garage guys, who joins the young man, and a woman with a rucksack and a tablet, who takes a seat at the far table beneath the hanging lamps.

'Watch her,' says Mrs Gataki. 'She is a journalist. Never trust them. They come in here wanting to hear our pain, they say, *our stories*, and then they go off and write about global warming. It's an insult to what we have endured and how we have been let down.'

I do not say anything. I look over at the woman, who is now glancing around the room. Her eyes stop on me for a second, and I nod; she nods back and turns her attention quickly to the tablet in her hands.

'I would like to speak to you about something,' I say to Mrs Gataki.

'Oh, yes?' She is cutting up her omelette and pauses to look at me with great interest.

'It's difficult,' I say.

'Try me.'

'I'm not really sure if here is the right place.'

She tilts her head, almost suspiciously, and I notice again the missing earring.

'Why don't you just begin the conversation, and we'll see?'

'Well, OK, it's about Mr Monk.'

'Hmm hmm?' she says, nodding and eating omelette.

'It's something that the police found by the tree where he died.'

I wait until she finishes chewing, then she wipes her mouth with a napkin and says, 'I see.' She lays her knife and fork over the omelette as if she has finished her meal, though she has only taken a bite, and says, 'Right. Well, in that case, let's go for a walk, shall we?' She grabs Maria's attention. 'My lovely,' she says, 'put these coffees in some takeaway cups for us, will you? We have to go somewhere – it's rather urgent.'

Maria gives her a quick raise of the eyebrows and takes the drinks, returning a few moments later with two cardboard cups. We take them and head out of the Kafeneon. I follow Mrs Gataki's lead. I see that she pauses for a second at the crossroads. We will either head up towards the burnt forest or down towards the sea.

I don't say anything, and she veers right so that we are heading down, past the burnt villas with their still-standing gates, through a narrow alleyway that leads down to the port. The land all the way down is black. The boats sit still and empty. There isn't a single person around. But the sea gleams beneath the midday sun.

We do not say a word to each other until eventually she stops walking and stands facing the water.

'I was in the water for hours,' she says. 'I imagine you were, too. We haven't spoken about it, have we?'

'No,' I say.

'We have a shared experience, and yet we have both remained quiet about it. Isn't it funny how we do that.'

It doesn't sound like a question, so I don't give her an answer.

'This is where he died,' she says, and I know she is talking about her husband. 'We were lucky. We managed to make it down to the water. Others didn't. But you know that. Why am I telling you things you already know?' She turns to look at me now, and I see that she is crying. I didn't hear it in her voice; there was not a crack or a tremor. But there is a tear running down her cheek, shining in the light.

Then she looks back at the sea and pats her face with her fingers, wiping away the tear. 'So, what was it that you found?'

'Well,' I say, 'it wasn't me as such. The police found a small gold heart-shaped earring by the chestnut tree where Mr Monk died.' I pause, before saying, 'I went to the station today. They've recorded his death as suicide. They have no other evidence. There were no fingerprints at the scene except mine. Nothing to go by. I didn't say anything at all about your earring. But I know that it is yours.'

She doesn't turn to face me; she does not move at all. In fact, we stay that way for what feels like a long time, and I can hear her breathing. Long, slow breaths.

Then she exhales deeply and says, 'I'm not going to lie to you, daughter. I love you, so I'll tell you the truth. If you would like to go to the police and tell them what I'm about to say, you are welcome to. However, not only will it amount to nothing, but at the moment I'm not sure I even care much about what happens to me. Perhaps I should have even been dead instead of my husband. He was seven years younger than me, and stronger, but there you go – that's life.'

Again, she turns to look at me, and her eyes are aflame.

Then she turns back to the sea. 'I didn't do anything much,' she says. 'I went to a hardware shop out of town and bought a long, thick rope. It was packed in plastic. I wore gloves, in case you are wondering. Then I went to his house very early one morning – the day you found him – and I handed him the rope. That is all I did. That is a promise.'

Her voice shakes, and I turn to look at her. I see that her entire body seems to be shaking, too, but I do not reach out to touch her.

'Was it only you?'

'No,' she says. 'It wasn't. But I won't tell you who was with me.'

She shoots me a look, and I nod. 'Then what happened?'

'He took the rope from us, and we left. We didn't even say anything to him. Not a single word passed between us.'

'Then how did your earring end up beneath the chestnut tree?'

'I felt horrible. I went home and tried to nap, but I had nightmares. I was walking through dark tunnels with no way out. One tunnel led to another. A right turn, and there was another tunnel. A left turn, and yet another. I woke up feeling terrible. I kept picturing his face when he opened the door.

'That afternoon, I went back to his house, but he wasn't there. I'm not sure what I would have said to him, had he been in. But there was no one at home. The door was open, and I went in. I called him, but there was no reply. I was scared of what I might find, but I forced myself to go into every room, checking … but he wasn't there. So, I headed into the forest. I searched for him, and then eventually, I found him sitting beneath the tree, the noose around his neck, the branch broken. I sat beside him for a while. I knew that he was definitely dead, that there was nothing I could do, so I quietly walked away.'

For a while, neither of us says anything. Seagulls fly over, disappearing into the distance. The sky is such a soft blue, and the sea so calm; the merest ripples catch the light. There is suddenly the sound of an engine, and a boat tears across the water, heading east, breaking up the surface of the sea.

'What was his face like,' I say, 'when he opened the door?'

'It's hard to describe,' she says, 'but I can see it clearly in my mind, and I will never forget it. There are some things that never fade, don't you think? When he opened the door, he had a rucksack on his shoulders, as if he was just about to head out, but he looked tired, worn out. And when I handed him the

319

rope, he just … accepted it. He nodded and took it from my hands. His eyes were gentle and sad, and … I can't really explain this, but it was like he forgave me for handing him the rope.'

Then she remains silent, and I know that she has nothing more to say. So we stand like that, me and her, unmoving, looking at the water where her husband had died.

But I remember Mr Monk. I can picture his eyes, full of *my* memories. I see him sobbing. I almost hear it.

The people, he said. *The people.*

The people who had died.

The people who gave him the rope.

The people who gave him the rope relied upon him to carry so much on his shoulders.

I feel my shoulders drop.

My heart drops.

Then I remember again my daughter, when she came up for breath, her face glistening with water. On every part of her skin, her cheeks and her gasping mouth and tightly shut eyes, red fire was reflected, as if she were made of flames. This is an image that will never leave me.

My daughter glistening all over with red and orange flames.

My daughter's entire face alight with water and fire, as if the world was burning upon her.

Before going home, I head back up the mountain and into the dead forest. I walk resolutely to the ancient chestnut tree. I am alone now, completely, without Rosalie, without another heartbeat. The quiet gets inside me. The wind blows.

I walk towards the tree. I run my hand along the alive side, feeling the grooves and crevices in the wood. Then I sit beneath its branches, in the spot where I found Mr Monk. I imagine the land before me for a second, through his eyes. Maybe he saw the ghosts of all the missing people; maybe he thought of his daughter. Lieutenant Makris let me off the hook – I will not be facing legal repercussions for what I did – but I will have to live with it.

The people, Mr Monk said, and I understand now what he could have meant: the people who died, or the people who handed him the rope. Now I, too, am one of the people Mr Monk spoke of: a victim and a perpetrator. I will always be this divided person – someone I barely recognise. Yes, Mr Monk started the fire. Yes, the fire brigade did not respond how they should have. Yes, the government underfunded them. *Yes*, Lazaros says, standing before me suddenly, taking off his wicker baseball cap and lowering his head to the ground.

I pick up a handful of dry earth and hold it in my palm towards him.

I suddenly remember one more thing he said, something I wish I could forget forever: *There is a ghost hovering above us, and it is not godly. It is the spirit of our own destructiveness.*

Lazaros fades and disappears.

Then I think of my great-grandfather sitting right here, so many years ago, playing music on his bouzouki after he had been ripped away from his home. I almost hear the notes in the silence, reaching me from long ago. Then I see the scar on Chara's back, the trunk winding up her spine and opening up like the branches of a strong tree across her shoulder blades.

I get up and stand back, looking at the huge, disfigured tree. I feel so small. Its left side, charred and black, is like melted tar. I see now that the right side looks like a person, dragging up a dying loved one or tugging up the dark side of itself from the ashes.

The Book of Fire

Once upon a time, a man came in from the garden with sunshine in his eyes and sat beside his wife at the kitchen table.

They sat in silence at first. She poured some tea into a mug for him. She saw that his hands were resting safely on his lap; the same position they had assumed when they were bandaged. But he caught her eye, and he lifted his hand and took hold of the mug. Then he brought the mug to his mouth and blew on the hot tea to cool it down. They sat like this, quietly, as he took one sip and then another. They didn't say a word to each other until he finished the tea and placed the mug back on the table.

Then, instead of putting his hands back on his lap, he shifted his chair around to face her, and he took both her hands in his. His palms felt soft, softer than they had ever felt, but with her thumb she felt the grooves of his scars. He held on to her and looked into her eyes.

He inhaled deeply, and on his exhale, he said, 'I'm sorry.'

It was as if the words spilt out from his soul. This was how the woman felt; this was how she heard them.

That was all. Just two words. But she didn't need anything more. In fact, she didn't need any words; all she wanted was to be able to look into his eyes and know that he was there.

She nodded, and he kissed her gently on the lips.

'I have something for you,' he said. He released her hands and opened the door of the pantry, and from it he brought out an instrument, which he held in his arms.

'I found this old bouzouki in my dad's basement,' he said. 'It's probably out of tune, though.'

It was so beautiful. The flat panel on top of the body was made of pale wood, and upon this was painted a scene from the forest: fir trees and pine trees and wildflowers and the glimmer of a stream.

'Did you paint this?' she said.

He nodded. 'I stayed up all last night. It's only small, so I could manage. And be careful, because it's not dry. But when it is, you can play for us again – if you want to, that is?'

'Thank you,' she said, and she could barely see the forest scene now through the fog of her tears, and she allowed him to place it in her hands, and she sat so still and held it.

When her daughter entered the kitchen on her crutches, the dog was by her side, watching her every step, and the baby jackal was behind them, eyes wide, ears perked up.

'I think he loves me,' the daughter said. 'He follows me everywhere I go.'

'It's because he knows you love him so much,' the woman said, and the girl smiled.

Then her dad picked up the sketchpad from the kitchen counter and tucked it beneath his arm.

'I have so much to do,' she said. 'Pappa is going to help me. Did you know that already?' She looked at her mother. And though it would have made sense for her to be beaming at this moment, her face was serious and determined.

'No,' the mother said. 'No, I didn't know. But I'm glad.'

'I want to go back to the chestnut tree, and I want to draw where the river used to run and where the animals used to roam. I want to sketch the hillside where our house was … There's so much to do.' Then she fell silent, and her eyes looked sad, but she turned to face the land through the open door, and using her crutches, careful not to rest her sore leg on the ground, she slowly began to head out, past the fig tree and through the garden.

At first, her father turned to follow her, but he paused to glance back at his wife.

'What's the matter?' he said.

She was sitting with the bouzouki still in her open hands.

'I know what happened to the man who started the fire,' she said.

'Yeah?'

'Some people in the village … they gave him a rope.'

He looked at her severely for what felt like a long time, then he nodded and looked away.

'The police have put the case to rest. Suicide.'

At the far end of the garden, just before the dead land began, the girl approached the gate. The dog was right by her side and the little jackal ran along behind, its golden fur and silver-scaled paws shimmering in the soft afternoon light.

'Well,' her husband said, 'if only it was that simple – because if it was that simple, we would have nothing left to worry about.'

The door closed behind him, and the woman got up, placed the bouzouki on the kitchen table and stood by the door to look out of the window.

Her husband caught up with their daughter. The dog stood on its hind legs, putting its paws onto his chest; it was so happy to have its companion back. The girl made sure that the little jackal stayed on the safe side of the fence, in the garden; it was not yet ready to venture further, and it sat there obediently, watching them head off, waiting for their return.

The girl carried a small sling bag, which probably contained charcoals and erasers. The dog ran ahead, and the sun shone upon them as they walked across the field together, where the wildflowers had been.

The mother sat alone now at the table and looked at the bouzouki that her husband had painted. She imagined picking it up and playing it, feeling the strings on her fingers and its vibration in her chest.

She thought about her daughter and her husband walking in the dead forest. She imagined them returning, her daughter's sketchbook full of drawings of what had come to be, of what might still come to be. She held in her hands the dying whispers of the past, the dying whispers of the future. The bag would probably be on her husband's shoulders by the time they returned, and her daughter would be dragging herself back on her crutches, exhausted and ready for dinner and a bath, but with the kind of passion and determination that she possessed before the fire. The dog, with muddy paws, would be running along ahead, and the jackal, waiting by the gate, would nip at the dog's feet as they walked down the path to the house. Then they would have dinner together, and later she would sit at the edge of her daughter's bed and trace the scar on her back and tell her it looked like the ancient tree in the ancient forest, where the girl's great-great-grandfather had sat, after a hundred-day journey, to eat berries and play his bouzouki.

And tomorrow would be another day.

The mother decided that it was time to close *The Book of Fire* and place it on the shelf.

Once upon a Harry Lime, there was a beautiful village inside an ancient forest on the slope of a mountain that looked down upon the sea.

24

NEO AND HIS FAMILY ARE coming to visit. This is the first time I will have seen them all since after the fire. I have prepared pastries, the kind my father-in-law used to make. I found his recipe book, the one that once belonged to Tasso's mum, and I have made baklava with crumbly pastry and pistachios, walnuts and pecans, cinnamon and cardamom – dripping with honey. I am proud of my creations. I could have picked up some pastries from Maria's Kafeneon, but I wanted the house to smell homely. And I wanted to feel close to Lazaros.

I slice the baklava into diamonds.

Chara is outside in the garden, sitting on the chair with the crutches by her side, watching her dad play ball with Rosalie. The little jackal is getting involved in the game in his own way. I can hear Chara calling, 'Neo, this way! No, this way, little Neo! He keeps running the wrong way, Pappa!'

And I can hear laughter – beautiful, rippling laughter. The sound makes my heart rest.

The doorbell rings. I take off my apron and head to the door and take a deep breath before opening it. Sophia and Alexandros stand at the door. She is holding a plant in her arms, and he has a bottle of red wine.

I welcome them into the house.

Sophia places the plant into my hands and kisses my cheek, squeezing my arm.

'Something smells delicious!' she says, beaming. She glances around. 'And it's great to see that you are settled here in this lovely home.'

'I'm so happy to see you both,' I say. 'But where is Neo?'

'Neo heard Chara laughing,' Alexandros says. 'He ran round the back.'

We walk through the living room to get to the kitchen, and just like everybody else, Sophia and Alexandros stop and stare at the paintings; they inhale as if they are taking in the smells of the real forest. Then I see Sophia exhale, in such away as if her anxiety has left, like she feels safe in the world again. It is as if the forest of the past has wrapped its arms around her.

Alexandros says quietly, 'Well,' and turns to face the painting of the great chestnut tree.

Tasso comes in from the garden; he looks flushed and fresh, and he smiles at the kind couple. He stretches out his arm and shakes Alexandros's hand. It is a firm shake, warm and thankful, and I see Tasso's black eyes twinkle.

'So,' Alexandros says and glances around at the paintings, 'I don't know what to say, but you are a very talented man, and I'm glad these paintings exist. But if only . . .' His sentence trails away unfinished.

329

They all sit around the kitchen table while I make Greek coffees and serve the baklava. I open the door and call Chara.

'We'll come in a bit!' she yells back.

I take a seat at the table. The smell of coffee fills the room.

'What are the kids doing?' Tasso says.

'Neo brought Chara some fresh olive pits to plant,' says Alexandros. 'He picked them last week, then he crushed the olives, soaked them, nicked the pits with bolt cutters. They are completely ready to be sowed. He even brought some fertiliser soil.'

'He's a good boy,' Tasso says.

I stand up with my coffee and look out of the window. Just beyond the gate at the end of the garden, where the forest used to begin, Chara and Neo are sitting on the ground, crouched over the soil. Rosalie and the little jackal sit on their hind legs, right beside them.

'I told Neo it would be hard work to grow a tree in these conditions,' Alexandros says, 'but he's never lacked determination. They'll have to clear any debris, get to the soil beneath – it will probably be barren soil, so they will need to saturate it and then enrich it with the fertiliser, manure and compost.'

My mind drifts out to the garden. I see Chara nudge Neo's shoulder at something he has said, and they both laugh. She digs into the soil with a spade, and he opens the bag of fertiliser and manure. Then I see him take something out of another small bag. He opens up his palm and Chara looks down. It must be the olive pits. She takes one, and, as if she

330

is holding a diamond, she raises it up to the sunlight and stares at it. Then she places it down into the soil.

'Come and join us!' I hear Tasso's voice. I realise that it is me he is calling, and I turn to face him. He is holding a deck of cards in his hands. 'How about a game of rummy?' he says, placing the cards in the middle of the table.

'And how about we open the bottle of wine?' Sophia says.

I fetch some wineglasses and take a seat. Alexandros pours the wine. Tasso shuffles the cards and begins to hand them out.

As the afternoon light flashes through the clouds, I see the scars on his hands, appearing like the roots of an uprooted tree.

Then I hear Chara's laughter again. It fills up the entire room, and I pick up my cards to play.

Acknowledgements

FIRSTLY, I WOULD LIKE TO thank all the people I interviewed in various parts of Greece who had been victims of wildfires and carried deep wounds, emotional, or physical, or both. Thank you to those people who told me their stories with such courage, thank you for sharing your memories, your opinions and thoughts. Thank you to Poly Lavda and her husband for showing me around the area and describing how things were before the fire.

Thank you to Dr Nikos Christidis at the Met Office for taking your time to speak with me and answer all my questions, thanks so much for your expertise and insight. Thank you to Peter Stott, Professor of Detection and Attribution at the University of Exeter and acting Director of the Met Office. Thank you for writing the wonderful and informative *Hot Air*, thank you for your time, all your insight and the immensely interesting conversations and for being so thorough and thoughtful. Thank you to Pierrette Thomet Stott, musician, artist and co-creator of Climate Stories, for the interview, for your fascinating thoughts and creativity, which made my brain buzz with ideas.

Thank you to the Conway Road writer's group, for being great friends, for your helpful critique and for all the wonderful Thursday night conversations and digressions.

Thank you to my family and friends for your constant support and belief. To my dad and Yiota in particular for the daily encouragement and love and to Uncle Chris and Auntie Tina, Louis and Katerina for always being there for me through thick and thin. Thank you Viktoria Kondratenko for being an amazing nanny and looking after little Evie, giving me some time to write. Thank you, Evie, you are a gift, you fill up my heart and inspire me. I researched this story when you were in my belly, I took you with me on my journeys, then I began to write while you slept in your crib. That is how the story began, with you sleeping soundly beside me.

Thank you to Kate Parkin, your opinion and passion means so much to me and always will.

Thank you to my publishers at Bonnier, in particular to Margaret Stead for not only being a brilliant editor but for always being such a rock. Thank you for all your time and effort, your insight and your lovely way of making suggestions and opening avenues of thought. Thank you to Arzu Tahsin for once again working on the manuscript with me, for all your editorial suggestions which always make such a difference. Thank you to Justine Taylor for your meticulous edits and sharp eye. Thank you to my publicists Beth Whitelaw and Eleanor Stammeijer for being such a pleasure to work with and for everything you do on a daily basis. Thank you to Ellie Pilcher for your creative marketing ideas.

Thank you to my magnificent agent Marianne Gunn O' Connor for all your hard work, your strength, your deep knowledge and instincts. Thank you also for being such a kind and caring person, for always being there for me, for always believing in me, thank you just for being you and being in my life. Thank you to Vicki Satlow for absolutely everything you do and for being amazing.

Thank you also to all the booksellers and librarians who have supported me and continue to support me. And to my readers, I have so much gratitude.

Every book I write changes me, so I would like to say thank you once again to everyone who opened my eyes to things happening in the world, helping me to understand and feel the human stories.

Author's note

AUGUST 2017. I WAS IN Athens, working at a refugee centre for women and children, people mostly fleeing Syria and Afghanistan – the experience that subsequently inspired me to write *The Beekeeper of Aleppo*. While I was there – consumed by the emotional impact of what was happening, being present as so many families flooded into Greece searching for safety – something else caught my attention, something that would keep coming back to haunt me.

One midsummer morning, I woke up and looked out of my window as usual. I drank a cup of coffee, preparing myself to go to work. But that morning, the sky was not a flawless summer-blue as usual – in the distance I could see thick smoke rising from what seemed to be a town or village not too far away. I turned on the TV and saw that firefighters were struggling to contain a fast-moving fire north-east of Athens. Hundreds of people were fleeing their homes. I felt vulnerable. Would the fire reach us? Where would we go if it did? How big was it? How ferocious? How much more powerful than us? Among the war and destruction – the consequences of which I was seeing in the faces of the children at The Hope Centre where I worked – among all this, behind the scenes, was another seemingly quiet threat, an expanding shadow – and there it was that morning, slowly consuming the sky. Wildfires are not uncommon in Greece, especially when there are scorching temperatures and dry winds but – as people kept telling me – things were getting worse, and later my research would confirm this. At the time, I was too involved with my volunteer work to pay much attention. I finished my coffee and headed for the metro to get to Victoria Square.

The following few years in London, as I heard about more and more wildfires on the news, I remembered looking out of the window that day and feeling for a moment how very small we are. The deadly 2018 California fires; the 2018 raging fire in Mati, Greece; the 2019–20 Black Summer fires in Australia – I have merely named a few of the fires that happened leading up to my research, but there are many more. These fires had become so intense because of the exceptionally dry conditions, lack of soil moisture due to drier winters those years, and sometimes earlier blazes. Some of these fires were getting so intense in size, duration and dimension that they were beyond our human control. But it was the fire on the island of Evia, Greece that really woke up my desire to write about this issue. More than 46,000 hectares went up in smoke – one of the worst wildfires in the county's history. Woods and meadows, pine forests, olive groves, beehives and livestock and houses – all gone. The scenes on TV were apocalyptic. Thousands of people fled their homes.

I felt compelled to write about it. However, I did not want to write a novel set in the near future, not a story about what might or could happen, but a tale of our times, a picture of what is already happening.

It was the brutal summer of 2021 that I decided to fly to Greece to begin my research. I was three months pregnant with Evie and fires were raging in Greece, Spain, France, Italy, Croatia and Cyprus. It was during this time that I heard people's stories. I went first to Mati and stayed there for a while, getting to know the locals, understanding what happened on that fateful day, seeing the landscape and hearing about what it used to be like. Imagining the forest that existed before the fire. I heard so many people's stories, young and old. I remember one man could not even speak to me, his eyes filled with tears, and he told me he had no words in a way that stayed with me more than all the words combined. That look in his eyes of utter sadness and loss. I met brave children who lived with permanent scars but had survived. Most people I spoke to still looked frightened to me, as if they no longer felt safe in the world. Feeling Evie growing inside me, I wondered what kind of world she would grow up in.

I prepared myself mentally to hear people's stories, like I always try to do. Whenever I start research like this, I say to myself to open my heart, to allow myself to feel, but to be careful not to break. This isn't always easy and not always possible, like when I was writing *The Beekeeper of Aleppo* and could not forget the children in the camps when I went back to London. What I was not expecting, however, was to learn so much and hear so much about the attribution of blame. I came to understand how desperately people needed to blame a tangible entity – a person, a group of people, the government. In this case there were many candidates – the man who started the fire; the fire brigade and police, who had made mistakes in their first response; the government for many reasons, including not cracking down on land speculation. And this was all justifiable. I knew that I too would be angry in their position for the things they were telling me, and that these issues needed to be explored, investigated and dealt with. What I was not expecting, however, was that any mention of the bigger issue, of climate change and global warming, was shut down immediately and completely. It was made clear to me by many that this was an unacceptable subject. Survivors felt that it had nothing to do with what they had suffered, that the people accountable needed to pay. 'But what if we are all accountable in some way?' I asked once, stressing the last two words. I got no response. Was I naive to ask this question? I continuously questioned myself. Was I insensitive?

But what if I understood what they were saying and could relate to it, while at the same time feeling that I also didn't want to forget the changing climate – because I knew that if we all forgot about it, especially if we ever experienced such devastation and trauma, that it would only get worse.

In all my travels and interviews, I realised how necessary it is for all of us to hold on to something tangible and that often it is a way of protecting ourselves from the immense difficulty of facing the bigger issue. Global warming became in a way like a dark shadow-reflection of ourselves, hovering around us, almost invisible. We could not talk about it, but it was there. We could not address it, but it was there. I realised how complex people's responses were and equally how complex my response was as an outsider. It was not black and white. And that is where the idea of Mr Monk came from. It is much easier to put all of the blame in the other.

While researching, I came across a word that stayed in my mind: *solastalgia,* coined by philosopher Glenn Albrecht. Essentially, it describes the feeling of distress, grief, depression, anxiety and longing caused by environmental change, experienced by people whose lands, homes or communities have been subject to adverse and unforeseen environmental changes. 'No More Walks in the Wood' by the Eagles gives a good sense of this feeling. It is something I imagine most of us can relate to. If we haven't experienced such catastrophic loss ourselves, it is not difficult to empathise, to imagine, to fear it. However, I have started to think that, in some way, so many of us are already feeling it on a daily basis, maybe without realising – we see and feel the smaller changes, the shifting seasons, flowers blooming at the wrong times, hotter summers, temperatures rising and warmer winters, and we know deep down, as hard as it sometimes is to hold on to, that the world, our world, is changing.

Christy Lefteri

Reading Group Questions

- What are the main themes of the novel?
- Do you agree with Irini's sense of shared responsibility at the beginning of the novel? What might this suggest about her state of mind?
- Which of the characters seem strongest at the start of the novel? Does this impression change by the end?
- How does Irini and Tasso's relationship change during the course of the novel?
- How important is the act of storytelling to the book? Whose story is left out of the novel?
- How do English and Greek culture and tradition interact in the book? How is this dual heritage visible in Chara?
- What role does painting and music play in the characters' lives – and their recovery?
- Could you consider the chestnut tree a character in this story?
- What characteristics do the animal characters share, specifically Rosalie the greyhound and the jackal? How do they help the family heal in the aftermath of the fire?

- The book clearly states that 'The fire had already been lit before'. How does the novel approach questions of climate change and environmental responsibility?

- Vassilios' father discusses how people turn to destruction and violence when they demonise the 'other'. How does the fire in the book exacerbate the othering of one or more characters?

- 'The entire earth is changing, and we have neglected our home'. How far do Irini's words summarise the novel as a whole?

- The question 'will it all be remembered?' haunts the narrative. How does the idea of legacy play a part in the story and does it make you consider your own personal legacy?

- How does the book approach mental health in the wake of trauma?

- Can reading a novel about the devastating consequences of climate change have a different emotional impact to that of the media and news?

For further exploration and inspiration into thinking about our environment and the effects of climate change on us all, check out Climatestories.org.uk

Founded by Professor Peter Stott and Pierrette Thomet Stott, and supported by a team of academics, experts, scientists, writers, musicians and artists, Climate Stories is a forum and educational hub where people can share climate stories through poetry, music, art, film and more, as well as attending workshops and events.

Sign up to
Christy Lefteri's Readers' Club

Scan the QR code below to join Christy Lefteri's Readers' Club and receive exclusive content from the bestselling author of *The Beekeeper of Aleppo*, *Songbirds* and *The Book of Fire*.

THE INTERNATIONAL
BESTSELLER

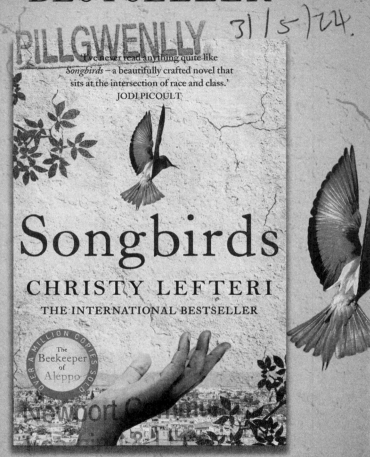

31/5/24.

PILLGWENLLY

'I've never read anything quite like
Songbirds – a beautifully crafted novel that
sits at the intersection of race and class.'
JODI PICOULT

Songbirds

CHRISTY LEFTERI
THE INTERNATIONAL BESTSELLER

OVER A MILLION COPIES SOLD

The
Beekeeper
of
Aleppo

Newport Community

Discover the illuminating follow-up to
The Beekeeper of Aleppo. Songbirds is an upliftin
story of love, loss and the enduring bond that
connects a mother and child, no matter
the distance.

Available now.